PENGUIN BOOKS
Patricia Grace
Collected Stories

Patricia Grace was born in Wellington in 1937. She is of Ngati Raukawa, Ngati Toa and Te Ati Awa descent. She has taught in primary and secondary schools in the King Country, Northland and Porirua. She now lives in Plimmerton. She is married with seven children.

Patricia Grace's stories have been published in a number of periodicals and anthologies. Her first collection of stories, *Waiariki*, was published in 1975 and won the Hubert Church Award for a first book of fiction for that year. Her first novel, *Mutuwhenua, The Moon Sleeps*, was first published in 1978 and was shortlisted for the New Zealand Book Awards. Her second collection of stories, *The Dream Sleepers*, was published in 1980.

She has also written three children's books: *The Kuia and the Spider* (1981), *Watercress Tuna and the Children of Champion Street* (1985), both illustrated by Robyn Kahukiwa, and *The Trolley* (1993), illustrated by Kerry Gemmill. *The Kuia and the Spider* won the Children's Picture Book of the Year award in 1982. She also wrote the text for *Wahine Toa* (1984), paintings by Robyn Kahukiwa.

Patricia Grace's second novel, *Potiki*, was published in 1986 and won the fiction section of the New Zealand Book Awards in 1987. Her third story collection, *Electric City and Other Stories*, was published in 1987, followed by *Selected Stories* in 1991. *Cousins*, a novel, published in 1992, was shortlisted for the fiction section of the New Zealand Book Awards. Her latest stories, *The Sky People*, were published in 1994.

PATRICIA GRACE

Collected Stories

PENGUIN BOOKS

For Kerehi Waiariki Grace

PENGUIN BOOKS

Penguin Books (N.Z.) Ltd, 182–190 Wairau Road, Auckland 10, New Zealand.
Penguin Books Ltd, 27 Wrights Lane, London W8 5TZ, England
Penguin Books: 375 Hudson Street, New York, N.Y. 10014, U.S.A.
Penguin Books Australia Ltd, 487 Maroondah Highway, Ringwood, Australia 3134
Penguin Books Canada Ltd, 10 Alcorn Avenue, Toronto, Ontario, Canada M4V 3B2

Penguin Books Ltd, Registered Offices: Harmondsworth, Middlesex, England

The stories in this book were first published as:
Waiariki and Other Stories, published by Longman Paul, 1975
The Dream Sleepers and Other Stories, published by Longman Paul, 1980
Electric City and Other Stories, published by Penguin Books, 1987

Copyright © Patricia Grace 1975, 1980, 1987

Designed by Richard King
Typeset by Egan-Reid Ltd, Auckland
Printed in China

Acknowledgements are due to *Landfall*, the *New Zealand Listener* and
Te Ao Hou, in which some of the stories in this book first appeared.

WAIARIKI
and
Other Stories

Contents

A Way of Talking

ROSE CAME BACK YESTERDAY; WE WENT DOWN TO THE BUS TO meet her. She's just the same as ever Rose. Talks all the time flat out and makes us laugh with her way of talking. On the way home we kept saying, 'E Rohe, you're just the same as ever.' It's good having my sister back and knowing she hasn't changed. Rose is the hard-case one in the family, the kamakama one, and the one with the brains.

Last night we stayed up talking till all hours, even Dad and Nanny, who usually go to bed after tea. Rose made us laugh telling about the people she knows, and taking off professor this and professor that from varsity. Nanny, Mum and I had tears running down from laughing; e ta Rose, we laughed all night.

At last Nanny got out of her chair and said, 'Time for sleeping. The mouths steal the time of the eyes.' That's the lovely way she has of talking, Nanny, when she speaks in English. So we went to bed and Rose and I kept our mouths going for another hour or so before falling asleep.

This morning I said to Rose that we'd better go and get her measured for the dress up at Mrs Frazer's. Rose wanted to wait a day or two but I reminded her the wedding was only two weeks away and that Mrs Frazer had three frocks to finish.

'Who's Mrs Frazer anyway?' she asked. Then I remembered Rose hadn't met these neighbours though they'd been in the district a few years. Rose had been away at school.

'She's a dressmaker,' I looked for words. 'She's nice.'

'What sort of nice?' asked Rose.

'Rose, don't you say anything funny when we go up there,' I said. I know Rose, she's smart. 'Don't you get smart.' I'm older than Rose but she's the one that speaks out when something doesn't please her. Mum used to say, 'Rohe, you've got the brains but you look to your sister for the sense.' I started to feel funny about taking Rose up to Jane Frazer's because Jane often says the wrong thing without knowing.

We got our work done, had a bath and changed, and when Dad came back from the shed we took the station-wagon to drive over to Jane's.

Before we left we called out to Mum, 'Don't forget to make us a Maori bread for when we get back.'

'What's wrong with your own hands,' Mum said, but she was only joking. Always when one of us comes home one of the first things she does is make a big Maori bread.

Rose made a good impression with her kamakama ways, and Jane's two nuisance kids took a liking to her straight away. They kept jumping up and down on the sofa to get Rose's attention and I kept thinking what a waste of a good sofa it was, what a waste of a good house for those two nuisance things. I hope when I have kids they won't be so hoha.

I was pleased about Jane and Rose. Jane was asking Rose all sorts of questions about her life in Auckland. About varsity and did Rose join in the marches and demonstrations. Then they went on talking about fashions and social life in the city, and Jane seemed deeply interested. Almost as though she was jealous of Rose and the way she lived, as though she felt Rose had something better than a lovely house and clothes and everything she needed to make life good for her. I was pleased to see that Jane liked my sister so much, and proud of my sister and her entertaining and friendly ways.

Jane made a cup of coffee when she'd finished measuring Rose for the frock, then packed the two kids outside with a piece of chocolate cake each. We were sitting having coffee when we heard a truck turn in at the bottom of Frazers' drive.

Jane said, 'That's Alan. He's been down the road getting the Maoris for scrub cutting.'

I felt my face get hot. I was angry. At the same time I was hoping Rose would let the remark pass. I tried hard to think of something to say to cover Jane's words though I'd hardly said a thing all morning. But my tongue seemed to thicken and all I could think of was Rohe don't.

Rose was calm. Not all red and flustered like me. She took a big pull on the cigarette she had lit, squinted her eyes up and blew the smoke out gently. I knew something was coming.

'Don't they have names?'

'What? Who?' Jane was surprised and her face was getting pink.

'The people from down the road whom your husband is employing to cut scrub.' Rose the stink thing, she was talking all Pakehafied.

'I don't know any of their names.'

I was glaring at Rose because I wanted her to stop, but she was avoiding my looks and pretending to concentrate on her cigarette.

'Do they know yours?'

'Mine?'

'Your name.'

'Well . . . Yes.'

'Yet you have never bothered to find out their names or to wonder whether or not they have any.'

The silence seemed to bang around in my head for ages and ages. Then I think Jane muttered something about difficulty, but that touchy sister of mine stood up and said, 'Come on, Hera.' And I with my red face and shut mouth followed her out to the station-wagon without a goodbye or anything.

I was so wild with Rose. I was wild. I was determined to blow her up about what she had done, I was determined. But now that we were alone together I couldn't think what to say. Instead I felt an awful big sulk coming on. It has always been my trouble, sulking. Whenever I don't feel sure about something I go into a big fat sulk. We had a teacher at school who used to say to some of us girls, 'Speak, don't sulk.' She'd say, 'You only sulk because you haven't learned how and when to say your minds.'

She was right that teacher, yet here I am a young woman about to be married and haven't learned yet how to get the words out. Dad used to say to me, 'Look out, girlie, you'll stand on your lip.'

At last I said, 'Rose, you're a stink thing.' Tears were on the way. 'Gee Rohe, you made me embarrassed.' Then Rose said, 'Don't worry, Honey, she's got a thick hide.'

These words of Rose's took me by surprise and I realised something about Rose then. What she said made all my anger go away and I felt very sad because it's not our way of talking to each other.

Usually we'd say, 'Never mind, Sis,' if we wanted something to be forgotten. But when Rose said, 'Don't worry, Honey, she's got a thick hide,' it made her seem a lot older than me, and tougher, and as though she knew much more than me about the world. It made me realise too that underneath her jolly and forthright ways Rose is very hurt.

I remembered back to when we were both little and Rose used to play up at school if she didn't like the teacher. She'd get smart and I used to be ashamed and tell Mum on her when we got home, because although she had the brains I was always the well-behaved one.

Rose was speaking to me in a new way now. It made me feel sorry for her and for myself. All my life I had been sitting back and letting her do the objecting. Not only me, but Mum and Dad and the rest of the family too. All of us too scared to make known when we had been hurt or slighted. And how can the likes of Jane know when we go round pretending all is well? How can Jane know us?

But then I tried to put another thought into words. I said to Rose, 'We do it too. We say, "the Pakeha doctor," or "the Pakeha at the post office", and sometimes we mean it in a bad way.'

'Except that we talk like this to each other only. It's not so much what is said, but when and where and in whose presence. Besides, you and I don't speak in this way now, not since we were little. It's the older ones – Mum, Dad, Nanny – who have this habit.'

Then Rose said something else. 'Jane Frazer will still want

to be your friend and mine in spite of my embarrassing her today; we're in the fashion.'

'What do you mean?'

'It's fashionable for a Pakeha to have a Maori for a friend.' Suddenly Rose grinned. Then I heard Jane's voice coming out of that Rohe's mouth and felt a grin of my own coming. 'I have friends who are Maoris. They're lovely people. The eldest girl was married recently and I did the frocks. The other girl is at varsity. They're all so *friendly* and so *natural* and their house is absolutely *spotless*.'

I stopped the wagon in the drive and when we'd got out Rose started strutting up the path. I saw Jane's way of walking and felt a giggle coming on. Rose walked up Mum's scrubbed steps, 'Absolutely spotless.' She left her shoes in the porch and bounced into the kitchen. 'What did I tell you? Absolutely spotless. And a friendly natural woman taking new bread from the oven.'

Mum looked at Rose then at me. 'What have you two been up to? Rohe I hope you behaved yourself at that Pakeha place?' But Rose was setting the table. At the sight of Mum's bread she'd forgotten all about Jane and the events of the morning.

When Dad, Heke and Matiu came in for lunch, Rose, Mum, Nanny and I were already into the bread and the big bowl of hot corn.

'E ta,' Dad said. 'Let your hardworking father and your two hardworking brothers starve. Eat up.'

'The bread's terrible. You men better go down to the shop and get you a shop bread,' said Rose.

'Be the day,' said Heke.

'Come on, my fat Rohe. Move over and make room for your daddy. Come on, my baby, shift over.'

Dad squeezed himself round behind the table next to Rose. He picked up the bread Rose had buttered for herself and started eating. 'The bread's terrible all right,' he said. Then Mat and Heke started going on about how awful the corn was and who cooked it and who grew it, who watered it all summer and who pulled out the weeds.

So I joined in the carryings on and forgot about Rose and Jane for the meantime. But I'm not leaving it at that. I'll find some way of letting Rose know I understand and I know it will be difficult for me because I'm not clever the way she is. I can't say things the same and I've never learnt to stick up for myself.

But my sister won't have to be alone again. I'll let her know that.

Toki

FROM THE NORTH HE CAME, TOKI, IN HIS YOUNG DAY. AH YES. A boaster this one, Toki the fisherman.

'They are all here, the fish,' he said. 'In the waters of the north. The tamure, the tarakihi, the moki, and the hapuku. And Toki, he has the line and the hand for all of them,' Toki from the north, Toki the fisherman.

But it was not as a fisherman we saw him then but as a boaster and a stranger, and looked upon with suspicion by many. And named Toki Fish by us since long ago days.

Long ago we had a mind for the same girl, Toki and I. A beautiful girl this, and looking my way till he came with his boasting ways. Promised to me, for it had been arranged between our families. Then he came, Toki, and her head was turned until I showed him as a boaster.

After the wedding of my eldest brother when all were gathered for singing and dancing, he began to boast again of days fishing, Toki. To scorn our ways and these waters of ours. And she listened with eyes down, the girl, which was a way of hers. Very jealous then I, and stood to speak.

'Well it may be,' I said, 'to catch many fish where fish are many. In the north they are plenty, the fish, and you wait with your hooks and your lines for them to come. A fisherman of skill catches fish where there are none to catch.'

'They are many or they are few, the fish,' said Toki. 'Still they come to me for I have the line and the hand.'

'Together then we, tomorrow,' I replied, and he knew my meaning as did those who listened.

'Not together, but one, then the other,' he.

'Together tomorrow to choose the place,' I. 'After that I go, and the next day you.'

17

They all spoke then, the old people, of days fishing, and much advice they gave to we of young days. But sat quietly, I, to wait for morning. Then rowed together past the point of crayfish rock and in a line with Poroti where green meets blue.

'Here then,' I said.

'So,' said Toki.

It was all there, the bait, when we returned, for all were eager to see who would be the fisherman of skill. To the rocks for crayfish they, for it is best bait in these parts.

Next morning then I, with many there early to see me go. Out to sea with the day just coming, pulling strong and straight. Around the point, then quickly to the chosen place to get down my line before sunrise.

Not one of the good fishing grounds this, and doubtful at the start. But as the day came in the tarakihi. A quick pull this, and knew many would follow because it is the way of the tarakihi. Eight hooks to my line, and counted eight before bringing it up. Fat they were, waving in the water as my hand pulled in my line. Quick to put on my bait again and put it at the bottom of the sea, for it feeds quickly the tarakihi. Four times to the surface with eight, and a good beginning. But the time after this, pulling the line, there came the heads of my tarakihi but not the bodies. Gone. The work of a hapuku this, and very excited then I.

Quickly to change the bottom hooks for a bigger size and tie the bait on firmly.

'Come to me, hapuku,' I said. 'Come to me, old man. Come to the line of Hotene. This is the line for you and this the bait.'

My hand felt the pull of the tarakihi many times but waited. Then away, the line, with the strong slow pull of the hapuku.

'Mine then,' I said, and brought him up. A big size, though it was not the grounds of the hapuku.

Then at the slacking of the water, rolled in my line to rest and prepare my spinner, for it is the time of the blind eel, this.

Not many more fish for me that day, but knew my catch

was good for such a place of chance. Home then, hard pulling with my paua-shell spinner flashing at the back of the boat, waiting for the eye of the kahawai. Round the corner it waited, the kahawai, and a spread of green and silver as it took the spinner.

A happy fisherman then, I, heading for home to the crowd on the beach. A lucky day this, and knew I'd not be beaten. But then it was, as I waited for the eighth wave to take me in, that I thought of what could happen. He sees all these fish of mine, Toki, and he will know he cannot equal in such a place chosen. He will go then, well out to sea, to the grounds of the hapuku. There to fish because his boast is strong.

Now in these parts the landing of a boat is not safe except to come in on the eighth wave. Watch for the biggest, then after this, turn your boat into the eighth. It is the right size this one to take your boat to the shallows safely. Kept from the ears of Toki, it would be my safeguard, this.

To the hills early next morning, and from there saw the little boat head straight for the deep. Glad then that I had kept the secret of the waves.

Many were there to watch him come in and so sat quietly to watch. No counting of waves Toki, but turned his boat into a breaker of small size which brought him halfway in. But then came the big one. A big one this, swelling and getting faster, up to the boat, then . . . crash!

Swamped, the boat, and Toki in the water with his catch around him as I had thought. Toki Fish we named him as he swam for shore and that has been his name since. All were happy for me to show him as a boaster, because all knew he had not gone to the chosen place to fish. And she came to my side once more, the girl, and is there still though old lady now, she.

He goes for the paua and the kina now, Toki. He throws his line from the beach for the shark, but no more in a boat he, for fear of what would be said. But a boaster still this one, a boaster still. It blows strong the wind from north.

At the River

S AD I WAIT, AND SEE THEM COME SLOW BACK FROM THE RIVER. The torches move slow.

To the tent to rest after they had gone to the river, and while asleep the dream came. A dream of death. He came to me in the dream, not sadly but smiling, with hand on heart and said, 'I go but do not weep. No weeping, it is my time.'

Woke then and out into the night to watch for them with sadness on me, sadness from the dream. And waiting, there came a morepork with soft wing beat and rested above my head. 'Go,' I said to the bird. 'He comes not with you tonight. He is well and strong. His time is not here.'

But it cried, the morepork. Its call went out. Out and out until the tears were on my face. And now I wait and I see the torches come, they move slow back from the river. Slow and sad they move and I think of him.

Many times have we come to this place for eels. Every year we come at this time. Our children come, and now our grand-children, his and mine. This is the river for eels and this the time of year.

A long way we have travelled with our tents and food stores, our lamps and bedding and our big eel drums. Much work for us today preparing our camp. But now our camp is ready and they have gone with the torches down river to the best eel place. And this old lady stays behind with her old kero-sene lamp and the camp fire dying, and the little ones sleeping in their beds. Too tired for the river tonight, too old for the work of catching eels. But not he. He is well and strong. No aching back or tired arms he. No bending, no sadness on him or thoughts of death like this old one.

His wish but not mine to come here this year. 'Too old,' I

said to him. 'Let the young ones go. Stay back we two and tend our kumara and corn.'

'This old body,' he said, 'it hungers for the taste of eel.'

'The drums will be full when they return,' I said. 'Let them bring the eels to us, as they would wish to do.'

'Ah no,' he said. 'Always these hands have fetched the food for the stomach. The eels taste sweeter when the body has worked in fetching.'

'Go then,' I said, and we prepared.

I think of him now as I await their return. 'My time is here,' he said in the dream, and now the bird calls out. And I think too of the young ones who spoke of him today in a new way, a way I did not like.

Before the night came they worked, all of them, to make their torches for the river. Long sticks of manuka, long and straight. Tins tied at the tops of the sticks, and in the tins rag soaked in oil. A good light they made as they left tonight for the river. Happy and singing they went with their torches. But I see the lights return now, dim. Dim and slow they come and sadly I await them.

And the young ones, they made their eel hooks. Straight sticks with strong hooks tied for catching eels. He smiled to see the eel hooks, the straight sticks with the strong hooks tied.

'Your hooks,' he said, 'they work for the hands?' But the young ones did not speak, instead bent heads to the work of tying hooks.

Then off, the young ones, to the hills for hare bait as the sun went down. Happy they went with the gun. Two shots went out and we awaited their return. The young ones, they came back laughing. Happy they came with the hare. 'Good bait this,' they said. 'Good bait and good hooks. Lots of eels for us tonight.'

But their nanny said to them, 'A hook is good for the eel but bad for the leg. Many will be there at the river tonight, your uncles, aunties, big cousins, your nanny too. Your hooks may take a leg in place of an eel. The old way, with the stick, and the bait tied is a safe way and a good way. You waste your time with hooks.'

But the young ones rolled on the ground. 'Ho Grandpa,' they called. 'You better watch your leg, tonight. The hook might get your leg, Grandpa.'

'And watch your hand, Grandpa, the eel might get your hand.'

'Bite your hand off, Grandpa. You better watch out.'

Did not like their way of talking to their nanny but he has patience with the young.

'You'll see,' he said. 'You want to know how to get eels then you watch your grandpa.'

They did not keep quiet, the young ones, after that. Called out to him in a way I did not like, but he is patient.

'Ah Grandpa, that old way of yours is no good. That way is old like you, Grandpa.'

'You might end up in the river with your old way of catching eels.'

Spoke sharply to them then in our own language.

'Not for you to speak in this manner. Not our way to speak like this. It is a new thing you are doing. It is a bad thing you have learned.'

No more talk from these two then, but laughing still, and he spoke up for them.

'They make their torches, the boys, and they make the hooks, and then they go to the hills for hare. They think of the river and the eels in the river, and then they punch each other and roll on the ground. Shout and laugh waiting for the night to come. The funny talk it means nothing.'

'Enough to shout and fight,' I said. 'Enough to roll on the ground and punch each other, but the talk needs to stay in the mouth.'

Put my head down then not pleased, and worked at my task of kneading the bread for morning.

Now I wait and stir the ashes round the oven while the morning bread cooks, and on the ashes I see my tears fall. The babies sleep behind me in the tent, and above me the bird cries.

Much to do after a night of eeling when the drum is full. From the fire we scrape away the dead ashes to put into the drum of eels. All night our eels stay there in the drum of ashes to make easier the task of scraping. Scrape off the ashes and with them come the sticky eel slime. Cut the eels, and open them out then ready for smoking. The men collect green manuka for our smoke drum. Best wood this, to make a good smoke. Good and clean. All day our smoke house goes. Then wrap our smoked eel carefully and pack away before night comes and time for the river again.

But no eels for us this night. No scraping and smoking and packing this time. Tonight our camp comes down and we return. The dim lights come and they bring him back from the river. Slow they bring him.

Now I see two lights come near. The two have come to bring me sad news of him. But before them the bird came, and before the bird the dream – he in the dream with hand on heart.

And now they stand before me, the boys, heads down. By the dim torch-light I see the tears on their faces, they do not speak.

'They bring your nanny back,' I say. 'Back from the river.' But they do not speak.

'Hear the morepork,' I say to them. 'It calls from the trees. Out and out it cries. They bring him back from the river, I see your tears.'

'We saw him standing by the river,' they say. 'Saw him bend, looking into the water, and then we saw him fall.'

They stand, the young ones in the dim torch-light with tears on their faces, the tears fall. And now they come to me, kneeling by me, weeping.

'We spoke bad to him,' they say. 'They were bad things we said. Now he has fallen and we have said bad things to him.'

So I speak to them to comfort them. 'He came to me to-night with hand on heart. "Do not weep," he said. "It is my time." Not your words that made him fall. His hand was on his heart. Hear the morepork cry. His time is here.'

And now we weep together, this old lady and these two young ones by her. No weeping he said. But we will weep a little while for him and for ourselves. He was our strength.

We weep and they return. His children and mine return from the river bearing him. Sad they come in the dim light of torches. The young ones help me to my feet, weeping still, and I go towards them as they come.

And in my throat I feel a cry well up. Lonely it sounds across the night. Lonely it sounds, the cry that comes from in me.

Transition

SEE WHAT THEY DO, THESE GRANDSONS AND GRANDDAUGHTERS of mine. Take these large stones from the river bed and put them here on the track where each day I walk. This is what they do, these mokopuna, and so to please them I walk with the bad leg that has in it a feeling of deadness. This way and that, round and about the big river stones to make these young ones happy.

Home from school they will say to me, 'Did you walk today, Nanny? Did you see our stones, our big river stones?'

'Yes,' I will say. 'Yes, I walked. This way and that. Round and about the stones making the old leg all tired.'

'Ah Nanny. Soon we will have your leg all better. Soon. You'll see, Nanny.'

And then seeing how pleased they are, I will be happy to have done this for them. Not much time left now to give happiness to these little ones. Soon this old light goes out.

And the mother too. This daughter of mine. Every morning this daughter gives me the work of kneading bread in order to get the lame hand strong once more. Sad this daughter. Sad to see this old one hobble about with one side lame. And sad this old one to see the daughter with yet another worry on her.

I tell her, never mind. Never mind this old one. Look to the young. Look to the years ahead.

And yet this one asks herself what future there is for these dear ones of hers.

And a great sadness comes.

What future on this little corner of land, once enough to support many but now in these days merely a worry and a trouble. The ground dry and hard, and great round stones where once a river flowed. A great sadness comes, for this old one knows that soon these ones must go away from this place. The city must claim these loved ones of hers, and in claiming take its price. But nowhere for this old one in such a new place. Her place is here, and so the daughter has a sadness on her.

'Come,' she says. 'Come with your children. We cannot leave you here. Before when you were well, though not even then happily. But now, since your illness?'

'Each day,' I say, 'I am a little stronger. Here I can walk along beside the river bed. Still I can take a hoe in one good hand, still I can roll the dough for new bread, and have others here beside me. My needs are few.'

But she is torn in two this daughter.

I say to her, 'Here is the place where I was born and here is where I die.'

And the mokopuna who listen say, 'Don't talk so funny, Nanny.' So I try to tell them there is nothing to fear.

'No need to fear a life ahead without an old nanny. This is just an old nanny with her light getting dim who likes to see her days go by in this house, on this poor dried out piece of land where she was born.'

Then the husband, father of these little ones, stands firm and says, 'We cannot leave you here and if you'll not come then we stay too. This wife of mine and these children would fret away in the town without their old lady.'

'Go,' I say. 'Here there is nothing.'

'And there?' he asks, and I know his meaning.

'The arrangements are made,' I say to him, 'and you must go.'

'Made before your illness,' he says, 'and now can be un-made.'

The mokopuna listen and are glad, and the daughter too.

'We can get along,' she says. 'We have till now, and shall. This is a better place, a freer place, and our hearts are here.'

Look then at this daughter of mine, ageing before her time with so much work, and this good son-in-law with the worry of bills to be paid and future needs to look to. Then the

26

children much too thin, and the older ones with little time for school work because of chores. A great sadness.

Yet suddenly all these ones of mine are smiling, laughing because the good son-in-law has said arrangements can be unmade, and they will stay here with the old nanny on the dried-up place.

'Ha Nanny,' they say. 'We will stay here with you now and make your leg better with our rocks. You'll see, Nanny.'

'And cook special food for you as the doctor said so you can live to a hundred.'

All at once this old one is laughing too. 'Better for an old nanny like this to keep her old habits and go away happy, than live to a hundred on dried-up kai.'

Away then happy to their jobs. Laughing, and happy to work till dark on this thirsting soil, and leaving this old one minding the days gone past. Not long now, for the light grows dim. Not long now will this old woman hold these ones here, for soon this light goes out. These ones of hers will go from this place with some sadness, remembering an old lady that once was their bond. But yet will depart with a new hope coming and a new life to make.

This old one awaits that time, which is not long away. Not long. Then this old body goes to this old ground, and the two shall be one, with no more to be given by one or by the other to those who weep.

And from the two – the land, the woman – these ones have sprung. And by the land and by the woman held and strengthened. Now, from knowing this, the old one in turn draws strength as the old light dims, as the time of passing comes.

The Dream

I T WAS STILL DARK WHEN RANIERA AWOKE FROM A DISTURBED
sleep. In the night the dream had come to him. Carefully
he groped back through the fuzz of his awakening, pushing his
thoughts back into the dark moments of oblivion. The dream
. . . what was it now? He had seen himself in his dream. Alone
– standing on the soft bank of a deep muddy creek. Stooping,
peering into the murky water, and something in his hand . . . a
rope.

Yes, a rope. Now it all came to him . . . the hinaki. His
hinaki, sucked deep into the soft grey mud, and himself pulling
on the rope knowing that the hinaki would be full of eels, because pulling took all his strength.

Slowly the wire cage had surfaced and he had seen that it
was full, not with several eels as he had thought, but with one
big eel – thick, black, coiled round in the hinaki like an inflated
inner tube.

And in the dream he had dragged his hinaki with the eel
in it up the bank, and tipped the eel out on the grass . . . the
biggest eel he had ever seen. He had seen himself stoop over
the eel, put a hand under each gill, and push his fingers around
its slimy girth until his fingers touched under the belly. Then
he had pointed his thumbs together over the eel's back and his
thumbs had just touched.

There the dream had ended – with him stooping over the
eel and measuring its girth with his hands. A hand on each side,
thumbs touching, fingers touching.

This, he felt, was the important part of his dream. What
did it mean? He felt under the pillow for his *Best Bets*, then
reached out to light the candle which was on a chair by the
bed.

Best Bets was open at the second leg. Slowly he read down the list of names, turning each carefully in his mind – looking for a connection with his dream.

Gay Ring
Prophecy
Gold Stripe
Fair Fellow

Nothing about eels there.

. . . Lonely Boy – lonely? Alone? He had been alone in his dream.

. . . Black Knight – the eel was black, the creek dark . . . Black Knight?

. . . Prophecy – hadn't he tried to prophesy what was in the hinaki? But he had been wrong, and that meant Prophecy wouldn't win. He scratched a line through Prophecy with the burnt match-head.

Blue Smoke
Dark Beauty
Royal Sun
Lucky Touch
Guardian
Foxwood.

He went over the dream again in his mind, then he put the book down, cupped his fingers together, tipped thumbs. A big eel. As big as that. There must be a winner there somewhere. He'd better get to town early to see Ben and the others, and they could all talk about the dream. Work it out. Must be a winner there somewhere.

'E Hika! He aha te moemoea?' called Ben as Raniera stepped from the taxi and waved to the driver.

'What's the dream?'

'E tama, he tuna.'

'Ei! Kia tika ra!'

'Yeh! A big one this eel. Ka nui te kaita!'

He showed Ben with his hands the size of the eel of his dream. And there under the white verandah of the TAB his

29

friends gathered to listen; Ben, Lucy, Monty, Hone, Ritimana, Haua.

Raniera told them how he had been stooping, looking into the mud. They watched him carefully as he showed them how he had pulled the hinaki in, pulled it up the bank, tipped the eel on to the grass.

'Wii!' he said. 'A big eel – that size.' And he showed them how he had measured it with his hands . . . fingers touching under the belly, thumbs touching over the back.

'Pai, good dream ne?' said Haua.

'E champion.'

They nodded, smiled, and turned the pages of *Best Bets*; studied the second leg.

'One eel,' said Lucy. 'Number one, Gay Ring. One eel. Number one.'

'Dark Beauty,' said Ben. 'A beauty eel. Dark. Dark Beauty!' One by one they gave their opinions and advice.

At last it was eleven o'clock, time to place bets for the double. Into the pastel-painted room they went and had a final look at the printed lists on the wall. Up to the window. Bets placed.

Raniera gave his numbers. 'Twelve,' he said. No trouble there. His daughter Rose had turned twelve two days ago. number twelve, Sunset Rose, but the second? 'Aee,' he sighed. One eel in the hinaki, and the eel coiled in a ring. Number one, Gay Ring, Must be. 'Twelve and one,' he said.

There was a hush in the bar as the race began. 'This ti-ime,' called the commentator. 'Off to a good start . . . Fair Fellow, Guardian, Gay Ring.'

Raniera, Ben, Monty, Hone, Ritimana and Haua drummed their fists on the bar.

'Na, Gay Ring.'

'Ho! A good start. Ka pai ne?'

Earlier that day they had heard Sunset Rose come in, and now they listened eagerly, certain that this was to be Raniera's lucky day. 'E champion, this dream,' they said.

As the race progressed they all pressed closely together at the bar, feet tapping, bodies rocking.

'Kia kaha! Gay Ring,' they called as Gay Ring went through to challenge the leading horse.

'My horse that one. My dream,' shouted Raniera.

But Gay Ring, after going into the lead and holding it for a short while, began to tire.

'Gay Ring dropping well back now,' called the commentator.

'Aue!'

'Kei whea Gay Ring?'

Shoulders drooped, elbows pressed onto the bar, heads shook slowly.

'And as they pass the post it's Lucky Touch half a length from Gold Stripe, two lengths to Lonely Boy . . .'

'E tama. Kei whea to moemoea? What happened to the dream?'

'Aue! No good.'

Once again out came *Best Bets*. Fingers down the list – Lucky Touch. Number ten. Lucky Touch.

'Aue!' said Ben, and he flicked his arms above his head. 'Number ten.' And as the others nodded, sighed, he explained. 'Five fingers on this hand. And five fingers on this hand.' He showed them his hands. 'E Ra,' he turned to Raniera. 'You put your hands around the tuna like this. Na? Five and five are ten – number ten. The fingers touched – Lucky Touch, the fingers touched.'

'Aee,' they agreed.

'Ko tera taku! I'll say!'

Raniera shook his head. 'Aue! Waste a good dream.'

'No dough for the Maori today,' said Monty. 'Ka hinga ta tatau crate.'

They all laughed.

'E ta, ko haunga to tuna,' said Ritimana slicing the air with his hand. 'Your eel stinks.'

'Na! Ka puta mai te piro,' called Haua, as the laughter rose.

Then Raniera spread his fingers wide, raised both arms

above his head. 'Whio!' he yelled. Down came his arms in a full arm sweep. 'Haunga!'

'Haunga!' they echoed, and their laughter swelled, burst, and filled the bar.

Holiday

YOU KNOW, I LOVE MY NANNY RETIMANA. EVERY HOLIDAYS I say to Mum and Daddy, I'm going to my Nanny Retimana's, and I pack my bag. And Mum and Daddy take me down to the railway station and put me in the railcar, and even though it's a long, long way to Nanny Retimana's place I don't care. I wouldn't care if Nanny lived on the other side of the world or up on the moon, I'd still go every holidays to see her.

Mum and Daddy put me in the railcar with some sandwiches and apples and comics, and they kiss me and tell me everything to do and everything not to do. Then they kiss me again and wave. And it is a little bit sad to go away from Mum and Daddy, especially when they worry and keep telling me this and that. But they shouldn't worry because I'm so happy to go to Nanny Retimana's and I know everything to do and everything not to do. And all the way in the railcar my Nanny Retimana's name keeps going round and round in my head like music – Nanny Retimana, Nanny Retimana. And Papa Retimana too of course. I love him too even though he cheeks me a lot.

Nanny and Papa have an old car, and Papa won't let anyone drive it but him. He goes everywhere in his old car. To town, to the pub, to football; to Wellington, Auckland, anywhere. One day he even went over the bank in it, with Nanny and my two aunties and Uncle Charlie, all the shopping and his beer and me. Roll, roll, bang the car went, and landed on its side on the creek road below the bank. And I was sitting on top of Auntie Materoa, who was on top of Uncle Charlie, who has a stiff leg. I was glad I wasn't underneath because you should see how fat Auntie Materoa and Uncle Charlie are.

None of us was hurt very much, but the eggs were all

smashed and Papa Retimana got hit on the back of the neck with a tin of golden syrup. And Auntie Kiri was all spooky because the bag of flour broke and she had white eyebrows and eyelashes and a white chin. And she was sneezing all the time.

We all had to climb up out of the window, which was a tight squeeze for everyone but me, and Uncle Charlie couldn't get out at all because of his stiff leg. So Auntie Kiri had to get back in and push him up while the others pulled. Auntie Kiri was still sneezing too, and it took a long time to get Uncle Charlie out.

Gee, and the car was all dented and the shopping was everywhere. Eggs, flour, rolled oats, potatoes. Everywhere. But, you know, Papa's beer was all right. Not one bottle was broken and Papa was really happy. Auntie Kiri looked at the beer and she looked at Papa's happy face and said, 'E ta! The devil looks after his own. Hard case all right.' But Papa didn't care about her teasing because he was so glad about his beer.

Nanny and Papa Retimana always come down in their car to meet me at the station. I watch out the window and I see the two of them there and I'm glad because they look just the same as ever. I get out of the railcar and I go and hug them both, and you know, Papa Retimana nearly breaks all my bones with his big hug. I ride all the way back to Nanny's place squashed between my Nanny and Papa, and they say to me, 'Ah you still skinny, Atareta', and they shake their heads. And they say, 'Ah your mummy been cutting your hair', and they shake their heads again. But I don't really think they mind how skinny I am. I don't think they're really angry about my short hair, they squeeze me all the way back to their place for thirty miles. And, you know, my name isn't Atareta at all. My name's Lynette. But Nanny says I look just like my Auntie Atareta, who lives way down the South Island and who I've never seen. And when my Auntie Atareta was little she used to sit on her legs with her feet sticking out at the sides the same as I do. Well that's what Nanny Retimana says, and Nanny Retimana, she calls me Atareta all the time.

When we come to Nanny and Papa's little house I see that

it's just the same as the last time and I feel really glad. I like Nanny and Papa Retimana's house, all painted white with the little paths running everywhere. The paths are all covered in stones and shells, and all the flower gardens are edged by big round river stones that Nanny and Papa have painted all colours. And it looks so cheerful always. I like arriving at Nanny and Papa's and seeing all the pretty paths and gardens, all the bright painted stones, and the little white house sitting in amongst it all.

When we get inside Nanny gets me a whole lot of kai out of the big pot on the stove so she can make me fat. And it's a wonder I'm not as fat as anything because I eat everything Nanny gives me, and I have bread and a big mug of tea as well. Papa cuts off thick slices of Nanny's bread for him and me. He puts thick butter on his bread and then he dips it in his tea. 'That's the way,' he says. 'Bread on butter and put it in the tea.' So I do it too and it's good, you know. It's a wonder I'm not as fat as anything.

After I've had my kai I go into Nanny's sitting room and look at all of her and Papa's photos.

'All your relations, Atareta,' Nanny tells me. And she talks to me about all my old nannies who are dead now, and my aunties and uncles and cousins. There are photos of me there too with Mum and Daddy, and one of Mum and Daddy's wedding. And some of Auntie Atareta and her husband and kids who live way down the South Island. Some of the photos are hard case too, like the one of my cousin Danny pulling an ugly face, and the one of Uncle Charlie asleep out on the grass and all you can see in the photo is Uncle's big puku sticking up.

I'm always glad to go to bed after my long journey in the railcar, so after Nanny and I have looked at all the photos I change and get into my bed with the three mattresses on and go fast asleep.

Most days there's just Nanny and Papa and me, and I help them with the work and talk a lot. I help Nanny with the dishes and we polish the lino, and sometimes we make jam or bottle some fruit.

I like to go out and help Papa too. We feed all the ducks, and Papa's old pig, and his two dogs, and in the afternoons we often go out to the gardens and work there.

But in the weekends we have to be quick with our jobs because that's when all my aunties and uncles and cousins start turning up. And my aunties look at me and say, 'Ah that's you, Atareta,' and they all kiss me and so do my uncles. Then all my cousins kiss me too, so it's no wonder I don't get fat after all because I'm sure I get worn out after a while. But I still like it. I like all my aunties and uncles and cousins coming.

And I get out and play with my cousins. We ride the horse or go swimming in the river, or slide down the hills and wear our pants out. We play all day long until dark, and when we go back inside we're so hungry we eat everything out of the big pot and all the bread as well. Nanny and Papa Retimana and our aunties and uncles all have some beer and laugh a lot and talk, and Auntie Materoa, well she can't stop laughing. She laughs all the time. She sounds just like a fire engine with her way of laughing, 'Eeee Hardcase, Hardcase, Eeeeee,' with tears all running down. Uncle Ben teases her and says, 'You lay an egg in a minute, Mattie.' And away Auntie Materoa goes again, 'Eeee Hardcase, Hardcase Eeeeee.'

Sometimes in the weekends instead of our aunties and uncles coming, we get in the car and go to one of their places. I like going to Auntie Kiri's place because it's not far from the beach. And you know, Auntie Kiri's house is really neat. It's flash. Auntie's place is all full of carpets and thick curtains and electric heaters, and a big TV, a deep-freeze, clothes drier, and stereogram. Auntie's house is so flash she won't let us kids inside until we've had a good wash under the hose.

We met Auntie in town one Friday and she told us to come back and stay with them so we did. It was raining that day. And when we got to Auntie's house Uncle Ben was sitting in the kitchen and Auntie's big clothes drier was rumbling away in the wash-house. Auntie was really pleased with Uncle for doing all her washing and putting it in the drier and she gave him a big kiss.

Then afterwards she went to get the clothes out and she started yelling her head off out in the wash-house, 'Parengo. Your stink parengo! Who told you to put your haunga seaweed in my drier?'

And Uncle said, 'How else do I dry my parengo in this weather?'

And we all ran out to the wash-house to look at Uncle's parengo in Auntie's drier. Auntie Materoa who was there too started up laughing as usual, 'Eeee Hardcase, Parengo Eeeeee,' screeching, looking into Auntie Kiri's drier.

Gee Auntie Kiri growled. She called Uncle a stink and a dead loss and a taurekareka. Then after a while she started up laughing too, and Auntie Kiri's laugh is nearly as bad as Auntie Materoa's, well that's what I think.

Auntie Kiri can growl, you know. She doesn't growl at us little kids though, only if we mess up her house, but she growls at her big grown-up kids, my big married cousins. They always come there and start looking in the cupboards and all round the house for Auntie's bread.

'You made a bread, Mum?' they say.

'You got any meat? Gee-ee, Macky forgot to get us a meat for the weekend.' And Auntie Kiri growls.

'Don't you come here looking for bread and meat you tahae things,' she growls. But I don't think she means it really because afterwards she goes and gets the bread from a tin in her wardrobe. And my big cousins all grin and say, 'Gee what a lovely bread, Mum. Cunning all right.' And Auntie Kiri looks pleased and says, 'Cunning yourself.'

She growls too if they come to her place untidy. Mostly my cousins make sure to change before they come to Auntie's, but one day Benjy came in his old kanukanu pants and Auntie went off at him.

'Haven't you got a decent pants?' she said. 'Can't that fat wife of yours sew a button on your pants. Where is she anyway? At home with her eyes on the TV the lazy. You bring your wife next time, and bring my mokopuna. You didn't bring my mokopuna to see me.'

37

Then Auntie made a funny noise at Benjy to show how bad he was, 'A-ack!'

Later that night when I was pretending to be asleep on the settee I heard Auntie saying, 'Come here, useless,' to Benjy, and I peeped through my eyelashes and saw her with a needle and cotton and a button, and she started sewing a button on my big cousin's pants. And Benjy was dancing up and down saying, 'Gee-ee, look out, Mum. Watch out you'll sew up my thing in a minute.' Rude ay?

But Auntie just said, 'Good job too,' and kept on sewing.

And of course Auntie Materoa started up screeching again. You know, Auntie Materoa's hard case with her laugh. I had to wriggle down under my blanket so no one would see my mouth grinning.

I like going to Auntie Materoa's too. I don't sleep on the settee at Auntie Materoa's, I just get in bed with all her kids. My cousins and I get up to all sorts at Auntie Materoa's. We have pillow fights, and use the beds for trampolines, and dress up in Auntie Materoa's clothes and put her shoes on. Four of us can fit in one of Auntie Materoa's dresses, that's how fat Auntie Materoa is. And nobody growls. Nobody takes any notice of us kids yelling and jumping around in the bedroom. Even when we sneak out in the kitchen and have a feed they take no notice at all. They all sit round in Auntie Materoa's sitting room and drink their beer and sing. And they dance and do the hula, even my Nanny Retimana who is quite old really. She does the hula and they all shout hard case things to her like:

'Good on you, aunt.'

'Swing it, kuia.'

'Watch out, ka makare to tarau,' and that's just about rude because it means Nanny might lose her pants if she does the hula too much.

Nanny Retimana doesn't care, she shouts out, 'Shut up, you fullas jealous, *E puru tai tama* . . .'

They all sing *E puru tai tama*, and start clapping and sometimes Uncle Charlie gets up and joins in the hula, and that sets Auntie Materoa off again because Uncle Charlie's got a stiff leg, 'Hardcase! Hardcase!' tears running down and us kids all looking round the door to watch Uncle Charlie and Nanny Retimana and some others doing the hula.

I enjoy myself at my Auntie Kiri's and Auntie Materoa's, but I'm always pleased to get back to Nanny's where we can be peaceful and quiet again, and I go round helping Nanny and Papa and play with the ducks and Papa's two dogs, or have a quiet ride on the horse.

And my holiday never seems very long. It's soon time to pack my bag again and get into Papa Retimana's old car – it's still got all the dents in too and there's a stain on the seat where all the syrup poured out – and Nanny and Papa take me to the station and put me in the railcar with some kai in a biscuit tin, and some pauas in a plastic bag from Auntie Kiri to take home to Mum and Daddy.

I wave to my Nanny and Papa Retimana out of the railcar window. I wave and wave until I can't see them any more, and I'm sorry to be going away from them. Then after a while I start thinking about Mum and Daddy waiting for me at the other end, but it seems a long, long way. I have a few sleeps, and I nibble at all the kai Nanny Retimana has packed for me. Then as I get nearer to home I start to feel excited because Mum and Daddy will be waiting at the station for me. Then I think what if they've changed? What if they're different or don't know me? And I worry and put my face to the window as the railcar comes in, and I see them both standing on the platform waiting for me. And I see they haven't changed. They're not different at all, and they do know me because they start smiling when they see my face at the window.

You know, I love Mum and Daddy. I pick up my bag and my tin of kai and my pauas in a plastic bag from Auntie Kiri, and I hurry out of the railcar and onto the platform. I hug Mum and Daddy and we go and get into our car. I sit between them on the front seat and they squeeze me all the way home to our place.

Waiariki

WHEN WE WERE LITTLE BOYS WE OFTEN USED TO GO around the beach for kai moana. And when we reached the place where the rocks were we'd always put our kits down on the sand and mimi on them so the shellfish would be plentiful.

Whenever the tides were good we would get our kits and sugar-bags and knives ready, then go up at the back of our place to catch the horses – Blue Pony, Punch, Creamy, and Crawford. And people who lived inland would ring and ask us about the tides. 'He aha te tai?' they'd ask over the phone – 'What time's the tide?' and we'd tell them. All morning the phone would ring; 'He aha te tai? He aha te tai?'

And on those days there would be crowds of us going round the beach on horses with our kits and knives, and when we arrived at the place for gathering shellfish we boys would mimi on our kits and sugar bags then wash them in the salt water, all of us hoping for plenty of kai moana to take home.

We never thought much about the quiet beauty of the place where we lived then. Not in the way I have thought about it since. I have many times wished I could be there, living again in our house overlooking the long curve of beach and the wide expanse of sea. We could climb up through the plantation behind our place to the clearings at the top and look away out for miles, and could feel as free as the seagulls that hung in the wind above the water. It was from this hill that I once saw a whale out off the point, sending up plumes of spray as it travelled out to the deep. And on another occasion from the same hill, we watched the American fleet go by, all the ships fully lit, moving quietly past in the dusk.

If we went down the gully and up on the hills at the left we could look back to where our old house had been, then down to the present dwelling with all the flower gardens and trees around it. And below the house by the creek were our big vegetable gardens which kept us busy all year round. One would have thought that with vegetable gardens to tend, our parents would not have had time for flowers. But flowers, shrubs and trees we had in abundance, and looking down from the hills, or from the beach below, the area round the house was always a mass of colour. But it is now, looking back, that I appreciate this more.

The bird tree was our favourite, with its scarlet flowers like red birds flying. Then there were the hibiscus of many different colours, the coral tree, kaka beak, and many varieties of coloured manuka and broom. And there was a big old rata under which one of our brothers was born, and named Rata for the tree.

In front of the house at the end of the lawn was a bank where scores of coloured cinerarias, black-eyed Susans, and ice plants grew, and beyond there was the summer house that my fathers and brothers built before I was born. This was where my father had all his hanging baskets crowded with ferns and flowers.

When I first left there to go away to school, and when I first realised what other people had in the way of money and possessions, I used to think how poor we children were. I used to think about it and feel ashamed that our patched clothing, much of it army surplus, was the best we had. And felt ashamed that the shoes that had been bought for me for high school were my first and only pair. It wasn't until many years later that I realised that we had many of the good things, and all the necessary things of life.

There were ten of us living in the house at the time I remember, but there were older children who had married and gone away. Seventeen children my parents had altogether, though not all lived. I can remember the day my youngest sister and her twin were born. Our mother had been away at one of the top gardens getting puha, and on our way home from school we could see her coming down the track on Craw-ford. And our father was standing by the gate with his hands on his hips, shaking his head.

'That one riding on a horse,' he was saying. 'That one riding on a horse.'

And Mum got down off the horse when she got home and said, 'Oh Daddy, I was hungry for puha.' Then she began walking round and round the house, pressing her hands into her sides, pressing her hands. Later she went to bed and Dad delivered the girl.

My big sister Ngahuia brought the new little sister Maurea out into the kitchen where it was warm and began washing her. Then Mum called out to Dad that there was another baby and at first he thought it was all teka. He thought she was teasing because he had growled about her riding on the horse. But when he went to her he knew she wasn't playing after all and went to help, but the boy was stillborn. Mum was sad then because she had been riding on the horse so close to her time, but my father was good to her and said no, it was because the boy was too small. They took the tiny body up to where the old place had been, and buried it there with the other babies that had not lived.

Maurea was never very strong and on most nights we went to sleep listening to the harsh sound of her coughing. That was until she was about five years old. Then our parents took her to an old aunt of ours who knew about sicknesses, and the old aunt pushed her long forefinger down our sister's throat and hooked out lump after lump of hard knotted phlegm. Maurea was much better from then on though still prone to chest complaints and has never been sturdy like the rest of us.

There were three different places where we went for kai moana. The first, about a mile round the beach, called Hua-papa, was a place of small lagoons and rock pools. The rocks here were large and flat and extended well out into the sea. This was a good place for kina and paua and pupu. We would ride the horses out as far as we could and tether them to a rock.

They would stand there in the sun and go to sleep. To get kina we would go out to where the small waves were breaking, in water about knee deep. We'd peer into the water, turning the flat stones over, and it wouldn't take long to fill a sugar-bag with kina. The paua were there too, as well as in the rock pools further towards shore. The younger children, who were not old enough to stand in the deeper water and not strong enough to turn the big rocks for paua and kina, would look about in the rock pools for pupu, each one of them hoping to find the biggest and the best.

The next place, Karekare, further round the beach, was also a good place for shellfish, but the reason we liked to go there was that there was a small lagoon with a narrow inlet, which was completely cut off from the sea at low tide. Often at low tide there were fish trapped there in the lagoon. And we children would all stand around the edge of the lagoon and throw rocks at the fish.

'Ana! Ana!' we'd yell.

'Patua! Patua!' hurling the stones into the water. And usually there would be at least one fish floating belly up in the lagoon by the time we'd finished. Whoever jumped in first and grabbed it would keep it and take it home.

One day after a week of rain we arrived at Karekare to find the water in the lagoon brown and murky, and even before we got down from the horses we could see two dozen or more fins circling, breaking the surface of the water. We all got off the horses and ran out over the rocks calling, 'Mango, Mango,' and scrambled everywhere looking for rocks and stones to throw. But my father came out and told us to put the rocks down. Then he walked out into the lagoon and began reaching into the water. Suddenly he threw his arms up, and there was a shower of water, and a shark came spinning through the air, 'Mango, Mango,' way up over our heads with its white belly glistening and large drops of water raining all over us. 'Mango, Mango,' we shouted. Then – smack! It landed threshing on the rocks behind us. So we hit it on the head with a stone to make sure of it, and turned to watch again. My father caught ten sharks this way, grabbing their tails and sending them arcing out over our heads to the rocks behind, with us all watching and shouting out 'Mango, Mango,' yelling and jumping about on the rocks.

The other place, Waiariki, is very special to me. Special because it carries my name which is a very old name and belonged to my grandfather and to others before him as well. It is a gentle quiet place where the lagoons are always clear and the brown rocks stand bright and sharp against the sky. This was a good place for crayfish and agar. Mum was the one who usually went diving for crayfish, ruku koura. She would walk out into the sea fully clothed and lean down into the water, reaching into the rock holes and under the shelves of rock for the koura. Sometimes she would completely submerge, and sometimes we would see just a little bit of face where her mouth was, sitting on top of the sea.

The rest of us would feel round in the lagoons for agar. Rimurimu we called it. For the coarse agar we would need to go out to where there was some turbulence in the water, to pluck the hard strands from the rocks. But the finer rimurimu was in the still parts of the lagoons and we would feel round for it with our feet and hands, and pick it and put it into our sugar-bags.

When our bags were full we would take the agar ashore and spread it on the sand to dry. Then we'd put it all into a big bale and tramp it down. We had a big frame of timber to hold the bale, and our own stencil to label it with. I don't know how much we were paid for a bale in those days. But I do remember once, after one of the cheques had arrived, my father went to town and came home in a taxi with a rocking-horse and two guitars. He handed me one of the guitars and I tuned it up and strummed on it, and I remember thinking that it was the most beautiful sound I had ever heard.

And another time my father brought home a radio, and after that our neighbours and relations used to come every week to listen to *Gentleman Rider* or the *Hit Parade*. And when the boxing or wrestling was on people would come from everywhere. We'd all squeeze into our kitchen and turn the radio up as loud as it would go. On the morning after the fights we boys would go down to the beach and find thick strands of bull kelp and make our own boxing belts and organise our own boxing or wrestling tournaments on the sand.

The horses were very useful to us then. They were of more use to us than a car or truck would have been. Besides using them for excursions round the beach we used them for every-day work, and when the rain came and flooded the creek our horses were the only means we had of getting to town. All of our wood for the range was brought down from the hills by the horses too.

On the days when we were to go for firewood we boys would go up back before breakfast and bring the horses down, and after breakfast we'd prepare the horses for the day's work. Dad would sort out all the collars and chains, and we'd go out into the yard, put the collars on the horses, and hook the long coils of chain onto the hames. Then we'd get together the axes and slashers and start out down and across the creek, and go up onto the scrub-covered hills about a mile from the house.

It was always the younger boy's job to trim the leaves and side branches from the felled manuka and stack the wood on to the track ready to be chained into loads for the horses to pull. One of the older boys who had been chopping would come down and wrap the short chains round the stacks, then hook the long chains from either side of the horses' collars on to each side of the load.

Once when I was about nine years old my father and mother were at the bottom of the hill stacking the wood into cords – we were selling wood then – for the trucks to come and take away to town. My older brothers were chopping and stacking at the top of the hill and my sisters and I were taking the horses down with the loads. I was on my way up the hill on Blue Pony and my sister was at the top hitching a load to Punch, who was a good willing horse but very shy. Erana accidentally bumped the chain spreader against Punch's leg and away he went. I saw Punch coming, bolting towards me with the chains flying, but it was too late to do anything. Punch knocked Blue Pony down, and I went hurtling out over the bank like Dad's mango thrown out of the lagoon.

I landed in scrub and fern and wasn't hurt. Everyone came running to look at me, but I got up laughing, and I remember my father saying, 'E tama, that one flying!' Then he went off to rescue Punch who was by then caught up in one of the fences by his chains.

On warm nights we used to like to go fishing for shark from the beach. Mangoingoi. We'd go down to the beach with our lines and bait and light a big fire there, and on some nights, especially when the sea was muddy after rain and we knew the sharks would be feeding close to the shore, there would be people spread out all along the beach, and four or five fires burning and cracking in the night.

We always used crayfish for bait, and because crayfish flesh is so soft we would bind it to our hooks with light flour-bag string. Then we would tie the ends of our lines to a log and prepare the remainder so that the full length of it would be used once it was thrown. We'd walk out into the sea then, twirling the end of the line with the hooks and horseshoe on it, faster and faster, then let it go. And the line would go zipping out over the sea, and sometimes by the fire's light we'd see the splash out off shore, where the horseshoe sinker entered the water.

We waited after that, sitting up on the beach with our lines tied to our wrists. We'd talk, or sometimes sleep, and after a long while, usually an hour or more, someone's line would shoot away with shark.

'Mango, Mango!'

'Aii he mango!'

And we would all tie our lines and go running to the water's edge, 'Mango, Mango,' to watch the shark being pulled in with its tail flapping and water splashing everywhere.

Mum used to cut the shark into thick pieces and boil it, then skin it. Then she'd put it into a pan to cook with onions, and we'd eat till we were groaning. Sometimes we would hang

46

strips of shark flesh on the line to dry, and when this had dried out we would put it in the embers of our outside fire to cook. There was one teacher at school who used to get annoyed when we'd been eating dried shark at lunchtime. He'd march around the classroom flinging the windows open and saying, 'You kids have been eating shark again. You pong.' And we'd sniff around at each other wondering what all the fuss was about.

Dad used to hang the shark liver on the line too, and let the oil drip into the stomach bag. Then he'd put the oil in a bottle and save it to treat the saddles and bridles with.

I went back to the old place last summer and took my wife and children with me for a holiday. I wanted them to know the quiet. I wanted them to enjoy the peace, and to do the things we used to do.

In most ways the holiday was all I hoped it would be. My parents still live there in much the same way as before, even though the house seems somewhat empty now with only the two of them and two grandsons living there. Most of the other families have moved away. The vegetable gardens are not as extensive now because there is not the need, but flowers and trees are as abundant as ever, and the summer house is still there with my father's ferns flourishing and the begonias blooming.

Electricity hasn't reached that far yet, so it is still necessary for the old people to bring the wood down from the hills, and I don't like to think of them doing this on their own with only two small boys to help.

My wife and children had a good holiday. We spent two days getting firewood so that there would be plenty there after we had gone. Punch, Blue Pony, Creamy and Crawford are all dead now, and the two horses that they use are getting old too. There are other younger horses on the hills, but with no one to break them in they are completely wild.

I took my family up on the hills and we sat looking out over the sea. I told them about the whale I had once seen out

47

past the point, and about the American fleet, all lit, going silently by.

And one night I took them down to the beach fishing. Mangoingoi. We caught a little shark too, and Mum cooked it for us in the old way and my father hung strips of it to dry and caught the oil in the stomach bag for the bridles and saddles.

Another day we all went round the beach for kai moana and, although the tides were good and the weather perfect, we were the only ones there on the beach that day. We visited all the favourite places and took something from each. And when we went to Waiariki, which even now I think of as my own special place, I told my children its name, and that it was special to me because I had that name and so had others before me. And my little boy said to me, 'Dad why can't we stay here forever?' because he has the name as well.

But when we arrived at the first place with our knives and bags and kits and dismounted from the horses, and looked out over the flat rocks of Huapapa which is the best place for kai moana, I felt an excitement in me. I wanted to reap in abundance. I wanted to fill the kits full of good food from the sea. And then, I wanted to tell my children to put their kits down on the sand and mimi on them so that we would find plenty of good kai moana to take home. I wanted to say this to them but I didn't. I didn't because I knew they would think it unclean to mimi on their kits, and I knew they would think it foolish to believe that by so doing, their kits would be more full of sea food than if they hadn't.

And when we left the rocks with our kits only half filled I felt regret deep in me. I don't mean that I thought it was because of my children not christening their kits as we stood on the beach that we were unable to fill our bags that day. There are several reasons, all of them scientific, why the shellfish beds are depleted. And for the few people living there now, there is still enough.

No. My regret came partly in the knowledge that we could not have the old days back again. We cannot have the simple things. I cannot have them for my children and we cannot have full kits any more. And there was regret in me too for the passing of innocence, for that which made me unable to say to my children, 'Put your kits on the sand little ones. Mimi on your kits and then wash them in the sea. Then we will find plenty. There will be plenty of good kai moana in the sea and your kits will be always full.'

And So I Go

*O*UR SON, BROTHER, GRANDCHILD, YOU SAY YOU ARE GOING AWAY *from this place you love, where you are loved. Don't go. We warm you. We give you strength, we give you love.*
These people are yours.
These hills, this soil, this wide stretch of sea.
This quiet place.

This land is mine, this sea, these people. Here I give love and am loved but I must go, this is in me. I go to learn new ways and to make a way for those who follow because I love.

My elders, brothers and sisters, children of this place, we must go on. This place we love cannot hold us always. The world is large. Not forever can we stay here warm and quiet to turn the soil and reap the sea and live our lives. This I have always known. And so I go ahead for those who come. To stand mid-stream and hold a hand to either side. It is in me. Am I not at once dark and fair, fair and dark? A mingling. Since our blue-eyed father held our dark-eyed mother's hand and let her lead him here.

But, our brother, he came, and now his ways are hers out of choice because of love.

And I go because of love. For our mother and her people and for our father. For you and for our children whose mingling will be greater than our own. I make a way. Learn new ways. So I can take up that which is our father's and hold it to the light. Then the people of our mother may come to me and say, 'How is this?' And I will hold the new thing to the light for them to see. Then take up that which is our mother's and say to those of our father, 'You see? See there, that is why.'

And brother, what of us. Must we do this too? Must we leave

*this quiet place at the edge of hills, at the edge of sea and follow you?
For the sake of our mother's people who are our own. And for our
father and because we love?*

You must choose but if you do not feel it in you, stay here
in warmth. Let me do this and do not weep for my going. I
have this power in me. I am full. I ache for this.

Often I have climbed these hills and run about as free as rain.
Stood on the highest place and looked down on great long waves
looping on to sand. Where we played, grew strong, learned our
body skills. And learned the ways of summers, storms and tides.
From where we stepped into the spreading sea to bathe or gather
food. I have watched and felt this ache in me.

I have watched the people. Seen myself there with them
living too. Our mother and our blue-eyed father who came
here to this gentle place that gives us life and strength.
Watched them work and play, laugh and cry, and love.

Seen our uncle sleeping. Brother of our mother. Under a
tree bright and heavy with sunned fruit. And beside our uncle
his newest baby daughter sleeping too. And his body-sweat ran
over her head in a new baptising. I was filled with strength.

And old Granny Roka sits on her step combing her granddaughter's hair, patiently grooming. Plaiting and tying the
heavy tangled kelp which is her pride. Or walk together on the
mark of tide, old Granny and the child, collecting sun-white
sticks for the fire. Tying the sticks into bundles and carrying
them on their backs to the little house. Together.

And seen the women walk out over rocks when the tide is
low, submerging by a hole of rock with clothes ballooning.
Surfacing with wine-red crayfish, snapping tails and clawing
air on a still day. And on a special day the river stones fired for
cooking by our father, our cousins and our uncles who laugh
and sing. Working all as one.

Our little brother's horse walks home with our little one
asleep. Resting a head on his pony's neck, breathing in the
warm horse stink, knees locked into its sides. Fast asleep on
the tired flesh of horse. And I ache. But not forever this. And
so I go.

And when you go, our brother, as you say you must, will you be warm? Will you know love? Will an old woman kiss your face and cry warm tears because of who you are? Will children take your hands and say your name? In your new life our brother will you sing?

The warmth and love I take from here with me and return for their renewal when I can. It is not a place of loving where I go, not the same as love that we have known.

> No love fire there to warm one's self beside
> No love warmth
> Blood warmth
> Wood and tree warmth
> Skin on skin warmth
> Tear warmth
> Rain warmth
> Earth warmth
> Breath warmth
> Child warmth
> Warmth of sunned stones
> Warmth of sunned water
> Sunned sand
> Sand ripple
> Water ripple
> Ripple sky
> (Sky Earth
> Earth Sky
> And our beginning)

And you ask me shall I sing. I tell you this. The singing will be here within myself. Inside this body. Fluting through these bones. Ringing in the skies of being. Ribboning in the course of blood to soothe swelled limbs and ache bruised heart.

You say to us, our brother, you will sing. But will the songs within be songs of joy? Will they ring? Out in the skies of being as you say? Pipe through bone, caress flesh wounding? Or will the songs within be ones of sorrow?

Of warmth dreams
Love dreams
Of aching
And flesh bruising.
If you listen will it be weeping that you hear?
Lament of people
Earth moan
Water sigh
Morepork cry of death?

My sisters, brothers, loved ones, I cannot tell. But there will be gladness for me in what I do. I ask no more. Some songs will be of joy and others hold the moan and sigh, and owl cry and throb of loneliness.

What will you do then, our brother, when the singing dirges through your veins, pressing and swelling in your throat and breast, pricking at your mind with its aching needles of sound?

What should I do but deny its needling and stealing into mind. Its pressing into throat and breast. I will not put a hand of comfort over body hardenings nor finger blistered veins in soothing. The wail, the lament shall not have my ear. I will pay the lonely body ache no mind. Thus I go.

I stand before my dark-eyed mother, blue-eyed father, brothers, sisters. My aunts and uncles and their children and these old ones. All the dark-eyed, light-eyed minglings of this place.

We gather. We sing and dance together for my going. We laugh and cry. We touch. We mingle tears as blood.

I give you my farewell.

Now I stand on a tide-wet rock to farewell you, sea. I listen and hear your great heart thud. I hear you cry. Do you too weep for me? Do you reach out with mottled hands to touch my brow and anoint my tear-wet face with tears of salt? Do not weep but keep them well. Your great heart beats I know for such as these. Give them sea, your great sea love. Hold them gently. Already they are baptised in your name.

As am I
And take your renewal where I go
And your love
Take your strength
And deep heart thud
Your salt kiss
Your caring.

Now on a crest of hill in sweeping wind. Where I have climbed and run. And loved and walked about. With life brimming full in me as though I could die of living.

Guardian hill you do not clutch my hand, you do not weep. You know that I must go, and give me blessing. You guard with love this quiet place rocking at the edge of sea . . .

And now at the highest place I stand. And feel a power grip me. And a lung-bursting strength. A trembling in my legs and arms. A heavy ache weighting down my groin.

And I lie on soil in all my heaviness and trembling. Stretch out my arms on wide Earth Mother and lay my face on hers. Then call out my love and speak my vow.

And feel release in giving to you, earth, and to you, sea, to these people.

So I go. And behind me the sea-moan and earth-cry, the sweet lament of people. Towards the goddess as she sleeps I go. On with light upon my face.

Huria's Rock

OLD NOW THESE BONES, AND ONE LEG WITH A STICK TO HELP it, old now. He sits, this old one with his stick, on the beach and the agar about him all spread to dry. It is good, the stick, to turn the spread agar, and to poke the ashes round the big camp oven.

She makes the camp oven bread, my daughter, in the morning early, early, as did the mother before her. Good bread, this of the camp oven, and the work of this old one to poke the ashes and turn the spread agar with the stick.

Too old now these bones and this leg for the work of young days, and so they go, those of young days, to collect the agar from the sea, while this old one he tends the fire and with the stick turns the agar to dry. His work, too, to guard the little one who sleeps there in the tent. A great-grandson this, who sleeps on his rug in the tent. He wakes, this young one, then it is the work of this old one to wave his stick for the mother to come and tend him. But no – sleeps the little one. Sleeps he.

Soon they will return, those who gather agar, with kits full and backs tired. Back to camp to rest and eat, then before nightfall to pick up the dried agar and tramp it into the bale. Then to get ready the beds in the tent and then to sleep, for it is much work this gathering of agar.

Many years now since last we came to camp and gather agar here. Young days then I, and the leg without a stick to help it. Two good legs then, and a back strong. Two good eyes, and the hands to pull the agar from the warm sea.

But a sad time that, when last we came to this place. Died here, my wife, when last we came. Drowned she, under crayfish rock, now named Huria's rock for her. No more to that rock since then for crayfish. We leave it to her, to Huria – it is her resting place.

It was large, the crowd that came that year for agar. A good tide that day – the day she died – and the top of crayfish rock showing above the water. Many were there gathering agar in shallow water, but Huria, she took her kit and started out to crayfish rock and took our boy with her. We who picked the agar could see the boy sitting on the rock with the kit, and many times Huria came to him with crayfish.

A good day for crayfish this, thought I. A good day and a good time.

Then looked again to the rock, and the boy he stood looking into the water. Waiting and looking, with the crayfish from the kit crawling about him on the rock.

To the rock then I, calling her name. The others, they left the agar and came behind me for they had seen the spilled crayfish, and the boy waiting and looking down into the sea.

A sad time this. Caught in a crack of the rock we found her, and much work it was to free her for we who mourned.

Lonely years since then for this old one who sits now on the beach. But she will come soon, Huria, for the old one with the stick. She will come for he who looks to her rock and thinks of her, while those of young days gather agar from the sea.

Look now, to Huria's rock, thinking of Huria, and now I see her sitting there on the rock. Look away then I, for they are old now, these eyes. But then back again to the rock and still she sits. It is Huria. She has come.

'For this old one?' I call. But her head is turned away.

'Huria, Huria,' but she looks not at me.

'It is time then, for this old one?' I say.

But she moves then, Huria. Puts out her hand to the tent. To the tent then I, quickly, with the stick working for the leg. Into the tent. But he sleeps, the little one, sleeps peacefully. Out then and looking to the rock, and still she sits, Huria, still she looks to the tent.

'Sleeping, the young one,' I call. 'Come not for the young but the old.'

56

Then stands Huria, and moves nearer, looking to the tent.

Quickly then I, to the lagoon where they gather agar, and wave my stick. She waves, the mother of the little one, and comes to me.

'He is sick, the little one. Go to your baby,' I say.

Drops the kit of agar then, and runs to the tent.

'He sleeps, Grandpa,' she calls from the tent.

'Go to him,' I say. 'He is sick. Huria, she comes for the little one.' I show her Huria but she does not see.

'You sit too much in the sun, Grandpa,' she says. 'And you think too much of Huria. It was wrong to come to this place for agar. It was bad to bring you here.'

'Huria she is close,' I say to her, and I pull her into the tent with me, to the little one.

Screams then, and pulls my stick from my hand.

'The spider, Grandpa – the katipo,' and beats at the blanket where sleeps the young one. Beats and beats the katipo with the stick. Picks up the little one then as he wakes and cries.

'Safe my baby,' she says. 'Our Grandpa has saved you. Safe now,' says she.

Out then I, to look for one who gave us warning. But gone, Huria. Gone she who helped the old one guard the young.

But tired, the old one. Tired. And soon she will be back, Huria, for the old one with the stick.

Soon she comes.

Valley

Summer

THE SUN-FILLED SKY WRAPS THE MORNING IN WARMTH. Already the asphalt has begun to shimmer with light and heat, and the children are arriving.

They spill out of the first bus with sandwiches and cordial, in twos and threes, heads together, strangely quiet. Uncertain they stand with bare feet warming on asphalt, clutching belongings, wondering. They are wondering what I will be like.

It is half past eight. I am watching from my kitchen window and see them glance this way, wondering. In a minute or two I will be ready to go over for them to look at me, but now they are moving away slowly, slapping feet on the warmed playground.

They are wondering what he will be like too. He is in his classroom already, sorting out names, chalking up reminders, and cleaning dead starlings from the grate of the chip-heater in the corner. They stand back from the glass doors and stare, and he comes out with the dead birds on a shovel and gives them to a big boy to take away and bury. They all stare, and the younger ones wonder if he killed the birds, but the older ones know that starlings get trapped in the chimneys every summer and have to be cleaned out always on the first day of school.

I pick up the baby and my bag and walk across. Their eyes are on me.

'Hullo,' I say, but no one speaks, and they hurry away to the middle room, which is Tahi's, because they know her. Some of them call her Mrs Kaa because they have been told to; others call her Auntie because she is their aunt; and others call her Hey Tahi because they are little and don't know so much.

At nine he rings the bell and makes a come-here sign with his arm. They see, and know what he wants, and walk slowly to stand on the square of concrete by the staffroom steps. They stand close together, touching, and he tells them his name and mine. Then he reads their names from a list and Tahi tells each where to stand. Soon we have three groups: one for the little room which is mine, one for the middle room which is hers, and one for the big room which is his.

We find a place for the sandwiches and cordial and then they sit looking at me and not speaking, wondering what I am like.

I put the baby on a rug with his toys. I put my bag by the table, then write my name on the board to show them how it looks. And I read it for them so they will know its sound. I write baby's name as well and read it too, but they remain silent.

And when I say good morning they look at one another and at the floor, so I tell them what to say. But, although some open their mouths and show a certain willingness, no sound comes out. Some of them are new and haven't been to school before and all of them are shy.

The silence frightens me, beating strongly into the room like sun through glass.

But suddenly one of them speaks.

He jumps up and points excitedly. Necks swivel.

'Hey! You fullas' little brother, he done a mimi. Na!'

And there is little Eru with a puddle at his feet. And there we are, they and I, with a sentence hanging in the sun-filled room waiting for another to dovetail its ending.

I thank him and ask his name but his mouth is shut again. The little girl in shirt and rompers says, 'He's Samuel.'

'Mop?' Samuel asks, and means shall I get the wet mop from the broom cupboard and clean up the puddle. Which is friendly of him.

'Yes please,' I say, but again he stands confused.

Shirt and rompers shoves him towards the door. 'Go,' she says.

He mops up the water and washes the mop at the outside tap. Then he stands on the soggy mop-strings with his warmed feet, and the water squeezes out and runs in little rivers, then steams dry.

Samuel wears large serge shorts belted with a man's necktie and there is one button on his shirt. His large dark eyes bulge from a wide flat face like two spuds. His head is flat too, and his hair has been clipped round in a straight line above his ears. The hair that is left sticks straight up as though he is wearing a kina.

Shirt and rompers tells me all the names and I write them on the board. Her name is Margaret.

> Samuel
> Margaret
> Kopu, Hiriwa
> Cowboy
> Lillian, Roimata
> Glen
> Wiki, Steven
> Marama, Evelyn
> Michael, Edie
> Hippy
> Stan.

We have made a poem. The last two are twins; I don't know how I'll ever tell them apart.

We find a place for everyone at the tables and a locker for each one's belongings, but although they talk in whispers and nudge one another they do not offer me any words. And when I speak to them they nod or shake their heads. Their eyes take the floor.

The play bell rings and I let them go. They eat briefly, swig at the cordial or go to the drinking taps. Then they pad across the hot asphalt to the big field where the grass is long and dry. Then they begin to run and shout through the long grass as though suddenly they have been given legs and arms, as though the voices have at that moment been put into them.

Ahead of them the grasshoppers flick up and out into the ever-heating day.

Hiriwa sits every morning at the clay table modelling clay. He is a small boy with a thin face and the fingers that press into the clay are long, and careful about what they do.

This morning he makes a cricket – female, by the pointed egg-laying mechanism on its tail. He has managed the correct angles of the sets of legs, and shows the fine rasps on the hind set by lifting little specks of clay with his pencil. Soon he will tell me a story so I can write for him; then later he will show the children what he has made and read the story for them.

We collected the crickets yesterday because we are learning about insects and small animals in summer. The crickets are housed in a large jar containing damp earth and stones and a wine biscuit. The book tells me that this is the way to keep crickets, and they seem content enough to live like this as they begin their ringing in the warmth of mid-morning.

Two weeks ago we walked down past the incinerator to where nasturtiums flood a hollow of ground at the edge of bush, covering long grass and fern beginnings with round dollar leaves and orange and gold honey flowers blowing trumpets at the sky.

The first thing was to sit among the leaves and suck nectar from the flowers, which wasn't why we had come but had to be done first. And it gave us a poem for the poem book too. Roimata, who finds a secret language inside herself, gave us the poem:

> I squeeze the tail off the nasturtium flower
> And suck the honey,
> The honey runs all round inside me,
> Making me sweet
> Like sugar,
> And treacle,

And lollies,
And chocolate fish.
And all the children lick my skin
And say, 'Sweet, sweet,
Roimata is a sweet, sweet girl.'

The next thing was to turn each flat nasturtium leaf carefully and look on the soft green underside for the pin-prick-sized butterfly eggs. We found them there, little ovals of yellow, like tiny turned-on light bulbs, and found the mint-green caterpillars too, chewing holes in their umbrellas.

The next thing was to put down the leaves they had picked and to begin rolling down the bank in the long grass, laughing and shouting, which wasn't why we had come but had to be done as well:

I rolled busting down the bank
On cold seagrass,
And I thought I was a wave of the sea,
But I am only a skinny girl
With sticking out eyes,
And two pigtails
That my Nanny plaits every morning
With spider fingers.

Now all the eggs have hatched, and every afternoon they pick fresh leaves for the caterpillars. Every morning we find the leaves eaten to the stems, and the table and floor littered with black droppings like scattered crumbs of burnt toast.

The caterpillars are at several stages of growth. Some are little threads of green cotton, and difficult to see, camouflaged by the leaf and its markings. Others are half grown and working at the business of growing by eating steadily all day and night. The largest ones are becoming sluggish with growth, and have gone away from food and attached themselves to the back of the room to pupate:

The caterpillar,
Up on the classroom wall,
Spins a magic house around itself
To hide from all the boys and girls.

Then yesterday on coming in from lunch we found the first of the butterflies, wing-beating the sun-filled room in convoy. We kept them for the afternoon, then let them out the window and watched them fly away:

Butterfly out in the sun,
Flying high by the roof,
'Look up there,' Kopu said.
'Butterfly. Na.
The best butterfly.
I want to be a butterfly flying.'

I said that he would tell me a story to write about his cricket. And that later he would show the children what he had made and read the story for them. But I turned and saw his arm raised and his fist clenched. His thin arm, with the small fingers curled, like a daisy stem with its flower closed after sundown. The fist came down three times on the carefully modelled insect. Head, thorax, abdomen. He looked at what he'd done and walked away.

'Why?' I asked, but he had no words for me.

'That's why, he don't like it,' Samuel told me.

'That's why, his cricket is too dumb,' Kopu said.

Those two have made a bird's nest out of clay and are filling it with little round eggs, heaping the eggs up as high as they will go.

'I made a nest.'

'I made some eggs.'

I made a cricket as best I could with my careful fingers. Then my flower hand thumped three times down on the cricket. Abdomen, thorax, head. And my cricket is nothing but clay.

63

Autumn

Autumn bends the lights of summer and spreads evening skies with reds and golds. These colours are taken up by falling leaves which jiggle at the fingertips of small-handed winds.

Trees give off crowds of starlings which shoot the valley with scarcely a wing beat, flocking together to replace warmth stolen by diminishing sun.

Feet that were soft and supple in summer are hardening now and, although it is warm yet, cardigans and jerseys are turning up in the lost-property box. And John, our neighbour, looks into his vat one morning and sees a single sheet of milk lining the bottom. He puts his herd out and goes on holiday.

Each day we have been visiting the trees – the silver poplar, the liquid amber, and the plum, peach, and apple. And, on looking up through the branches, each day a greater patch of sky is visible. Yet, despite this preoccupation with leaves and colours and change, the greater part of what we see has not changed at all. The gum tree as ever leaves its shed bark, shed twigs, shed branches untidily on its floor, and the pohutukawa remains dull and lifeless after its December spree and has nothing new for this season.

About us are the same green paddocks where cows undulate, rosetting the grass with soft pancake plops; and further on in the valley the variegated greens of the bush begin, then give way to the black-green of distant hills.

They have all gone home. I tidy my table, which is really a dumping ground for insects in matchboxes, leftover lunches and lost property. Then I go out to look for Eru. The boys are pushing him round in the wood cart and he is grinning at the sky with his four teeth, two top and two bottom, biting against each other in ecstasy.

Tahi is in the staffroom peeling an apple. She points the knife into the dimple of apple where the stem is and works the knife carefully in a circle. A thin wisp of skin curls out from the blade. She peels slowly round and down the apple, keeping the skin paper-thin so that there is neither a speck of skin on the apple nor a speck of apple flesh left on the skin. Nor is there a ridge or a bump on the fruit when she has finished peeling. A perfect apple. Skinless. As though it has grown that way on the tree.

Then she stands the apple on a plate and slashes it down the middle with a knife as though it is nothing special and gives me half.

'Gala Day in five days' time,' she says.

'Yes,' I say. 'They'll want to practise for the races.'

'We always have a three-legged and a sack.'

Then Ed comes in and picks up the phone. 'I've got to order a whole lot of stuff for the gala. Gala in five days' time.'

We wake this morning to the scented burning of manuka and, looking out, see the bell-shaped figure of Turei Mathews outlined by the fire's light against the half-lit morning. He stands with his feet apart and his hands bunched on his spread waist, so that his elbows jut. With his small head and his short legs, he looks like a pear man in a fruit advertisement, except that he has a woman's sunhat pulled down over his ears.

Beside him Ron and Skippy Anderson are tossing branches into the flames and turning the burning sticks with shovels. We hear the snap, snap of burning tea tree and see the flames spread and diminish, spread, diminish – watch the ash-flakes spill upwards and outwards into lighting day.

Yesterday afternoon Turei, Ron and Skippy brought the truckload of wood and the hangi stones and collected the two wire baskets from the hall. They spat on their hands, took up the shovels, and dug the hole, then threw their tools on the back of the truck and went.

Yesterday Ed and the boys put up the tents, moved tables and chairs, and set up trestles. The girls tidied the grounds, covered tables with newspaper, and wrote numbers in books for raffles.

We were worried by clouds yesterday. But now on waking

we watch the day lighting clear; we pack our cakes and pickles into a carton and are ready to leave.

By eight o'clock the cars and trucks are arriving and heaving out of their doors bags of corn, kumara, potatoes, pumpkin, and hunks of meat. Women establish themselves under the gum tree with buckets of water, peelers and vegetable knives. Turei and his helpers begin zipping their knives up and down steel in preparation for slicing into the pork. Tahi is organising the cakes and pickles and other goods for sale, Eru is riding in the wood cart, and Ed is giving out tins for raffle money. I take up my peeler and go towards the gum tree.

Roimata's grandmother is there.

'It's a good day,' she says.

'Yes,' I say. 'We are lucky.'

'I open these eyes this morning and I say to my mokopuna, "The day it is good." She flies all around tidying her room, making her bed, no trouble. Every smile she has is on her face. I look at her and I say, "We got the sun outside in the sky, and we got the sun inside dancing around." I try to do her hair for her. "Hurry, Nanny, hurry," she says. "Anyhow will do." "Anyhow? Anyhow?" I say. "Be patient, Roimata, or they all think it's Turei's dog coming to the gala."'

Opposite me Taupeke smokes a skinny fag, and every now and again takes time off from peeling for a session of coughing. Her face is as old as the hills, but her eyes are young and bird-like and watchful. Her coughing has all the sounds of a stone quarry in full swing, and almost sends her toppling from the small primer chair on which she sits.

'Too much this,' she explains to me, pointing to her tobacco tin. 'Too much cigarette, too much cough.'

And Connie next to her says, 'Yes, Auntie. You take off into space one of these days with your cough.'

She nods. 'Old Taupeke be a sputnik then. Never mind. I take my old tin with me. No trouble.'

Hiriwa's mother is there too. She is pale and serious-looking and very young. Every now and again Hiriwa comes and stands beside her and watches her working; his small hands

66

rest lightly on her arm, his wrist bones protrude like two white marbles. I notice a white scar curving from her temple to her chin.

Tahi comes over and says, 'Right, give us a spud,' then spreads her bulk on a primer chair and begins her reverent peeling. A tissue-thin paring spirals downward from her knife.

'How are you, Auntie? How are you, Connie? How are you, Rita? Gee, Elsie, you want to put your peel in the hangi and throw your kumara away.'

'Never mind,' says Elsie. 'That's the quick way. Leave plenty on for the pigs.'

'Hullo, Auntie, hullo, ladies. How are all these potato and kumara getting on?' asks Turei. He takes off his sunhat and wipes the sweat from his neck and head.

'Never mind our potato and kumara,' Tahi says. 'What about your stones? Have you cooks got the stones hot? We don't want our pork jumping off our plates and taking off for the hills.'

'No trouble,' Turei says. 'The meal will be superb. Extra delicious.'

'Wii! Listen to him talk.'

'You got a mouthful there Turei!'

'Plenty of kai in the head, that's why,' he says.

'And plenty in the puku too. Na, Plenty of hinu there, Turei.'

'Ah well. I'm going. You women slinging off at my figure I better go.'

He puts his hat on and pats his paunch. 'Hurry up with those veges. Not too much of the yakkety-yak.' He ambles away followed by a bunch of kids and a large scruffy dog.

The sacks are empty. We have peeled the kumara and potatoes, stripped and washed the corn, and cut and skinned the pumpkin. The prepared vegetables are in buckets of water and we stand to go and wash our hands.

But suddenly we are showered with water. We are ankle deep in water and potatoes, kumara, pumpkin and corn. Connie, who hasn't yet stood, has a red bucket upside down

67

on her lap and she is decorated with peelings. Turei's dog is running round and round and looks as though he has been caught in a storm.

'Turei, look what your mutt did,' Tahi yells, and Turei hurries over to look, while the rest of us stand speechless. Taupeke's cigarette is hanging down her chin like an anaemic worm.

'That mutt of mine, he can't wait for hangi. He has to come and get it now. Hey, you kids. Come and pick up all this. Come on, you kids.'

The kids like Turei and they hang around. They enjoy watching him get the hangi ready and listening to him talk.

'They're the best stones,' he tells them. 'These old ones that have been used before. From the river these stones.'

The boys take their shirts off because Turei wears only a singlet over his big drum chest.

'How's that, Turei?' they ask, showing off their arm muscles.

'What's that?' he says.

'What you think?'

'I seen pipis in the sand bigger than that.'

'You got too much muscles, Turei.'

'Show us, Turei.'

'Better not. Might be you'll get your eyes sore.'

'Go on,' they shout.

So he puts the shovel down, and they all watch the big fist shut and the thick forearm pull up while the great pumpkin swells and shivers at the top of his arm.

'Wii na Turei! Some more, Turei.'

'You kids don't want any kai? You want full eyes and empty pukus?'

'Some more, Turei. Some more.'

But Turei is shovelling the white-hot stones into the hangi hole. 'You kids better move. Might be I'll get you on the end of this shovel and stick you all in the hole.'

He makes towards them and they scatter.

The prepared food is covered with cloths and the

baskets are lowered over the stones. Steam rises as the men turn on the hose. They begin shovelling earth on to the covered food.

'Ready by twelve,' one of them says.

'Better be sweet.'

'Superb. Extra delicious.'

'Na. Listen to the cook talk.'

Over at the chopping arena the men finish setting up the blocks and get ready to stand to. The crowd moves there to watch as the names and handicaps are called. Hiriwa stands opposite his father's block-watching.

Different, the father. Unsmiling. Heavy in build and mood. Blunt fingered hands gripping the slim-handled axe.

Hiriwa watches for a while, then walks away.

The choppers stand to and the starter calls 'Go' and begins the count. The lowest handicapped hit into their blocks and as the count rises the other axemen join in. The morning is filled with sound as voices rise, as axes strike and wood splits. White chips fly.

By three o'clock the stalls have done their selling. The last bottle of drink has been sold, many of the smaller children are asleep in the cars and trucks, and the older ones have gone down to the big field to play. Some of the tents are down already and the remains of the hangi have been cleared away. At the chopping arena the men are wrenching off the bottom halves of the blocks from the final chop and throwing split wood and chips on to the trucks.

Turei's dog is asleep under a tree. Finally the raffles are drawn.

Joe Blow wins a bag of kumara which he gives to Ed. Ed wins a carton of cigarettes which he gives to Taupeke. And Tahi wins a live sheep which she tries to put into the boot of her car but which finds its feet and runs out the gate and down the road, chased by all the kids and Turei's dog.

The kids come back and later the dog, but the sheep is never seen again.

I said to Nanny,
'Do my hair anyhow,
Anyhow,
Anyhow,
Today the gala is on.'
But she said, 'Be patient, Roimata,
They'll think it's Turei's dog.'

Winter

It rains.
The skies weep.
As do we.

Earth stands open to receive her and beside the opened earth we stand to give her our farewell.

'Our auntie, she fell down.' They stood by the glass doors touching each other, eyes filling. Afraid.

'Our auntie, she fell.'

And I went with them to the next room and found her lying on the floor, Ed bending over her, and the other children standing, frightened. Not knowing.

'Mrs Kaa, she has fallen on the floor.'

Rain.

It has rained for a fortnight, the water topped the river banks then flowed over. The flats are flooded. Water stirred itself into soil and formed a dark oozing mud causing bare feet to become chapped and sore and hard.

Like sky people crying,
Because the sun is too lazy
And won't get up,
And won't shine,
He is too lazy.
I shout and shout,

'Get up, get up, you lazy,
You make the sky people cry.'
But the sun is fast asleep.

The trees we have visited daily are bare now, clawing grey-fingered at cold winds. Birds have left the trees and gone elsewhere to find shelter, and the insects that in other seasons walk the trunks and branches and hurry about root formations have tucked themselves into split bark and wood-holes to winter over.

Birds have come closer to the buildings, crowding under ledges and spoutings. We have erected a bird table and every morning put out crumbs of bread, wheat, bacon rind, honey, apple cores, and lumps of fat. And every day the birds come in their winter feathers, pecking at crumbs, haggling over fruit, fat and honey. Moving from table to ground to rooftop, then back to table.

On John's paddock the pied stilts have arrived, also in search of food, standing on frail red legs, their long thin beaks like straws, dipping into the swampy ground.

'Our auntie, she has fallen.'

I took them out on to the verandah where they stood back out of the rain, looking at the ground, not speaking. I went to the phone. Disbelief as I went to the phone.

An emptiness and an unbelieving.

Because they had all been singing an hour before, and she had been strumming the guitar. And now there was a half sentence printed on the board with a long chalk mark trailing, and a smashed stick of chalk on the floor beside her.

Because at morning break she'd made the tea and he'd said, 'Where's the chocolate cake?' Joking.

'I'll run one up tonight,' she'd said. 'But you'll have to chase the hens around and get me a couple of eggs. My old chooks have gone off the lay.'

'Never mind the eggs,' he'd said. 'Substitute something, like water.'

'Water?' It had put a grin on her face.

'Water?' It had brought a laugh from deep inside her and soon she'd had the little room rocking with sound, which is a way of hers.

Or was. But she lay silent on the schoolroom floor and he came out and spoke to them.

'Mrs Kaa is very sick. Soon the bus will come to take you home. Don't be frightened.' And there was nothing else he could say.

'Our auntie, she fell down.'

Standing by the glass doors, the pot-bellied heater in the corner rumbling with burning pine and the room steaming. She had laughed about my washing too, that morning. My classroom with the naps strung across it steaming in the fire's heat.

'I'm coming in for a sauna this afternoon. And a feed. I'm coming in for a feed too.'

Each morning the children have been finding a feast in the split logs that the big boys bring in for the fire. Kopu and Samuel busy themselves with safety pins, digging into the holes in the wood and finding the dormant white larvae of the huhu beetle.

'Us, we like these.'

And they hook the fat concertina grubs out on the pins and put them on the chip-heater to cook.

Soon there is a bacon and roasted peanut smell in the room and the others leave what they are doing and go to look. And wait, hoping there will be enough to go round.

Like two figures in the mist they stood by the doors behind the veil of steam, rain beating behind them. Large drops hitting the asphalt, splintering and running together again.

Eyes filling.

'Mrs Kaa, she fell down.'

Gently they lower her into earth's darkness, into the deep earth. Into earth salved by the touch of sky, the benediction of tears. And sad the cries come from those dearest to her. Welling up, filling the void between earth and sky and filling the beings of those who watch and weep.

'Look what your mutt did, Turei.'

'We always have a three-legged and a sack.'

'Water?' the room rocking with sound, the bright apple skinless on a plate, smashed chalk beside her on the floor.

'A sauna and a feed.'

'Our auntie.'

'Mrs Kaa . . .'

It is right that it should rain today, that earth and sky should meet and touch, mingle. That the soil pouring into the opened ground should be newly blessed by sky, and that our tears should mingle with those of sky and then with earth that receives her.

And it is right too that threading through our final song we should hear the sound of children's voices, laughter, a bright guitar strumming.

Spring

The children know about spring.

Grass grows.

Flowers come up.

Lambs drop out.

Cows have big bags swinging.

And fat tits.

And new calves.

Trees have blossoms.

And boy calves go away to the works on the trucks and get their heads chopped off.

The remainder of the pine has been taken back to the shed, and the chips and wood scraps and ash have been cleaned away from the corner. The big boys make bonfires by the incinerator, heaping on them the winter's debris. Old leaves and sticks and strips of bark from under the pohutukawa and gum, dry brown heads of hydrangea, dead wood from plum, peach and apple.

Pipiwharauroa has arrived.

'Time for planting,' he calls from places high in the trees. 'Take up spade and hoe, turn the soil, it's planting time.'

So we all go out and plant a memorial garden. A garden that when it matures will be full of colour and fragrance.

Children spend many of their out-of-school hours training and tending pets which they will parade at the pet show on auction day. They rise early each morning to feed their lambs and calves, and after school brush the animals, walk them, and feed them again.

Hippy and Stan have adopted Michael, who hangs between them like an odd-looking triplet. The twins have four large eyes the colour of coal, four sets of false eyelashes and no front teeth. They are a noisy pair. Both like to talk at once and shout at each other, neither likes to listen. They send their words at each other across the top of Michael's head and land punches on one another that way too.

Bang!

'Na Hippy.'

Bang!

'Na Stan.'

Bang!

'Serve yourself right, Hippy.'

Bang!

'Serve yourself right, Stan.'

Bang!

'Sweet ay?'

Bang!

'Sweet ay?'

Until they both cry.

Michael is the opposite in appearance, having two surprised blue eyes high on his face, and no room to put a pin head between one freckle and the next. His long skinny limbs are the colour of boiled snapper and his hair is bright pink. Without his shirt he looks as though the skin on his chest and the skin on his back is being kept apart by mini tent poles. His neck swings from side to side as Hippy punches Stan, and Stan punches Hippy. And Michael joins in the chorus. 'Na Hippy! Sweet? Sweet Stan ay? Serve yourself right.' And when they both cry he joins in that as well.

New books have come, vivid with new ink and sweet with the smell of print and glue and stiff bright paper.

We find a table on which to display the books, and where they can sit and turn the pages and read. Or where I can sit and read for them and talk about all the newly discovered ideas.

'Hundreds of cats, thousands of cats, millions and billions and trillions of cats.'

'Who goes trip trap, trip trap, trip trap over my bridge?'

'Our brother is lost and I am lost too.'

'Run, run, as fast as you can, you can't catch me I'm the gingerbread man.'

Hiriwa makes a gingerbread man with clay, and Kopu and Samuel make one too.

Out of the ovens jump the gingerbread men, outrunning the old woman, the old man, the cat, the bear. 'That's why, the gingerbread man is too fast.' Then is gone in three snaps of the fox's jaws. Snip, Snap, Snap. Which is sad they think.

'Wii, the fox.'

'Us, we don't like the fox.'

'That's why, the fox is too tough.'

'Cunning that fox.'

Then again the closed hand comes down on clay. Snip. Snap. Snap.

He writes in his diary, 'The gingerbread man is lost and I am lost too.' One side of his face is heavy with bruising.

On the day of the pet show and auction his mother says to me, 'We are going away. Hiriwa and I. We need to go, there is nothing left for us to do. By tomorrow we will be gone.' I go into the classroom to get his things together.

The cars and trucks are here again. The children give the pets a drink of water and a last brush. Then they lead the animals in the ring for the judges to look over, discuss, award prizes to. Some of the pets are well behaved and some are not. Patsy's calf has dug its toes in and refuses to budge, and Patsy looks as though she is almost ready to take Kopu's advice. Kopu is standing on the sideline yelling, 'Boot it in the puku, Patsy. Boot it in the puku.' And when the judges tell him to go away he looks put out for a moment. But then he sees Samuel and they run off together, hanging on to each other's shirts calling, 'Boot it in the puku. Boot it in the puku,' until they see somebody's goat standing on the bonnet of a truck, and begin rescue operations.

Inside the building, women from WDFF are judging cakes and sweets and arrangements of flowers. I go and help Connie and the others prepare lunch.

'Pity we can't have another hangi,' Connie says.

'Too bad, no kumara and corn this time of the year,' Elsie says. 'After Christmas, no trouble.'

Joe Blow stands on a box with all the goods about him. He is a tall man with a broad face. He has a mouth like a letter box containing a few stained stumps of teeth which grow out of his gums at several angles. His large nose is round and pitted like a golf ball, and his little eyes are set deep under thick grey eyebrows which are knotted and tangled like escape-proof barbed wire. Above his eyebrows is a ribbon width of corrugated brow, and his hair sits close on top of his head like a small, tight-fitting stocking stitch beanie. His ears are hand sized and bright red.

'What am I bid, ladies, gentlemen, for this lovely chocolate cake? Who'll open the bidding?

Made it myself this morning, all the best ingredients.

What do I get, do I hear twenty-five?

Twenty I've got. Thirty I've got.

Forty cents.

Forty-five.

Forty-five. Forty-five. Gone at forty-five to my old pal Charlie, stingy bugger. You'll have to do better than that, mates. Put your hands in your pockets now and what do I get for the coffee cake? Made it and iced it myself this morning. Walnuts on top. Thirty.

I have thirty. Thirty-five here.

Forty-five. Advance on forty-five come on all you cockies, take it home for afternoon tea.

Fifty I have, keep it up friends.

Fifty-five. Sixty, now you're talking.

Sixty-five, sixty-five, seventy.

Seventy again. Seventy for the third time. Sold at seventy and an extra bob for the walnuts, Skippy my boy.

Now this kit of potatoes. What am I bid?'

'Do we keep the kit?' someone calls.

'Did I hear fifty? Fifty? Fifty I've got. Any advance on fifty?'

'Do we keep the kit too?'

'Seventy-five I've got. Come on now, grew them myself this morning. Make it a dollar. A dollar I've got.'

'What about the kit?'

'One dollar fifty I've got. One seventy-five. Make it two. Two we've got. Two once, two twice, two sold. Sorry about the kit darling we need it for the next lot.' He tips the potatoes into her lap and gives the kit to one of his helpers to refill.

'Two geranium plants for the garden. Two good plants. What do I get? Come on Billy Boy, take them home for the wife. Make her sweet.'

'I already got something for that.'

'That's had it man, say it with flowers.'

'I got much better.'

'Skiting bugger. Twenty-five I've got. Thirty I've got. Advance on thirty? Forty. Forty. Forty again. Forty, sold!

Now here's one especially for Turei. Filled sponge decorated with peaches and cream. Come on cook, I'll start you at forty.

Forty cents, ladies, gents, and Charlie, from our friend Turei at the back. And forty-five at the front here, come on, Turei. Sixty?

Sixty. And seventy up front.

Eighty. Ninety.

One dollar from the district's most outstanding hangi

maker and a dollar twenty from the opposition.

One dollar fifty. Two? Two up front. Two fifty from the back. Two fifty, two fifty . . . Three.

Three we have. Come on, friend.

Three fifty. What do you say, Turei?

Five. Five from the back there.

Five once, five twice, five sold. One cream sponge to Turei, the best cook in the district. Thank you, boys.

Time's getting on, friends. What do you say to a leg a mutton, a bunch a silver beet, a jar a pickle, a bag a spuds, there's your dinner. A dollar? Two? Two ten, twenty, fifty, seventy. Two seventy. Two seventy, two seventy, no mucking around, sold.

Another kit of potatoes. I'll take them myself for fifty. Will you let me take them home for fifty? Seventy. Seventy to you, eighty to me. Ninety to you, a dollar to me. Dollar twenty, Okay, one fifty. Let me have them for one fifty? One fifty to me, ladies and gents and Charlie. One seventy-five? Okay, one ninety. Two? Two we have once, two we have twice, two for the third time, sold. All yours, boy, I've got two acres of my own at home.

Here we are, friends, another of these lovely home-made sponges. What do you say, Turei . . . ?'

But Turei is away under the gum tree sharing his cake with a lot of children and his dog.

And back again to summer, with all the children talking about Christmas and holidays, their pockets bulging with ripe plums.

The branches of the pohutukawa are flagged in brilliant red, and three pairs of tuis have arrived with their odd incongruous talking, 'See-saw, Crack, Burr, Ding. See-saw, See-saw, Ding.' By the time they have been there a week they are almost too heavy to fly, their wings beat desperately in flight in order to keep their heavy bodies airborne.

On the last day of school we wait under the pohutukawa for the bus to arrive, and a light wind sends down a shower of nectar which dries on our arms and legs and faces in small white spots.

They scramble into the bus talking and pushing, licking their skins. They heave their belongings under the seats and turn to the windows to wave. Kopu and Samuel who are last in line stand on the bus step and turn.

'Goodbye,' Kopu says, and cracks Sam in the ribs with his elbow.

'Goodbye,' Samuel says and slams his hands down on top of his kina and blushes.

As the bus pulls away we hear singing. Waving hands protrude from the windows on either side. Hippy, Michael and Stan have their heads together at the back window, and Roimata is there too, waving, chewing a pigtail –

> I am a tui bird,
> Up in the pohutukawa tree,
> And a teacher and some children came out
> And stood under my tree,
> And honey rained all over them,
> But I am a tui bird,
> And when I fly
> It sounds like ripping rags.

Smoke Rings

THE CHEQUE ARRIVED THIS MORNING – FORTY-ONE CENTS. Forty-one, that's my money for Athletic Park. It comes at about this time every year, and when I see the brown envelope with the window and all my long names printed on it, I know what it is and I dump it straight into the rubbish bin. Forty-one cents!

I know I could've given it to the kids to take down to the shops and spend, or I could've bought myself a packet of cigarettes. But no, every year when that money arrives I chuck it out, and that's my own way of quietly protesting. Well, who wants it anyway?

Even if I am broke.

I needed a smoke too, and I still do. I've been working hard all morning trying not to think about wanting a cigarette, and trying not to think about how broke I am. But smoke or not, broke or not, I can do without their money, and that's why I tossed the cheque out, envelope and all.

Well it's no wonder I'm broke. We've had George and his crowd for a fortnight, and George and them eat a lot so it's no wonder.

We got a telegram from George from down south the Friday before last; he's my brother. The telegram said, 'Meet Rangatira tomorrow morning George.'

You never know what to expect when you get a telegram from him. Last January we got a message, 'Meet plane two o'clock George.' It was one o'clock when it arrived, so we hurried out to the airport and found one of George's little kids sitting on her bag in tears because we weren't there to meet her – that's George.

Then we got another telegram about two months ago with

the same message, 'Meet plane two o'clock George.' The kids and I were home on our own and Rangi was away fishing somewhere out by Mana Island in a boat. Gee, it cost me four dollars twenty for a taxi to the airport, and when I got there it was a tin of mutton birds. Twenty-two mutton birds sealed in a kerosene tin.

Ah well, one thing about my brother, he always thinks of us when the mutton birds are in season.

But when this last telegram arrived, 'Meet Rangatira tomorrow morning George,' we knew it wouldn't be mutton birds because it was the wrong time of year. We didn't think it would be one of the kids travelling all the way from Gore overland, and then from Christchurch overnight in the Rangatira – though you never know with George.

So we all went down at seven a.m., walked on to the wharf, and there they all were coming down the gangway. All of them.

I stood there and bawled when I saw George and Peka and all the kids getting down off the Rangatira. I hadn't seen my brother and his family for six years. I stood there and bawled.

We squashed them into our car, seven of them with two big suitcases and a carton, Rangi and our three, and me with our fourth all but due, trying to keep my big bulk out of everyone's way.

Then when we arrived home we had to squeeze them all into our house. We cooked up a big breakfast and sat all the kids on the stairs with their plates on their laps. George, Peka, Rangi and I sat round the table to eat and we wagged our tongues until they were ready to drop off. That first night we stayed up all night talking, and most other nights too. It's no wonder I'm tired now they've gone.

These houses here all have inside stairs. We're all propped on the side of the hill with gorse sneaking in through our top fences as soon as our backs are turned. The ones this side of the road have living areas downstairs, and bedrooms, bathroom and toilet upstairs. So every time you need to go to the loo you hike up the stairs, which isn't so good when you're in this condition and needing to go every half-hour. But it's good here, we like it. We'll buy this place one day, later on, when we get rich.

We took them sight-seeing all round Wellington. Round the hills and all the bays. And we showed them Parliament and the fountain, the buildings, the Terrace, the Quay, the Basin, the park. And George put his head out of the window when we got to Athletic Park and yelled out, 'See that blade of grass in the middle there, that's mine.'

The kids were all proud of him for owning some of Athletic Park. But when he said that, it reminded me about the money.

'Now I know why you're so rich,' I said. 'You been saving all your cheques from your land.'

And George blew his cool. 'Forty-one bloody cents. I wouldn't use it for toilet paper. I wouldn't wipe my bum on it.'

And Peka pointed out that it wouldn't be big enough for that anyway, not with the size of George's fat bum.

And then George mentioned that, well, he'd put it up someone's one of these days and that it wouldn't be before time, and the kids were all proud of him.

Rangi's just as bad as George. If it hadn't been for Rangi I'd never have thought of throwing the cheque away in the first place, I mean who knows? But that's Rangi. Big ideas. He thinks a lot.

And now here I am scrubbing, polishing, washing, cleaning, sweating, making myself sore and tired, just so I can fill up the emptiness from having them all gone.

Ah well, my house is clean and shiny. Everything's done. Bathroom shines, washing's out, floors and windows sparkling. The whole place is like a telly advert for liquid something.

And I could sit down and put my inflated legs up if . . . but keep on, it's the only thing to do. Upstairs, one foot dragging after the other. Out the back door, four leaden steps to the line. All dry. Pull out the pegs and let them drop. Usually there is some pleasure in this bringing in of bright sheets and warm dry clothes, but not today. Arms and back aching. Legs swollen. Body as heavy as a kit of pipis.

And there on the edge of vision the incinerator. Papers need burning but no matches. Two steps away . . . but I pull the basket behind me. Inside and start folding. Plug in the iron and spread the cloth over the table, I could lay my head on it and sleep. Sheets in one pile, towels, underwear, shirts . . .

Or I could leave it and . . .

But no, shirts, underwear, tea-towels, socks. I could . . .

I see my hand go out slowly, the switch goes up. Two hands now, folding the cloth in half, in half again. Then my pumped-up legs take me slowly towards the door. Hand on the handle. Turn. Open. Out.

Four uphill steps, legs wobble. Change direction, two more steps and begin scratching the papers aside – Weetbix box, Purex roll, plastic container, supermarket bag, ripped-up beer carton, envelope. My hand takes up the envelope and I drift towards the house like the girl on telly who bites chocolate and is wafted through mists, over hills and streams, dressed in a plume of . . . smoke. Hurry. Comb through hair, go to the loo, sandals, downstairs, out.

Stepping out the Crescent in full sail, the envelope warm in my hand and all my long names looking out through its window.

Pre-schools out on their trikes. Brrrm, brrrm, faces clamped in concentration. Wheels spinning. Or do they stand. Still. Is the reeling, wheeling, spinning in my head.

'Where you going?'

'Shop.'

'What for?'

'Smokes.'

'Hey you kids, hey you kids, you know what. She's going to the shop. She's getting smokes.'

Why not? Rangi and his big ideas. Power poles, spiking skyward, two more poles to go. Rolling forward on pneumatic legs. So what if George (one more pole) wouldn't (almost there) wipe his (there and in) bum.

Take it from the envelope and put it on the counter. That's

the worst of having a husband and a brother with big ideas. The till rings.

Out again, the box fitting the palm of my hand, hot slime feel of cellophane. Drop the one cent change into a pocket and step the Crescent in reverse. George wouldn't expect . . . flesh and blood . . . for want of a fag . . .

'Where you going?'

'Home.'

'What for?'

'Smoke.'

'Hey you kids, hey you kids, you know what . . .'

Quickly home, inside and up the stairs, go to the loo, sandals off, turn the element on high and rip the cellophane open. Lean over the reddening coil and draw in, draw in. Mouth fills. Swallow. I walk into the sitting room, smoke seeping from my nose and mouth. Ears . . . Eyes . . .

I lay back with my feet up, puffing and blowing, room spinning. Poof, I go; one for Rangi. Poof; one for George. Poof, poof; two for me.

Then I get up and walk about the room blowing streamers in every direction. Big ideas.

I blow a double smoke ring out of my eyeballs, my hand finds my pocket and turns the one cent over for good luck.

Parade

YESTERDAY I WENT WITH HOANI, LENA, AND THE LITTLE ones up along the creek where the bush begins, to cut fern and flax. Back there at the quiet edge of the bush with the hills rolling skyward and the sound of the sea behind me I was glad I had come home in response to Auntie's letter. It was easy, there, to put aside the heaviness of spirit which had come upon me during the week of carnival. It was soothing to follow with my eyes the spreading circles of fern patterning the hills' sides, and good to feel the coolness of flax and to realise again the quiet strength of each speared leaf. It was good to look into the open-throated flax blooms with their lit-coal colours, and to put a hand over the swollen black splitting pods with the seed heavy in them.

And I thought of how each pod would soon cast aside its heaviness and become a mere shell, warped and empty, while that which had been its own heaviness would become new life. New growth and strength.

As we carried the bundles of fern and flax that we had collected and put them into the creek to keep fresh for the morning I was able to feel that tomorrow, the final day of the carnival, would be different from the ones recently passed when realisation had come to me, resting in me like stone.

'Please come for the carnival,' Auntie's letter had said. And the letter from my little cousin Ruby: 'Please come, Matewai. We haven't seen you for two years.' I had felt excitement in me at the thought of returning, being back with them. And I came for the carnival as they had asked.

It was easy this morning to feel a lightness of spirit, waking to a morning so warm and full-scented, with odours rising to the nostrils as though every morning comes from inside the earth. Rich damp smells drenched every grass blade, every seeded stalk, and every cluster of ragwort, thistle and black-berry. Steaming up through the warming rosettes of cow dung. Stealing up the stems of lupin and along the lupin arms, out on to the little spread hands of lupin leaves.

And a sweet wood smell coming from the strewn chips and wood stack by the shed. A tangle of damp stinks from the fowl-yard and orchard, and from the cold rustiness of the cow-holed swamp. Some of the earth morning smells had become trapped under the hot bodies of cows, and were being dispensed, along with the cows' own milk and saliva smells, from the swinging bellies and milk-filled udders as the animals made their way poke-legged to the milking sheds. That was what it was like this morning.

And there was a breath of sea. Somewhere – barely dis-cernible since evening had been long forgotten and the night had been shrugged aside – somewhere the sea was casting its breath at the land. It was as though it were calling to the land, and to us as we woke and walked into the day, 'I'm here, I'm here. Don't forget about me.'

The sun fingered the ridges of hills as we pulled the flax and fern from the creek and began to decorate the truck for the parade. We worked quickly, tying and nailing the fronds and leaves into place. And when we had finished, Uncle Hirini drove the truck in under some trees where the sun could not reach it, while we went inside to change into our costumes.

Auntie had sent all the children to wash in the creek, and as I watched them from the window it was like seeing myself as I had been not very long ago. As if it were my own innocence that they cast on to the willow branches with their clothes. Light had filtered through the willow branches on to the creek's surface, spreading in small pools to the creek banks and on to the patches of watercress and shafts of reed.

The sun had put a finger on almost everything by now. It had touched our houses and the paddocks and tree tops, and stroked its silver over the sea. The beach stones were warming from the sun's touching, and black weed, thrown up by the sea, lay in heaps on the shore drying and helpless in the sun's relentless stroking.

I watched the bodies falling into water warmed from the sun's touching, and fingers, not his, squeezing at large bars of yellow soap. Fingers spreading blistery trails of suds up and over legs and arms. Bodies, heads, ears. 'Wash your taringas.' Auntie from the creek bank. Backsides, frontsides, fingers, toes. Then splashing, diving, puffing and blowing in this pool of light. Out on to the banks, rubbing with towels, wrapping the towels around, scrambling back through the willows, across the yard where the sun caught them for a moment before they ran inside to dress. It was like seeing myself as I had been such a short time ago.

Auntie stood back on the heels of her bare feet, puffing at a cigarette, and looking at me through half shut eyes. Her round head was nodding at me, her long hair which she had brushed out of the two thick plaits which usually circled her head fell about her shoulders, and two more hanks of hair glistened under her armpits. The skin on her shoulders and back was pale in its unaccustomed bareness, cream coloured and cool looking. And there was Granny Rita stretching lips over bare gums to smile at me.

'Very pretty, dia. Very pretty, dia,' she kept saying, stroking the cloak that they had put on me, her old hands aged and grey like burnt paper. The little ones admiring, staring.

Setting me apart.

And I stood before them in the precious cloak, trying to smile.

'I knew our girl would come,' Auntie was saying again. 'I knew our girl would come if we sent for her.'

We could hear the truck wheezing out in the yard, and Grandpa Hohepa who is bent and crabby was hurrying everyone along, banging his stick on the floor. 'Kia tere,' he kept on saying. 'Kia tere.'

The men helped Granny Rita and Grandpa Hohepa on to the truck and sat them where they could see, then I stepped on to the platform which had been erected for me and sat down for the journey into town. The others formed their lines along each side of the tray and sat down too.

In town, in the heat of late morning, we moved slowly with the other parade floats along the streets lined with people. Past the railway station and shops, and over bridges and crossings, singing one action song after another. Hakas and pois.

And as I watched I noted again, as I had on the other carnival days of concerts and socials, the crowd reaction. I tried not to think. Tried not to let my early morning feelings leave me. Tried not to know that there was something different and strange in the people's reaction to us. And yet I knew this was not something new and strange, but only that during my time away from here my vision and understanding had expanded. I was able now to see myself and other members of my race as others see us. And this new understanding left me as abandoned and dry as an emptied pod of flax that rattles and rattles into the wind.

Everyone was clapping and cheering for Uncle Hirini and my cousin Hoani who kept jumping from the truck to the road, patterning with their taiaha, springing on their toes and doing the pukana, making high pipping noises with their voices. Their tongues lolled and their eyes popped.

But it was as though my uncle and Hoani were a pair of clowns. As though they wore frilled collars and had paint on their noses, and kept dropping baggy pants to display spotted underwear and sock suspenders. As though they turned cartwheels and hit each other on the head, while someone else banged on a tin to show everyone that clowns have tin heads.

And the people's reaction to the rest of us? The singing, the pois? I could see enjoyment on the upturned faces and yet it occurred to me again and again that many people enjoyed zoos. That's how I felt. Animals in cages to be stared at. This one with stripes, this one with spots – or a trunk, or bad breath, the remains of a third eye. Talking, swinging by the tail, walking in circles, laughing, crying, having babies.

Or museums. Stuffed birds, rows of shells under glass, the wing span of an albatross, preserved bodies, shrunken heads.

Empty gourds, and meeting houses where no one met any more.

I kept thinking and trying not to think, 'Is that what we are to them?' Museum pieces, curios, antiques, shells under glass. A travelling circus, a floating zoo. People clapping and cheering to show that they know about such things.

The sun was hot. Auntie at the end of the row was beaming, shining, as though she were the sun. A happy sun, smiling and singing to fill the whole world with song. And with her were all the little sunlets singing too, and stamping. Arms out, fingers to the heart, fists clenched, hands open, head to one side, face the front. Piupius swinging, making their own music, pois bobbing. And voices calling the names of the canoes – Tainui, Takitimu, Kurahaupo, Te Arawa . . . the little ones in the front bursting with the fullness of their own high voices and their dancing hands and stamping feet, unaware that the crowd had put us under glass and that our uncle and cousin with their rolling eyes and prancing feet wore frilled collars and size nineteen shoes and had had pointed hats clapped down upon their heads.

Suddenly I felt a need to reach out to my auntie and uncle, to Hoani and the little ones, to old Rita and Hohepa.

We entered the sports ground, and when the truck stopped the little ones scrambled down and ran off to look for their mates from school. Auntie and Hoani helped Granny Rita and Grandpa Hohepa down. I felt older than any of them.

And it was hot. The sun threw down his spinnings of heat and weavings of light on to the cracked summer earth as we walked towards the pavilion.

'Do you ever feel as though you're in a circus?' I said to Hoani who is the same age as I am. He flipped onto his hands and walked the rest of the way upside down. I had a feeling Hoani knew what I was talking about.

Tea. Tea and curling sandwiches. Slabs of crumbling fruit cake, bottles of blood-warm fizz, and someone saying, 'What're you doing in that outfit?' Boys from cousin Lena's school.

'Didn't you see us on the truck?' Lena was saying.

'Yeh, we saw.' One of the boys had Lena's poi and was swinging it round and round and making aeroplane noises.

Mr Goodwin, town councillor, town butcher, touching Uncle Hirini's shoulder and saying, 'Great, great,' to show what a great person he himself was, being one of the carnival organisers and having lived in the township all his life amongst dangling sausages, crescents of black pudding, leg roasts, rib roasts, flannelled tripe, silverside, rolled beef, cutlets, dripping. 'Great.' He was Great. You could tell by the prime steak hand on Uncle's shoulder.

Uncle Hirini believed the hand. Everyone who saw the hand believed it too, or so it seemed to me. They were all believers on days such as these.

And the woman president of the CWI shouting at Granny Rita as though Granny were deaf or simple. Granny Rita nodding her head, waiting for the woman to go away so she could eat her cake.

It was stuffy and hot in the hall with the stale beer and smoke smell clinging to its walls and floor, and to the old chipped forms and sagging trestle tables. Bird dirt, spider webs, mice droppings. The little ones had had enough to eat and were running up and down with their mates from school, their piupius swinging and clacking about their legs. Auntie rounding them all up and whispering to go outside. Auntie on her best behaviour wishing those kids would get out and stop shaming her. Wanting to yell, 'Get out you kids. Get outside and play. You spoil those piupius and I'll whack your bums.' Auntie sipping tea and nibbling at a sandwich.

We began to collect the dishes. Squashed raisins, tea dregs. The men were stacking the trestles and shifting forms. Mrs President put her hands into the soapy water and smiled at the ceiling, smiled to show what sort of day it was. 'Many hands make light work,' she sang out. We reached for towels, we reached for wet plates to prove how right she was.

Outside, people were buying and selling, guessing weights and stepping chains, but I went to where Granny Rita and

Grandpa Hohepa were sitting in the shade of a tree, guarding the cloak between them.

More entertainment. The lines were forming again but I sat down by old Rita and Hohepa out of the sun's heat.

'Go,' Granny Rita was saying to me. 'Take your place.'

'I think I'll watch this time, Nanny.'

'You're very sad today, dia. Very sad.'

Granny Rita's eyes pricking at my skin. Old Hohepa's too.

'It's hot, Nanny.'

A crowd had gathered to watch the group and the singing had begun, but those two put their eyes on me, waiting for me to speak.

'They think that's all we're good for,' I said. 'A laugh and that's all. Amusement. In any other week of the year we don't exist. Once a year we're taken out and put on show, like relics.'

And silence.

Silence with people laughing and talking.

Silence with the singing lifting skyward, and children playing.

Silence. Waiting for them to say something to me. Wondering what they would say.

'You grow older, you understand more,' Granny Rita said to me.

Silence and waiting.

'No one can take your eyes from you,' she said. Which is true.

Then old Hohepa, who is bent and sometimes crabby, said, 'It is your job, this. To show others who we are.'

And I sat there with them for a long time. Quiet. Realising what had been put upon me. Then I went towards the group and took my place, and began to stamp my feet on to the cracked earth, and to lift my voice to the sun who holds the earth's strength within himself.

And gradually the sun withdrew his touch and the grounds began to empty, leaving a flutter of paper, trampled heads of dandelion and clover, and insects finding a way into the sticky sweet necks of empty bottles.

The truck had been in the sun all afternoon. The withered

curling fern and drooping flax gave it the appearance of a scaly monster, asleep and forgotten, left in a corner to die. I helped Granny Rita into the cab beside Grandpa Hohepa.

'This old bum gets too sore on those hard boards. This old bum wants a soft chair for going home. Ah lovely, dia. Move your fat bum ova, Hepa.' The old parched hand on my cheek. 'Not to worry, dia, not to worry.'

And on the back of the truck we all moved close together against the small chill that evening had brought in. Through the town's centre then along the blackening roads. On into the night until the road ended. Opening gates, closing them. Crossing the dark paddocks with the hills dense on one hand, the black patch of sea on the other. And the only visible thing the narrow rind of foam curling shoreward under a sky emptied of light. Listening, I could hear the shuffle of water on stone, and rising above this were the groans and sighs of a derelict monster with his scales withered and dropping, making his short-sighted way through prickles and fern, over cow pats and stinging nettle, along fence lines, past the lupin bushes, their fingers crimped against the withdrawal of the day.

I took in a big breath, filling my lungs with sea and air and land and people. And with past and present and future, and felt a new strength course through me. I lifted my voice to sing and heard and felt the others join with me. Singing loudly into the darkest of nights. Calling on the strength of the people. Calling them to paddle the canoes and to paddle on and on. To haul the canoes down and paddle. On and on –

> Hoea ra nga waka
> E te iwi e,
> Hoea hoea ra,
> Aotea, Tainui, Kurahaupo,
> Hoea hoea ra.
>
> Toia mai nga waka
> E te iwi e,
> Hoea hoea ra,

Mataatua, Te Arawa,
Takitimu, Tokomaru,
Hoea hoea ra.'

THE
DREAM SLEEPERS
and
Other Stories

Contents

The Dream Sleepers

THE HOUSES SIT ON THEIR HANDKERCHIEFS, AND EARLY IN the morning begin to sneeze. They do not sneeze in unison but one at a time, or sometimes in pairs or threes, sometimes in tens or dozens. The footpaths and roads beyond the borders of the handkerchiefs quicken with the aftermath of sneezing.

The very earliest were the silent ones, quiet light tracing their movements from bedrooms, past sleepers who had not yet begun to dream their waking-up dreams, to bathrooms, to kitchens. The lights went out behind them, noiseless doors shut as they made their ways to the pick-up points, or got into taxis that would take them to the trains.

Juliet's mother was one of the three o'clockers. She hoped Bill would hear the alarm at six, and that Juliet would be ready for school and have breakfast ready by the time she got back at eight. Francie's grandmother was one, she hoped they would all get the jobs done quickly at work this morning, and that Elaine would empty the Hoover and wipe the chair legs without being told. Junior's sister was one, and she wanted someone she didn't yet know, to love her.

Juliet's mother and Francie's grandmother knotted their headscarves under their chins, turned their jacket collars up and walked together to the pick-up point. Junior's sister hurried to catch up to them thinking that they were old women and that they sometimes told her not to go on her own down the subway. But she enjoyed sitting in the van with them, smoking and listening to them have the driver on. Their gossip was good, and if she had a party she would invite them to it.

The five o'clockers were the next ones, a little less silent, putting lights on and off and turning on music. Putting the jug on and heating up food if there was time. But still, the sleepers, the ones who would eventually get to dreaming, had not yet arrived at that time. Some of the babies were awake already, mewing for food and dry clothes.

Neville woke his mother and put the baby's bottle in the jug to warm before he left for the delivery round. Dean's sister walked to the mall dairy where she made sandwiches until seven, and Pele's brother met Neville at the bus stop and they ran together to the corner where they could see the truck already on its way up the hill.

At seven the dream sleepers began flickering their eyelids, but the eight o'clock starters were already out on the footpaths, or in cars or buses. The lights of the street had just gone out.

At eight Juliet poured tea for her mother then went into the bedroom where she tied her cardigan round her waist making a large knot on her stomach with the ends of the sleeves, and letting the rest hang down like an apron over her backside. She toed her way into a pair of jandals and went across to meet Francie.

Francie was wearing a denim cap that she had snatched from Pele the day before. Her grandmother was seeing them all off to school before going back to bed, and her father had just got up for ten o'clock start. She and Juliet went to the dairy for chippies and gum.

Pele wanted the hat back but not because it was his. He had pulled the hat from Junior's pocket earlier in the week, and now he needed it to cover up his haircut. He sat on the footpath to wait for Francie, or someone with a hat. He could see Neville and Dean coming and they were going to be smart about his hair. They were pushing Valerie to school in her wheelchair.

'Hey you, Pele, you got a kina.'

'Who said?'

'Man I can see. I got eyes.'

'So what?'

'So you got a kina, Pele boy.'

'Smart you. Fif former.'

A dog came to sniff at him so he sat it down by him to wait. He hoped Francie and Juliet hadn't gone past already, but he thought they would be at the shops buying chippies and chewing gum. There were kids everywhere, and dogs. His dog ran away to watch a fight. It stood in the middle of the road with its ears up; a bus nosed up to it so it sidled away.

'Francie, Francie. Give us the hat.'

'Nah. It's not yours, Pele.'

'Give it, Francie.'

'Do you want some chippies, Pele?'

'No I want the hat.'

'What for?'

'I want it.'

'Who gave you the kina, Pele?'

'My sister, so what?'

'So take the hat then.'

'I got some smokes, Francie.'

'Any matches?'

'We can run after Junior for some matches.'

'So a business letter is more formal, isn't it, than a letter to a friend? What do you think that word means – "formal"? If you got an invitation to a ball or something and your invitation said "Dress formal", how would you dress?'

'Dress up.'

'Yes?'

'Dress up in your good things.'

'Right. How would the boys dress?'

'Suits and all that.'

'Ties.'

'Like poofters.'

'Church clothes.'

'Hair cut like Pele. Hey Pele, you sucker.'

'Okay. What about the girls?'

'Long skirts and . . . '

'Beads and that.'

'And platforms and fur coats.'

'All right. What about "informal"?'

'Jeans and jandals.'

'T-shirts.'

'Good, you've got the idea. Now about letters. Last week we did the sort of letter you would write to a friend – an informal letter. Now today . . .'

Today there were concrete block walls and holes in the lino just as there had been the day before. Sparrows had been in shitting on the ledges and there was a door somewhere that kept slamming. Va was passing sparkles to Nga, and Peter had nearly finished drawing the snake that coiled round and round from the back of his hand to his elbow. There was an old moustache on the poster of Elvis but the blacked-out tooth was new and so were the pencil holes in the eyes.

'So there you are. Your address, top right-hand corner. Business address – "The Personnel Officer, New World Supermarket", et cetera – below on the left . . .'

'Buy a bigga blocka cheese . . .'

'Then below that, "Dear Sir" . . .'

'How a-are ya?'

'Then you start . . .'

'I'm all ri-ight.'

'All right, no more nonsense, get on with it. Pele, you shouldn't be wearing that hat in class, should you?'

'Sir, he can't help it his sister gave him a Kojak.'

'There's still plenty of hair on his head.'

'She gave him a kina.'

'All right, come on now, you've got fifteen minutes before lunch. I'll come round and help anyone who needs it.'

('Dear Sir, I am a fourteen-year-old girl and I would like . . . *to be allowed down to the town centre on late shopping nights.*'

'I saw your advertisement in the paper . . . *and today is like yesterday.*'

'I am reliable and I work hard and I . . . *can sing and dance.*'

'I am a boy aged fourteen . . . *and for lunch I'll buy two doughnuts, a coffee bun, and a Coke.*'

'I would like a job for the holidays . . . *and my mother will die soon.*'

'I can come to an interview . . . *Then she walked away*
Quietly so afraid
Smiling
But no doubt
Crying
Her heart out
. . .'

'Yours faithfully . . . *Crying*
Her heart out
She really just wants
To stay . . .')

'The bell, sir.'

'I know.'

'We don't want to be last down the canteen.'

'I've got to go home and put the meat in . . .'

'All right, we'll have a look at those again tomorrow.'

Tomorrow there would be corridors to walk and steps to go down just as there were today. There'd be a group in the courtyard playing kick square, someone walking on the roof, and people waiting in rows in the canteen. There'd be more pie and doughnut bags to step on or over, and there'd be a swing door somewhere slamming back and forth. There'd be another message or two to read on the concrete block walls, and perhaps one to write. There was one to be written if only you could know what it was.

'So now just copy down that section into your books where it says "Our Heritage", showing all the things that have been handed down to us by the people of Ancient Greece, on page sixteen.'

'What for?'

'Why do we have to copy it down?'

'Who's that calling out? Page sixteen – if you work quickly

and quietly you'll get it finished by the time the bell goes.'

'What for? If we want to read about it we can read out of this book here. We don't have to write it all out.'

'I asked you not to call out, and if you have time you can draw a picture of one of these urns here, on page eighteen, or these coins at the bottom of the page . . .'

'It's a waste of time.'

'Now look I've had enough of this calling out, you're the one who's wasting time. Get started or you'll still be here when the bell goes.'

'Not me, I start work at four . . .'

'Not me either, I'm going home to get ready . . .'

'And that boy there, Pele, get that hat off.'

'He can't, miss, he's sister gave him a kina.'

'Now you heard me, get it off, you're supposed to be in uniform. That's not part of your uniform . . .'

'But miss, we all haven't . . .'

'None of us is in uniform.'

'See Juliet with her jandals on and Va with a T-shirt and Junior with a green jersey . . .'

'Besides, it's very bad manners, now get it off.'

'Who said it's bad manners?'

'Hey Pele boy, you got bad manners.'

'No I hafn't, I got a kina.'

'Hey Pele, you forgot to say "Peel-eeze".'

'You forgot to say "Tha-ank you".'

'Now stop all this nonsense. None of you have got any manners whatsoever, and I'm waiting for you, Pele, to get that hat off.'

'He can't, miss, it's stuck on his head.'

'He's whole head'll come off, miss.'

'Hey, miss, it's nearly bell time.'

'Come here, Pele. I'm going to see Mr Sutton about you in a minute.'

'What for, miss?'

'For being rude and ill-mannered, now give me that hat.'

'I hafn't got it, miss.'

Because he has taken it off and passed it behind him to Juliet who passed it back to George. George toed it across to Francie who stared at the wall and passed it to Nga who passed it to Va.

'Well where is it, what did you do with it?'

'I don't know, miss, it's gone.'

'Don't you lie to me, you've given it to someone. Where is it, Juliet?'

'I don't know, miss.'

'Now someone in this room has got it and whoever it is had better own up very quickly.'

And Va passed it to Peter, who passed it to Junior, who sits by the door.

'Well, I've had enough of this class and its rudeness and nonsense, and no one is leaving this room until I get that hat . . .'

'Except me, I'm going to work at four . . .'

'Except no one, now you can all just sit there and . . .'

'And I'm catching the bus . . .'

'All right I'll wait, and you'll all wait. No one leaves this room until I find out who's got the hat . . .'

People of Ancient Greece had ideas and coins and urns and acting and poetry, and messages on walls. Wall messages told truths, and you could look there if you wanted to know what was in your mind and heart. A door was slamming to and fro, and in the corridor Neville was trundling Valerie along to get her down the steps before three o'clock. Junior opened the door and tossed the hat.

'What are you doing, who said you could open the door? No one's to move until I get the hat, and I'm going to see Mr Sutton about this class . . .'

'Hey miss, the bell's gone . . .'

'No one's to move and no one's leaving this room . . .'

'Except me . . .'

'And me . . .'

'I go to work at four . . .'

'I catch the bus . . .'

'I watch telly and I peel potatoes . . .'
'I go to Peter's for a smoke . . .'
'We go to "Friendship" . . .'
'We go on a truck to collect rags and paper . . .'
'There's going to be trouble over this, you'll all be in trouble, the whole class . . .'

And I run to catch up to Neville and Valerie, running down the steps, jumping three at the bottom, fast past the parked cars and down the drive. Valerie has long white hair but her neck's on one side and her legs are no good.

'Vala-rie, Vala-rie, I want the hat back.'
'You look neat, Pele, with your haircut.'
'Give us it, Valerie.'
'But you look neat, Pele, ay Neville?'
'He looks like a kina.'
'Give me it, Valerie.'
'Take it then, get it off my head.'
'Hey Valerie, hey Neville and Dean, you want a smoke?'
'Have you got matches?'
'Junior's got matches.'
'You wait for Junior then catch us up.'
'Hey dog, hey dog, come here and wait by me.'

Between Earth and Sky

I WALKED OUT OF THE HOUSE THIS MORNING AND STRETCHED my arms out wide. Look, I said to myself. Because I was alone except for you. I don't think you heard me.

Look at the sky, I said.

Look at the green earth.

How could it be that I felt so good? So free? So full of the sort of day it was? How?

And at that moment, when I stepped from my house, there was no sound. No sound at all. No bird call, or tractor grind. No fire crackle or twig snap. As though the moment had been held quiet, for me only, as I stepped out into the morning. Why the good feeling, with a lightness in me causing my arms to stretch out and out? How blue, how green, I said into the quiet of the moment. But why, with the sharp nick of bone deep in my back and the band of flesh tightening across my belly?

All alone. Julie and Tamati behind me in the house, asleep, and the others over at the swamp catching eels. Riki two paddocks away cutting up a tree he'd felled last autumn.

I started over the paddocks towards him then, slowly, on these heavy knotted legs. Hugely across the paddocks I went almost singing. Not singing because of needing every breath, but with the feeling of singing. Why, with the deep twist and pull far down in my back and cramping between the legs? Why the feeling of singing?

How strong and well he looked. How alive and strong, stooping over the trunk steadying the saw. I'd hated him for days, and now suddenly I loved him again but didn't know why. The saw cracked through the tree setting little splinters of warm wood hopping. Balls of mauve smoke lifted into the air. When he looked up I put my hands to my back and saw him understand me over the skirl of the saw. He switched off, the sound fluttered away.

I'll get them, he said.

We could see them from there, leaning into the swamp, feeling for eel holes. Three long whistles and they looked up and started towards us, wondering why, walking reluctantly.

Mummy's going, he said.

We nearly got one, Turei said. Ay Jimmy, ay Patsy, ay Reuben?

Yes, they said.

Where? said Danny.

I began to tell him again, but he skipped away after the others. It was good to watch them running and shouting through the grass. Yesterday their activity and noise had angered me, but today I was happy to see them leaping and shouting through the long grass with the swamp mud drying and caking on their legs and arms.

Let Dad get it out, Reuben turned, was calling. He can get the lambs out. Bang! Ay Mum, ay?

Julie and Tamati had woken. They were coming to meet us, dragging a rug.

Not you again, they said, taking my bag from his hand.

Not you two again, I said. Rawhiti and Jones.

Don't you have it at two o'clock.

We go off at two.

Your boyfriends can wait.

Our sleep can't.

I put my cheek to his and felt his arm about my shoulders.

Look after my wife, he was grinning at them.

Course, what else.

Go on. Get home and milk your cows, next time you see her she'll be in two pieces.

I kissed all the faces poking from the car windows then stood back on the step waving. Waving till they'd gone. Then turning felt the rush of water.

Quick, I said. The water.

Water my foot; that's piddle.

What you want to piddle in our neat corridor for? Sit down. Have a ride.

Helped into a wheelchair and away, careering over the brown lino.

Stop, I'll be good. Stop, I'll tell Sister.

Sister's busy.

No wonder you two are getting smart. Stop . . .

That's it, missus, you'll be back in your bikini by summer. Dr McIndoe.

And we'll go water-skiing together. Me.

Right you are. Well, see you both in the morning.

The doors bump and swing.

Sister follows.

Finish off, girls. Maitland'll be over soon.

All right, Sister.

Yes, Sister. Reverently.

The doors bump and swing.

You are at the end of the table, wet and grey. Blood stains your pulsing head. Your arms flail in these new dimensions and your mouth is a circle that opens and closes as you scream for air. All head and shoulders and wide mouth screaming. They have clamped the few inches of cord which is all that is left of your old life now. They draw mucus and bathe your head.

Leave it alone and give it here, I say.

What for? Haven't you got enough kids already?

Course. Doesn't mean you can boss that one around.

We should let you clean your own kid up?

Think she'd be pleased after that neat ride we gave her. Look at the little hoha. God he can scream.

They wrap you in linen and put you here with me.

Well anyway, here you are. He's all fixed, you're all done. We'll blow. And we'll get them to bring you a cuppa. Be good.

The doors swing open.

She's ready for a cuppa, Freeman.

The doors bump shut.

Now. You and I. I'll tell you. I went out this morning. Look, I said, but didn't know why. Why the good feeling. Why, with the nick and press of bone deep inside. But now I know. Now I'll tell you and I don't think you'll mind. It wasn't the thought of knowing you and having you here close to me that gave me this glad feeling, that made me look upwards and all about as I stepped out this morning. The gladness was because at last I was to be free. Free from that great hump that was you, free from the aching limbs and swelling that was you. That was why this morning each stretching of flesh made me glad.

And freedom from the envy I'd felt, watching him these past days, stepping over the paddocks whole and strong. Unable to match his step. Envying his bright striding. But I could love him again this morning.

These were the reasons each gnarling of flesh made me glad as I came out into that cradled moment. Look at the sky, look at the earth, I said. See how blue, how green. But I gave no thought to you.

And now. You sleep. How quickly you have learned this quiet and rhythmic breathing. Soon they'll come and put a cup in my hand and take you away.

You sleep, and I too am tired, after our work. We worked hard you and I and now we'll sleep. Be close. We'll sleep a little while ay, you and I.

Mirrors

S O OUT UNDER A HANGING SKY WITH MY NECK IN DANGER
from the holes in my slippers. Hey slippers. Watch out now,
we've both seen younger days remember. Hurry me down to
the end of the drive for the milk. Milk. Then turn me and we'll
scuff back inside together to where the heater's plugged,
pressing a patch of warmth into the corner where I'll sit with
my back to the window, drinking tea. By gee.

Woke early this morning into shouldered silence with light
just signing in, and thought how it was, how it could be, to sit
silent in a silent house, in a warm corner drinking tea. Just me.

Or instead, I thought, I could as usual sleep. And wake in
an hour to the foot thuds and voice noise. Doors and drawers,
and perhaps with his arm reaching to turn me towards him.
But my feet made up my mind. Poking from under the covers
ready to find the floor, dangling. Two limp fillets of cod. How
did you get like that, feet? That shape, that colour – haven't
seen you since the summer and don't know you lately. We
found the floor and poked you into these two grinners, or
gaspers. Shuffled to the wardrobe for a gown and then to the
bathroom to wash.

Six drops no more, and only to keep the record straight.
Because I nag them in the mornings. In the mornings I issue
lists – to flush the toilet, to wash, to comb. Not to swing on
chairs, to grab, eat like pigs, fight. But none of that this early
morning. No lists, no nagging. This next half hour's mine.
Only six I promise, a quick flick is all.

Into the kitchen. Plug the heater, plug the jug. What shall
it be, coffee or tea? What do you say slippers? – your tongues
hang out like mine.

Yes tea, but you see, no milk.

Can't spoil the cup for want of. Milk. And it'll only take a moment, unplug the jug. Step quietly, sleep has ears remember. Trip me and it'll be the end of you two I promise, trippers. Turn handle and out. Out under a sky filled and sagging.

Dog next door is up before me and in a bad mood this morning. Anyway I don't want to talk to him, I'm hurrying. He turns his back and huffs, snuffing the ground, big-footing through silvered grass and scaring a bird. That was perhaps finding a snail to take and knock on stone. Leaving little specked brown shell pieces splintered on rock, and the morsel gone.

And cat prints ahead of me too. Cautious stars in the soft soil where the garden begins – she's dug a hole there perhaps, somewhere among the rusting silver beet and the holed cabbages. Somewhere in the early hours she excreted precisely, covered, and walked away. Perhaps. After roaming the darkness, pressing out soft stars on to the whole length and breadth of the night, that's right. Eyes specked like cut onion.

Quickly now. And remember I've come only for want of a few drops. Of milk. So I'll keep my mind on it. The corner waits warm and quiet. A nudge of a switch will set the jug uttering. So go. No time for star gazing. Get flapping, flappers, it'll rain. See how the sky reaches down. See its uncertainty – there a rinsing-water colour that's not the telly ad kind with *diamanté* bubbles rising and good enough to drink, but which is the real kind, yes. From the tub full of jeans, or load of jerseys and socks – and there, shot through with green, brown, black and purple. Growing and shrinking. Pocked and pimpled like mould. And I will sit warm listening to it, alone, the rain plunging, if I hurry. In a warm corner with my throat scalded by the flowing of hot liquid.

Here now, and I can reach into the box. For milk. Turn my back and go. No need this morning to look past the gate, over the road to the sea, to see, to determine its mood, find out about the island. They'll both be there mid-morning, tomorrow, next year, so go. But no, the gulls rise screaming.

See how they beat their wings into the wind this morning, their legs dangle useless like shreds of red or yellow balloon before they tuck them out of sight.

And now my eyes are spiked, winkled out from their sockets on bright pins, and swivelling. See how the horizon is buckled by the waves' leaping, and how the waves ride in bumper to bumper each side of the island, then forget which way to go. Face each other snarling. Pounce and fall back, chop and slap.

Kung Fu Fighting,
Yes, Yes,
Kung Fu Fighting,
Yes, Yes.

The island like the old dog grouching, in a bad mood this morning.

But nearer to shore the waves remember and reassemble, find the right curve and come gnashing in like great grinning mouthfuls of teeth. Heaping wads of weed on to the shore and tossing out white sticks. And further along they climb stacked rocks and splinter into marbled drops, wind hanging, then slow motion falling. Fingering in over ledges and into crevices, then evacuating as small stones roll and spin.

And this afternoon the children will walk there, take up the white sticks and stir the weed heaps to spark the small firework displays of leaping sand fleas.

They'll turn the tessellating stones for sticky fish which will play dead even after being pressed quite firmly with prising thumbs. They'll look into the rioting water for new things because once there was a netted glass ball from Japan, and once a bag of drowned cats, and once a corked bottle which could have contained a message but didn't. Once there was a condom floating, rim upward, which didn't look so out of place really and could have been a herring or a cod, open mouthed, coming to the surface to feed.

And they'll yell out over the water I wish it was summer.
I want to come in.
Wish it was summer.

I wish.

Summer.

I want I want.

I wish.

And they'll see their words curl in under the waves' furl and watch the words hurled back fragmented at their feet retreating.

And now there is the first drop, on the back of my hand as I turn. Hurry now. Safely do you hear. Next door's plum has one white flower and twig ends groaning. She'll be home tomorrow with her new baby and a bagful of black knitting.

I'm going, she'd yelled. But I came back for my knitting. And she had waved a plastic bag of needles and black skeins. So this minute while others sit in bed making white shells and fans, and loop up row upon row of holes in two-ply on twelves, she turns out an enormous black jersey cabled and twisted, for her husband who will be ashamed to have anything so wonderful. He will give it away and she will be pleased about the story she has to tell. There will be two flowers tomorrow perhaps, or more.

The next drop now, and there look. Damn dog. Hurry. I'm going to hit him hard with a bottle of milk. He sets himself at the top of the path, by the front door. He closes his eyes, hunches his shoulders and lowers his hind quarters as the stool elongates from under his tail. Hangs, as I come yelling, my neck in jeopardy. Slowly drops, coiling back on itself like a suicidal scorpion. He doesn't look at me, doesn't hear, but lowers his tail, lifts his head and walks off. His morosity parcelled away.

And all I wanted was a half hour I tell you, not great rain bullets fired at me as I look for a spade, not skin lumping from the cold and a mess to clean. Only a warm few minutes and breathing in and out, drinking tea. Time to look at the folds in the curtains and to watch the grey reels of darkness rotating in the room's corners and growing paler. A time to be you see.

But now they'll be up. Opening and closing. Peeing, washing. Dressing. And he'll be on the march, opening windows.

Letting fresh air in, instead of warm in bed. And I could have, if I'd thought, stayed. I'd have been warm right now and still asleep perhaps. Could have turned to him and we'd have coupled quite lazily. Warmly. Shared a quiet half hour, if.

But instead I make a vee-shaped hole with two thrusts of the spade while the rain assaults and the flesh bulges. Damn dog. Sat and shat. Then walked away, quite simply that.

Now look you've trodden in it, you'll feed the fire true you two. You're done for. I shunt what's left of dog into the vee and cover. I whip you two off and run with you under the dispatching sky and throw you into the incinerator. Goodbye. Then hose the wretched feet blueing under the sudden slam of water.

And now I step in onto the mat, gasping, and they have come to look at me.

Why?

Did you run round in the rain?

Barefooted?

In a dressing gown?

In pyjamas?

And leave the heater on?

And a cup. Waiting?

I'm in a mood, like dog – and island – and won't answer.

They stare, then the boys go back to their hunt for football jerseys. Two diving in the washing and the other hanging from a shelf in the hot-water cupboard. And I won't help them, won't say folded on the top shelf. Up there. The two little ones will not take their eyes away from my mood. They stare.

So at last I tell them grumpily I trod in it and had to hose my feet. And throw my slippers in the incinerator. Dog bog.

Dog bog? Their faces flower.

What colour was it?

We found a white one once.

On the footpath outside the shop.

We took half each.

To draw with.

On the road.

But it broke.

And fell into crumbs.

They want me to laugh but I'm flinging off clothes and rubbing my hair. Why should I laugh? Why don't they leave me alone? Pickers. Naggers.

And the other two will get up soon and yell about the noise that's going on. They'll turn on their music and grumble.

In the kitchen and lounge the back windows are open and fresh air pours in. He is striding, but stops to look at me, and at the mood I'm in.

Your feet, he says. Put something on them. Slippers.

She burnt them.

She trod in dog shit and now her slippers are in the incinerator.

For burning.

Burning.

He is all washed and combed and vigorous looking; the jug steams and he has made the porridge. His eyes are full of what he will do this morning zipped into an oilskin and booted to the knees. Mirrored I see two barrow loads of seaweed for the garden, forked out, spread and reeking. A trench for the kitchen scraps and two new rows of cabbage plants.

Now the three boys are in, geared for their games.

Burning?

Your slippers?

Why?

Waiting for me to break silence, to cry perhaps, or laugh.

He gone out and returned with a pair of his socks, his fingertips touching over the ball that the socks have been rolled into.

Put them on. We'll feed these ones and have a cup of tea before the other two get up. Grumbling. Turning their songs up loud.

And along with the seaweed and the scrap trench and the planted cabbages, I see mirrored I missed you this morning. And could have had a half hour quiet, together.

We play at ten.

The three of us. At ten.
If the rain stops.
And this afternoon I'm going down the beach.
To see.
To find something from Japan.
I wish I saw.
The dog.
Bog.
So I pull the socks over the two fillets of feet, purpled, and shut two windows.

On the plum tree. Next door, I say. There's one new flower. And twig ends all ready to heave.

Beans

EVERY SATURDAY MORNING IN THE WINTER TERM I BIKE INTO town to play rugby. Winter's a great time. We live three miles out of town and the way in is mostly uphill, so I need to get a good early start to be in town by nine. On the way in I don't get a chance to look around me or notice things very much because the going is fairly hard. Now and again where it gets a bit steep I have to stand up on the pedals and really tread hard.

But it's great getting off to rugby on a Saturday morning with my towel and change on the carrier, and pushing hard to get there by nine. It's great.

By the time I get to the grounds I'm really puffing and I know my face is about the colour of the clubhouse roof. But I'm ready to go on though. I can't wait to get on the field and get stuck into the game; I really go for it. I watch that ball and chase it all over the place. Where the ball goes I go. I tackle, handle, kick, run, everything. I do everything I can think of and I feel good. Sometimes it's cold and muddy and when I get thrown down into the mud and come up all mucky I feel great, because all the mud shows that I've really made a game of it. The dirtier I get the better I like it because I don't want to miss out on anything.

Then after the game I strip off and get under the shower in the club-room, and sometimes the water is boiling hot and sometimes cold as anything. And whatever it is, you're hopping up and down and getting clean, and yelling out to your mates about the game and saying is it hot or cold in your one.

I need a drink then. I get a drink from the dairy across the road and the dairy's always jammed full of us boys getting drinks. You should hear the noise, you should really hear it.

The going home is one of the best parts of all. I hop on my bike and away I go, hardly any pushing at all. Gee it's good. I can look about me and see everything growing. Cabbages and caulis, potatoes and all sorts of vegetables. And some of the paddocks are all ploughed up and have rows of green just showing through. All neat and tidy, and not much different to look at from the coloured squares of knitting my sister does for girl guides. You see all sorts of people out in the gardens working on big machines or walking along the rows weeding and hoeing: that's the sort of place it is around here. Everything grows and big trucks take all the stuff away, then it starts all over again.

But, I must tell you. Past all the gardens about a mile and a half from where I live there's a fairly steep rise. It's about the steepest part on the way home and I really have to puff up that bit. Then I get to the top and there's a long steep slope going down. It's so steep and straight it makes you want to yell and I usually do. That's not all though. Just as you start picking up speed on the down slope you get this great whiff of pigs. Poo. Pigs. It makes you want to laugh and shout it's such a stink. And as I go whizzing down the stretch on my bike I do a big sniff up, a great bit sniff, and get a full load of the smell of pigs. It's such a horrible great stink that I don't know how to describe it. We've got a book in our library at school and in it there's a poem about bells and the poem says 'joyous'. 'The joyous ringing of bells' or 'bells ringing joyously', something like that. Well 'joyous' is the word I think of when I smell the pigs. Joyous. A joyous big stink of pigs. It's really great.

It's not far to my place after I've taken the straight. When I get home I lean my bike up against the shed and I feel really hot and done for. I don't go straight inside though. Instead I flop myself down on the grass underneath the lemon tree and I pick a lemon and take a huge bite of it. The lemons on our tree are as sour as sour, but I take a big bite because I feel so good. It makes me pull awful faces and roll over and over in the grass, but I keep on taking big bites until the lemon is all gone, skin and everything. Then I pick another lemon and eat that all up too because I don't want to miss a thing in all my life.

We have an old lady living next to us. She's pretty old and she doesn't do much except walk around her garden. One day I heard her say to Mum, 'He's full of beans that boy of yours. Full of beans.'

Letters from Whetu

Dear Lenny,

> Be like Whetu o te Moana,
> Beat Boredom,
> Write a Letter.

How slack finding myself the only one of the old gang in the sixth form. How slack and BORING. And it's so competitive round here – No chance of copying a bit of homework or sharing a few ideas. Everyone's after marks and grades coz that's what counts on ACCREDITING DAY and Nobody Never tells Nobody Nothing – No Way. ACCREDITING DAY – it's ages away yet everyone's in a panic. It's like we're all going to be sorted out for heaven or hell, or for DECIDING DAY, and I really don't know what it's all for. I've thought and thought but just don't get it. I tell yuh it just doesn't add up. Must tell you about DECIDING DAY inaminnit.

See . . . it seems we get put through this machine so that we can come out well-educated and so we can get interesting jobs. I think it's supposed to make us better than some other people – like our mothers and fathers for example, and some of our friends. And somehow it's supposed to make us happier and more FULFILLED. Well I dunno.

I quite like Fisher. I kind of appreciate her even though she thinks she, and she alone, got me through S.C. last year, and even though she thinks I've got no brayne of my own.

Little does she know that I often wish now that I'd fayled. How was I to know I'd be sitting here alone and so lonely learning boring things. Why do we learn such boring things? We learned boring things last year and now we're learning boring things again. I bet this letter's getting boring.

I sometimes do a bit of a stir with Fisher, like I say 'yous' instead of 'you' (pl.). It always sends her PURPLE. The other day I wrote it in my essay and she had a BLUE fit. She scratched it out in RED and wrote me a double underlined note – 'I have told you many times before that there is no such word as "yous" (I wonder if it hurt her to write it). Please do not use (yous heh heh) it again.' So I wrote a triple underlined note underneath – 'How can I yous it if it does not exist?' Now that I think of it that's really slack – what lengths I go to, it's really pathetic. I mean she's OKAY, but I'm a bit sick of being her honourable statistic, her minority person MAKING IT.

I'll tell you something else, that lady sure does go on. And on. And on. She's trying to make us enjoy KM. Kay Em is what she calls Katherine Mansfield, as though she and KM were best mates. Well I suppose Fisher could be just about old enough to have been a mate of KM's . . . . I'll tell you what she's doing. She's prancing about reading like she's gonna bust. Her lips are wobbling and popping, and she's sort of poised like an old ballet dancer. She does a couple of tip-toes now and again. Sometimes she flaps the book about and makes circles in the air with it. I don't think she'll burst into tears.

Do you know what? When she waves and flaps the book about she doesn't stop 'reading', so I suppose that means she knows her KM off by heart, bless her HART (Halt All Racist Tours), punctuation and all. I don't think her glasses will quite fall off – Beat Boredom, wait and hope for Fisher's glasses to fall off and cut her feet to ribbons.

Gee I enjoyed our day at the beach last weekend, and us being all together again first time for ages. Andy looks great. All those hours in the sea and those big waves lopping over us. Hey why don't we save up and get us a surfboard?

I got my beans when I got home though, boy did I get my

beans. Yes, and we'll take some food next time, and some togs and towels (to save our jeans from getting so clean). What about this weekend, but we'd have to contact Andy. Anyhows think on it. Really neat. It wuz tanfastic bowling round in those breakers hour after hour.

And what about those new songs we made up – haven't done that since fourth form. Soon as I got home, after having my ears laid back by Mum and Dad, I went and wrote that second song down so we wouldn't forget it. I like it, I really do. I'm writing out a copy for each of us and I'm sending Andy's with his letter which I'll write period 4. I'm writing letters to all of you today. Gonna post them too, even though I see you all at lunchtime (except Andy).

Can't remember the words to that first song, there must've been about twenty verses, and what rubbish. I can remember the 'Shake-a Shake-a' and the 'Culley bubba' bits, and I remember Iosefa's verse,

> Tasi lua tolu fa,
> Come a me a hugga hugga,
> Shake-a Shake-a Shake-a,
> Culley bubba longa-a long-a.

And

> Tangaroa Tangaroa,
> Little fish belong-a he a,
> Shake-a Shake-a . . .

Then there was another one about a shitting seagull – well never mind. Great music you and Andy made for it though, and only the waves to hear.

She's still flapping, and poncing, and I swear there's a tear in her eye.

And yes. I said I was going to tell you about DECIDING DAY. Went to the library on Monday, and opened a book which I started reading in the middle somewhere. Well this story is all set in New Zealand in the future ay, and there's been a world war and wide devastation.

There are too many people and they're short of stuff – goods, manure, natural resources and all that, so it's been agreed that all the cripples, mentals, wrinklies and sickies have to be sorted out and killed, then recycled. DECIDING DAY is the day the computer comes up with who's human and who's 'animal'. They're going to make them (the dead mentals, etc.) into energy, and use their skins for purses, etc. The kid down the road becomes your new knife handles, buy a bottle of drink and it's your granny stoppered inside ready to fizz. Turn on your light and there's your nutty uncle. After that there'll be a perfect society and a life of ease so they reckon. Neat story?

After DECIDING DAY the fires are going for weeks and weeks, and there's smoke and stink everywhere. The remaining people (not very many coz the computer doesn't find too many 'humans') try to make out they can handle it, but they can't. They can't hack it at all, and they want to chunder over and over, or fall about mad screaming.

Well e hoa. Fisher's winding down, and period one almost over. Love talking to you, not bored at all. See you lunchtime but you won't get this til next week. Gonna get me some envelopes and stamps and do some lickin'.

Arohanui,
Whetu o te Moana.
(I was named after a church.)

Mathematics,
Room 68,
Period 2,
Friday.

Dear Ani,

The new maths teacher is really strange. He never calls the roll but just barges in, goes straight to the rolling blackboard and starts writing. At the same time as he's writing he's mumbling into his whiskers and flinging the board up. His

124

face is only about six inches from the board and you keep thinking he might catch his nose in it. I think he's half blind.

When he gets to the end of the rolling board he starts rubbing out with his left hand and keeps on scribbling his columns and numbers with his right. At the same time he keeps up his muttering and his peering. All he needs now is a foot drum and some side cymbals. When the bell goes he turns round as if he's just noticed us, his specs are all white and chalky and his whiskers are snowy, and he has a tiny pyramid of chalk pinched between his finger and thumb, all that's left of a whole stick. What a weird-o. Then he yells out page numbers and exercise numbers for homework and says, 'Out you go. Quickly.' As we go out he's cleaning his bi-fokes and getting out a new piece of chalk ready for the next lot of suckers. No wonder I'm no good at maths (not like Lenny who's got a mthmtcl brayne. What say we save up for a srfbrd and Lenny can be the treasurer).

Trust you to get stuck halfway up the cliff. Hey I got really scared looking at you, then I got wild with the boys just leaving you there and doing all that Juliet stuff with the guitar. Wasn't til I started up to help you that they decided to come up, and even so they were only assing round.

Then it was really beautiful up on that ledge after all. Wasn't it? You forget, living here. Living here you never really see the sun go down, or you don't think of it as being anything really good. Sometimes if you're outside picking up the newspaper or the milk bottles you see the sky looking a bit pink, or else it just gets dark and you know it's happened. But you don't think 'The sun's going down,' you only think 'It's getting dark.' Mostly we have the curtains over the windows because of people going past, and you think they might LOOK IN, or something TERRIBLE like that. And what if one of them HAD A GUN, and aimed it at you? What if there was a loud bang, and a little hole in the window the size of a peanut, and a big one in your head the size of an orange? What a splash of colour, what a sunset and a half that would be.

Yes and anyway we need the curtains over the windows

because of telly being on. Telly is a sort of window too, with everything always on the other side of the glass. After a while you don't know the difference between 'looking out' and 'looking in'. Well you know what I mean fren, you don't ever think how it is sitting halfway up a cliff making up songs, with the sun dropping behind an island.

You weren't scared anymore once we all got up there, and the sun settled at the head of the island like a big bloodshot eye just for a sec. Then it dropped behind like a trick ball.

You don't ever think of the sky slapped all over red and orange, and the sea smothered in gold-pink curls. When you think back you can see it all again but can't quite feel the same, like your skin is stretching tight over your body, like your eyes are just holes and it's all pouring in.

Well what a climb down in the dark, then the hunt in the dark for shoes. If we hadn't had to look for our shoes we'd have caught an earlier train home. God I got my beans when I got home. Then of course there was that long wait in the greasy shop for our greasies. I was *starving*.

When we were little we always used to go to the beach – every low tide even in the cold weather. But now that us kids have grown up I don't think Dad likes it anymore. Anyway he's so busy and on so many committees – marae committee, P.T.A., Tu Tangata, District Council – and Mum's almost as bad. We're never home together these days, especially now that Hepa's flatting and Amiria's married. As for Koro, he's never in one place for a day. He gets called north south east west, if not to a tangi then to a land meeting, if not to a land meeting then to a convention. Well it's no wonder we never get to the beach or see each other much.

Er um! Hepa turned up on Saturday, so Dad went and got Amiria and John. Er! Koro was back from Auckland, so, er, I was the only one not home. And NOBODY knew where I was. Tricky huh? Well we didn't know we were going to the beach did we? We started out to meet beautiful Andy off the train and ended up getting the next train north.

Hey old chalk-chewer is yelling out page numbers, he's

remembered we're here. He looks like a sort of constipated old Santa – I'd better end this letter inaminnit.

Yes Dad cracked a fit and I took a good bit of flak from Mum as well. They were all dressed to go out and they'd been waiting hours for me. Of course what Dad really thought was that I was out getting myself pooped, it's what they all think but won't say. Ding Dong. Got to bed midnight. Or was that the time we got home, heh heh?

The beach. It beats late shopping nights by a long way. Gotta go. I'm the only one left, goodbye fren. Writing to Iosefa next period. See you lunchtime, but you won't get this til next week.

> Much love,
> Yours ake, ake, ake,
> Star.
> > (I'm a Star
> > I'm a Star
> > I'm a Mon*star*.)

> Geography,
> Room 3,
> Period 3,
> Friday.

Dear Sef,

I write to you amid a show of topographical maps, aerial photos, fault lines and air masses. What a circus. Lattimer arrives loaded with books which he bangs on to a table. Then he starts spouting – So you SEE, so you SEE – producing his cross-sections, graphs, map keys, land formations like tricks out of a hat. After a while he bounces round the room dealing out worksheets and slamming books down in front of us, creating his own earthquakes.

Writing to Ani I remembered how we always used to go downtown on late shopping nights. She and I used to make up all sorts of excuses so we'd be allowed to go, and so did you.

You used to tell your mother you were going on a training run, then you'd run into town and we'd all meet and spend our money on take-aways and junk. Then we'd hang round the fountain with the other kids and hope a fight might start up between our college and the one up the line. We always knew who was out to get who, and who was ripping off what from where. The night we caught the taxi home (with Lenny's money) you had to run up and down the road to get puffed and sweaty before you went inside. I got home wet from you throwing half the fountain on me. We'd all swapped clothes as usual.

Well parents get upset about funny things. Wasn't allowed downtown for ages and ages and used to feel really slacked off on late-shopping-nite-nites because I wanted to be out there having FUN, that was winter. Hey what babies we were, running round, hiding in doorways and hoping all the time that something really awful would happen.

Yes, Lattimer's got a great act there. Maybe we should all crouch on our desks like circus tigers and spring from table to table and roar, and swipe the air with our paws.

What about the time we took your little cousins to the zoo, and Andy got smart to the ape and it went haywire. Then Andy walked away whistling and looking at the sky. Remember the ducks zooming in, and the tiger that turned its bum round at feed time and pissed on the people. And Ani pissed herself laughing. Oh Ani, what a roly-poly, what a ball. Ani's really neat.

Well the ape was bouncing all over its cage with its big open mouth as pink as undercoat paint, baring his old smoker's teeth and trying to wrench the bars apart. Then he began snatching and grabbing at his own arm, his own shoulder, his own head, and at the same time he kept opening his mouth and slamming it shut, and putting his bottom teeth almost up his nose. His eyes were as black as print and glinting like flicked pins.

Our mate Lenny looked at the ape and said, 'Honey baby, come to my pipi farm and I'll give you a gink at my muscles.'

Spare it! Poor monkey, with its thumbs on back to front. The palms of its hands looked like old cow turds.

I really wonder about Lattimer. The way he throws himself about the room you'd think he was really trying to knock the walls down and make a run for it, or perhaps he wants to give himself a crack on the head so he can be pulled out by the feet.

Anyway he's all right – busts out in a sick grin every so often. Remember Harris (harass) and her screwed-up face, and how she used to walk in and shove open all the windows because we all stank. I really wanted to walk out that time Andy left, if only I'd had the guts. Everytime she got on to him I felt like dying, even before I knew Andy properly. She'd never believe what Andy's really like, she was just so scared of him, of his looks, of the way he talks, of his poor clothes. Most of all she must have realised Andy had her taped, over and over, although he never said anything. On that last day I reckon it was his quietness and his acceptance that got to her. She was screwed up with hate, and screaming. Writing to Andy next period and won't forget to tell him about Palmer's DISGUISE.

Sometimes I can't hack the thought that I didn't follow Andy down the road that day, instead of sitting here waiting to 'realise' my 'potential'. Hey Sef, when and how does potential become whatever it's meant to become? I mean, Mum and Dad have all these IDEAS, they're both getting their THRILLS over my education and I reckon I'll be sitting behind a desk FOREVER.

Funny though, if it had been either one of them they'd have gone out the door with Andy without thinking twice, because they really know what's important. It's only me they've got under glass. Anyhows I'll leave it before I start thinking what a sucker I am.

And now I'll talk about the beach. Nex' time we'll take all our gears, especially FOOD. If you're wrkng next wknd, or if Ani's wrkng, or if Andy can't come, we'll go another time. Soon. But gee, Sef, the dropping sun and the bleeding sky and those great fat humping seas, the seagulls . . .

I often dream about flying, and sometimes in the dream

I'm afraid of what I'm doing, and other times I'm so happy and free flying about, up above everyone and everything, going anywhere I want . . . If I wasn't me I'd be a seagull belting out over the sea and throwing myself at any storm, ANY STORM. What would you be, e hoa, if you weren't you?

Gotta go Iosefa, he's snapping up all his books and handouts, and now, slurp, they're all back in the trick box. Howzat? See ya lunchtime, which is now.

Much love from,
Star of the Sea.

History,
Room 42,
Period 4,
Friday.

Dear Andy,

Great to see you on Sunday, you and your old guitar. I hardly remember going to the beach, only being there. When we came to meet you off the train we didn't quite expect to find ourselves on the next one heading north. Suddenly we were off the train again and legging it to the beach all those miles. But it seemed no distance, the road just rolled away under us and only our talking tongues were in a sweat. Hey that neat car, 'You got the Mercedes, I got a Benz' (according to Len). I've been writing letters all morning as part of my anti-boredom campaign.

What I want to tell you is that Iosefa has got a black eye. On Tuesday, Palmer, who is the new VICE principal, disguised himself (as a flasher) and pounced on Lenny, Iosefa and some other boys who were all puffing up large on the bank by the top field. True. He put on an old raincoat, ankle length no less (a real flasher's job), and one of those work caps that have advertisements printed on them – Marple Paints. The boys thought it was a member of the public taking a short-cut to the road so didn't take much notice. Instead it was old P ready to pounce, wearing his usual greaser's grin.

All the letters went home to parents as usual – 'Dear . . . , I wish to bring to your notice that your son/daughter . . . was discovered (!!!) smoking in the school grounds on . . . (date, etc., etc.).'

Iosefa got thumped by his old man, and Lenny's mum screwed up the letter and laughed her wrinkled old head off. On Wednesday Palmer's blackboard was covered with compliments – 'Palmer's a wanker' and all the usual things. Someone drew a spy glass with a gory eye looking through. And you know Rick Ossler? His old man came up and shook 'the letter' in Palmer's face and called him a Creeping Jesus. Well I laughed and laughed. Never heard that expression before, but when I told Mum she said it was an oldie.

Anyway enough of that. Neat fun sitting up on that ledge singing up large, we must've been there for hours. Every now and then I'd think of all our mates from fourth form days, and how we'd all go over to D6 and sing and act like fools, and make up funny songs.

But Angie and Brian, Willy, Judy, Vasa, Hariata, lots of others . . . I was thinking too of how we all used to terrorise the town on late-shopping-nite-nites. Wonder what they're all doing now?

Before I went to bed on Saturday (and after I'd had my ears blasted for being back late), I wrote down the words of our song so we wouldn't forget them. It seems there are things to know about our songs, even the rubbish ones, things we don't really know yet. There are so many things to know, and I really envy you because you're learning some of them. I want to know important things, and also I want to know what's important.

Slitting the throat of a sheep and hanging it up kicking seems to be a real thing, like picking watercress, and even though it's something you can do and I can't, I still want to know about it. Even though I wouldn't want to cut the belly and haul the guts out I know it must sometimes be all right to have blood on your hands. Or if not blood then dirt, or shit –

on the outside where you can see it. You see I've got this bad idea that I'm sitting here storing all the muck up inside me, getting slowly but surely shit ridden. As for you, you've never held any shit, ever, and never will.

But other things, so many things. I mean, I want to know what goes on in houses, especially in houses on hills with trees round them. What do the people there say to each other? What do they laugh about and what do they eat? Are their heads different from them being up higher? Do they chew gum, how can I know?

Are girls who work in clothes shops just like me, or do their faces fall away when night comes, and does someone hang them limp on a rack until morning? Does central heating dry people out and make them unable to face the weather? Well I could go on and on.

E hoa, I want to walk all over the world but how do I develop the skills for it sitting in a plastic bag fastened with a wire-threaded paper twist to keep the contents airtight. You sit cramped in there, with your head bowed, knees jack-knifed up under your chin.

If I walked round the world I'd wear two holes in my face in place of eyes and let everything pour in. I reckon I could play an alpine horn.

The other day two fifth formers bought pot from the care-taker then potted him. And a lot of fourth formers are getting high from sniffing cleaner fluid which they pour on their sleeves. Peter got his arm blown up when his mate lit a cigarette, and now he's in hospital (luckily). Were we *that* suicidal two years ago, screaming round town in our jackets wishing to see someone slit from eye to knee with a knife?

I saw a girl nick a bottle of the stuff from a stand in McKenzies yesterday but I didn't do anything. There were two rows of it on a glass shelf at 89c a bottle.

And now the bell rings and we're almost through the day. No more letters to write, but next period (last one) I'll write out THE SONG for everyone (see yours below). If I write slow enough it might use up the hour.

Well, dear friend, write back straight away and tell us when you can come down again. WE'VE GOT PLANS, and WE SEND OUR LOVE.

Yours 4 eva,
Whetu.

Sky love earth
Shine light
Fall rai-ai-ain,
Earth give life
Turn breast
To chi-i-ild.

Child
Steal light
Turn away rai-ai-ain,
Thrust bright
Sword
Deep into ea-ea-earth.

Mother bleed
Your child
Die,
Bleed mother
Child
Already dead.
                    W-o-te-M.

It Used to be Green Once

WE WERE ALL ASHAMED OF OUR MOTHER. OUR MOTHER always did things to shame us. Like putting red darns in our clothes, and cutting up old swimming togs and making two – girl's togs from the top half for my sister, and boy's togs from the bottom half for my brother. Peti and Raana both cried when Mum made them take the togs to school. Peti sat down on the road by our gate and yelled out she wasn't going to school. She wasn't going swimming. I didn't blame my sister because the togs were thirty-eight chest and Peti was only ten.

But Mum knew how to get her up off the road. She yelled loudly, 'Get up off that road, my girl. There's nothing wrong with those togs. I didn't have any togs when I was a kid and I had to swim in my nothings. Get up off your backside and get to school.' Mum's got a loud voice and she knew how to shame us. We all dragged Peti up off the road before our mates came along and heard Mum. We pushed Peti into the school bus so Mum wouldn't come yelling up the drive.

We never minded our holey fruit at first. Dad used to pick up the cases of over-ripe apples or pears from town that he got cheap. Mum would dig out the rotten bits, and then give them to us to take for play-lunch. We didn't notice much at first, not until Reweti from down the road yelled out to us one morning, 'Hey you fullas, who shot your pears?' We didn't have anywhere to hide our lunch because we weren't allowed school bags until we got to high school. Mum said she wasn't buying fourteen school bags. When we went to high school we could have shoes too. The whole lot of us gave Reweti a good hiding after school.

However, this story is mainly about the car, and about Mum and how she shamed us all the time. The shame of rainbow darns and cut-up togs and holey fruit was nothing to what we suffered because of the car. Uncle Raz gave us the car because he couldn't fix it up any more, and he'd been fined because he lived in Auckland. He gave the car to Dad so we could drive our cream cans up to the road instead of pushing them up by wheelbarrow.

It didn't matter about the car not having brakes because the drive from our cowshed goes down in a dig then up to the gate. Put the car in its first gear, run it down from the shed, pick up a bit of speed, up the other side, turn it round by the cream stand so that it's pointing down the drive again, foot off the accelerator and slam on the handbrake. Dad pegged a board there to make sure it stopped. Then when we'd lifted the cans out on to the stand he'd back up a little and slide off down the drive – with all of us throwing ourselves in over the sides as if it were a dinghy that had just been pushed out into the sea.

The car had been red once because you could still see some patches of red paint here and there. And it used to have a top too, that you could put down or up. Our uncle told us that when he gave it to Dad. We were all proud about the car having had a top once. Some of the younger kids skited to their mates about our convertible and its top that went up and down. But that was before our mother started shaming us by driving the car to the shop.

We growled at Mum and we cried but it made no difference. 'You kids always howl when I tell you to get our shopping,' she said.

'We'll get it, Mum. We won't cry.'

'We won't cry, Mum. We'll carry the sack of potatoes.'

'And the flour.'

'And the bag of sugar.'

'And the rolled oats.'

'And the tin of treacle.'

'We'll do the shopping, Mum.'

But Mum would say, 'Never mind, I'll do it myself.' And after that she wouldn't listen any more.

PATRICIA GRACE

How we hated Wednesdays. We always tried to be sick on Wednesdays, or to miss the bus. But Mum would be up early yelling at us to get out of bed. If we didn't get up when we were told she'd drag us out and pull down our pyjama pants and set our bums on the cold lino. Mum was cruel to us.

Whoever was helping with the milking had to be back quickly from the shed for breakfast, and we'd all have to rush through our kai and get to school. Wednesday was Mum's day for shopping.

As soon as she had everything tidy she'd change into her good purple dress that she'd made from a Japanese bedspread, pull on her floppy-brimmed blue sunhat and her slippers and galoshes, and go out and start up the car.

We tried everything to stop her shaming us all.

'You've got no licence, Mum.'

'What do I want a licence for? I can drive, can't I? I don't need the proof.'

'You got no warrant.'

'Warrant? What's warrant?'

'The traffic man'll get you, Mum.'

'That rat. He won't come near me after what he did to my niece. I'll hit him right over his smart head with a bag of riwais and I'll hit him somewhere else as well.' We could never win an argument with Mum.

Off she'd go on a Wednesday morning, and once out on the road she'd start tooting the horn. This didn't sound like a horn at all but more like a flock of ducks coming in for a feed. The reason for the horn was to let all her mates and relations along the way know she was coming. And as she passed each one's house, if they wanted anything they'd have to run out and call it out loud. Mum couldn't stop because of not having any brakes. 'E Kiri,' each would call. 'Mauria mai he riwai,' if they wanted spuds; 'Mauria mai he paraoa,' if they wanted bread. 'Mauria mai he tarau, penei te kaita,' hand spread to show the size of the pants they wanted Mum to get. She would call out to each one and wave to them to show she'd understood. And when she neared the store she'd switch the motor off, run into

136

the kerbing and pull on the handbrake. I don't know how she remembered all the things she had to buy – I only know that by the time she'd finished, every space in that car was filled and it was a squeeze for her to get into the driver's seat. But she had everything there, all ready to throw out on the way back.

As soon as she'd left the store she'd begin hooting again, to let the whole district know she was on her way. Everybody would be out on the road to get their shopping thrown at them, or just to watch our mother go chuffing past. We always hid if we heard her coming.

The first time Mum's car and the school bus met was when they were both approaching a one-way bridge from opposite directions. We had to ask the driver to stop and give way to Mum because she had no brakes. We were all ashamed. But everyone soon got to know Mum and her car and they always stopped whenever they saw her coming. And you know, Mum never ever had an accident in her car, except for once when she threw a side of mutton out to Uncle Peta and it knocked him over and broke his leg.

After a while we started walking home from school on Wednesdays to give Mum a good chance of getting home before us, and so we wouldn't be in the bus when it had to stop and let her past. The boys didn't like having to walk home but we girls didn't mind because Mr Hadley walked home too. He was a new teacher at our school and he stayed not far from where we lived. We girls thought he was really neat.

But one day, it had to happen. When I heard the honking and tooting behind me I wished that a hole would appear in the ground and that I would fall in it and disappear for ever. As Mum came near she started smiling and waving and yelling her head off. 'Anyone wants a ride,' she yelled, 'they'll have to run and jump in.'

We all turned our heads the other way and hoped Mr Hadley wouldn't notice the car with our mother in it, and her yelling and tooting, and the brim of her hat jumping up and down. But instead, Mr Hadley took off after the car and leapt in over the back seat on top of the shopping. Oh the shame.

But then one day something happened that changed everything. We arrived home to find Dad in his best clothes, walking round and grinning, and not doing anything like getting the cows in, or mending a gate, or digging a drain. We said, 'What are you laughing at, Dad?' 'What are you dressed up for? Hey Mum, what's the matter with Dad?'

'Your dad's a rich man,' she said. 'Your dad, he's just won fifty thousand dollars in a lottery.'

At first we couldn't believe it. We couldn't believe it. Then we all began running round and laughing and yelling and hugging Mum and Dad. 'We can have shoes and bags,' we said. 'New clothes and swimming togs, and proper apples and pears.' Then do you know what Dad said? Dad said, 'Mum can have a new car.' This really astounded and amazed us. We went numb with excitement for five minutes then began hooting and shouting again, and knocking Mum over.

'A new car!'

'A new car?'

'Get us a Packard, Mum.'

'Or a De Soto. Yes, yes.'

Get this, get that . . .

Well, Mum bought a big shiny green Chevrolet, and Dad got a new cowshed with everything modernised and water gushing everywhere. We all got our new clothes – shoes, bags, togs – and we even started taking posh lunches to school. Sandwiches cut in triangles, bottles of cordial, crisp apples and pears, and yellow bananas.

And somehow all of us kids changed. We started acting like we were somebody instead of ordinary like before. We used to whine to Dad for money to spend and he'd always give it to us. Every week we'd nag Mum into taking us to the pictures, or if she was tired we'd go ourselves by taxi. We got flash bedspreads and a piano and we really thought we were neat.

As for the old car – we made Dad take it to the dump. We never wanted to see it again. We all cheered when he took it away, except for Mum. Mum stayed inside where she couldn't watch, but we all stood outside and cheered.

We all changed, as though we were really somebody, but there was one thing I noticed. Mum didn't change at all, and neither did Dad. Mum had a new car all right, and a couple of new dresses, and a new pair of galoshes to put over her slippers. And Dad had a new modern milking shed and a tractor and some other gadgets for the farm. But Mum and Dad didn't change. They were the same as always.

Mum still went shopping every Wednesday. But instead of having to do all the shopping herself she was able to take all her friends and relations with her. She had to start out earlier so she'd have time to pick everyone up on the way. How angry we used to be when Mum went past with her same old sunhat and her heap of friends and relations, and them all waving and calling out to us.

Mum sometimes forgot that the new car had brakes, especially when she was approaching the old bridge and we were coming the opposite way in the school bus. She would start tooting and the bus would have to pull over and let her through. That's when all our aunties and uncles and friends would start waving and calling out. But some of them couldn't wave because they were too squashed by people and shopping, they'd just yell. How shaming.

There were always ropes everywhere over Mum's new car holding bags of things and shovel handles to the roof and sides. The boot was always hanging open because it was too full to close – things used to drop out on to the road all the time. And the new car – it used to be green once, because if you look closely you can still see some patches of green paint here and there.

Journey

HE WAS AN OLD MAN GOING ON A JOURNEY. BUT NOT REALLY so old, only they made him old buttoning up his coat for him and giving him money. Seventy-one that's all. Not a journey, not what you would really call a journey – he had to go in and see those people about his land. Again. But he liked the word Journey even though you didn't quite say it. It wasn't a word for saying only for saving up in your head, and that way you could enjoy it. Even an old man like him, but not what you would call properly old.

The coat was good and warm. It was second-hand from the jumble and it was good and warm. Could have ghosts in it but who cares, warm that's the main thing. If some Pakeha died in it that's too bad because he wasn't scared of the Pakeha kehuas anyway. The pakeha kehuas they couldn't do anything, it was only like having a sheet over your head and going woo-oo at someone in the lavatory . . .

He better go to the lavatory because he didn't trust town lavatories, people spewed there and wrote rude words. Last time he got something stuck on his shoe. Funny people those town people.

Taxi.

It's coming, Uncle.

Taxi, Uncle.

They think he's deaf. And old. Putting more money in his pocket and wishing his coat needed buttoning, telling him it's windy and cold. Never mind, he was off. Off on his journey, he could get round town good on his own, good as gold.

Out early today, old man.

Business, young fulla.

Early bird catches the early worm.

It'll be a sorry worm, young fulla, a sorry worm.

Like that is it?

Like that.

You could sit back and enjoy the old taxi smells of split upholstery and cigarette, and of something else that could have been the young fulla's hair oil or his b.o. It was good. Good. Same old taxi same old stinks. Same old shop over there, but he wouldn't be calling in today, no. And tomorrow they'd want to know why. No, today he was going on a journey, which was a good word. Today he was going further afield, and there was a word no one knew he had. A good wind today but he had a warm coat and didn't need anyone fussing.

Same old butcher and same old fruit shop, doing all right these days not like before. Same old Post Office where you went to get your pension money, but he always sent Minnie down to get his because he couldn't stand these old-age people. These old-age people got on his nerves. Yes, same old place, same old shops and roads, and everything cracking up a bit. Same old taxi. Same old young fulla.

How's the wife?

Still growling, old man.

What about the kids?

Costing me money.

Send them out to work, that's the story.

I think you're right, you might have something there old man. Well here we are, early. Still another half-hour to wait for the train.

Best to be early. Business.

Guess you're right.

What's the sting?

Ninety-five it is.

Pull out a fistful and give the young fulla full eyes. Get yourself out on to the footpath and shove the door, give it a good hard slam. Pick me up later, young fulla, ten past five. Might as well make a day of it, look round town and buy a few things.

Don't forget, ten past five.

Right you are, old man, five ten.

People had been peeing in the subway, the dirty dogs. In the old days all you needed to do to get on to the station was to step over the train tracks, there weren't any piss holes like this to go through, it wasn't safe. Coming up the steps on to the platform he could feel the quick huffs of his breathing and that annoyed him, he wanted to swipe at the huffs with his hand. Steam engines went out years ago.

Good sight though, seeing the big engines come bellowing through the cutting and pull in squealing, everything was covered in soot for miles those days.

New man in the ticket office, looked as though he still had his pyjamas on under his outfit. Miserable looking fulla and not at all impressed by the ten-dollar note handed through to him. A man feels like a screwball yelling through that little hole in the glass and then trying to pick up the change that sourpuss has scattered all over the place. Feels like giving sourpuss the fingers, yes. Yes he knows all about those things, he's not deaf and blind yet, not by a long shot.

Ah warmth. A cold wait on the platform but the carriages had the heaters on, they were warm even though they stank. And he had the front half of the first carriage all to himself. Good idea getting away early. And right up front where you could see everything. Good idea coming on his own, he didn't want anyone fussing round looking after his ticket, seeing if he's warm and saying things twice. Doing his talking for him, made him sick. Made him sick them trying to walk slow so they could keep up with him. Yes he could see everything. Not many fishing boats gone out this morning and the sea's turning over rough and heavy – Tamatea that's why. That's something they don't know all these young people, not even those fishermen walking about on their decks over there. Tamatea a Ngana, Tamatea Aio, Tamatea Whakapau – when you get the winds – but who'd believe you these days. They'd rather stare at their weather on television and talk about a this and a that coming over because there's nothing else to believe in.

Now this strip here, it's not really land at all, it's where we used to get our pipis, any time or tide. But they pushed a hill down over it and shot the railway line across to make more room for cars. The train driver knows it's not really land and he is speeding up over this strip. So fast you wait for the nose dive over the edge into the sea, especially when you're up front like this, looking. Well, too bad. Not to worry, he's nearly old anyway and just about done his dash, so why to worry if they nose dive over the edge into the sea. Funny people putting their trains across the sea. Funny people making land and putting pictures and stories about it in the papers as though it's something spectacular, it's a word you can use if you get it just right and he could surprise quite a few people if he wanted to. Yet other times they go on as though land is just a nothing. Trouble is he let them do his talking for him. If he'd gone in on his own last time and left those fusspots at home he'd have got somewhere. Wouldn't need to be going in there today to tell them all what's what.

Lost the sea now and coming into a cold crowd. This is where you get swamped, but he didn't mind, it was good to see them all get in out of the wind glad to be warm. Some of his whanaungas lived here but he couldn't see any of them today. Good job too, he didn't want them hanging round wondering where he was off to on his own. Nosing into his business. Some of the old railway houses still there but apart from that everything new, houses, buildings, roads. You'd never know now where the old roads had been, and they'd filled a piece of the harbour up too to make more ground. A short row of sooty houses that got new paint once in a while, a railway shelter and a lunatic asylum and that was all. Only you didn't call it that these days, he'd think of the right words in a minute.

There now, the train was full and he had a couple of kids sitting by him wearing plastic clothes, they were gog-eyed stretching their necks to see. One of them had a snotty nose and a wheeze.

On further it's the same – houses, houses – but people have to have houses. Two or three farms once, on the cold hills, and a rough road going through. By car along the old road you'd always see a pair of them at the end of the drive waving with their hats jammed over their ears. Fat one and a skinny one. Psychiatric hospital, those were the words to use these days, yes, don't sound so bad. People had to have houses and the two or three farmers were dead now probably. Maybe didn't live to see it all. Maybe died rich.

The two kids stood swaying as they entered the first tunnel, their eyes stood out watching for the tunnel's mouth, waiting to pass out through the great mouth of the tunnel. And probably the whole of life was like that, sitting in the dark watching and waiting. Sometimes it happened and you came out into the light, but mostly it only happened in tunnels. Like now.

And between the tunnels they were slicing the hills away with big machines. Great-looking hills too, and not an easy job cutting them away, it took Pakeha determination to do that. Funny people these Pakehas, had to chop up everything. Couldn't talk to a hill or a tree these people, couldn't give the trees or the hills a name and make them special and leave them. Couldn't go round, only through. Couldn't give life, only death. But people had to have houses, and ways of getting from one place to another. And anyway, who was right up there helping the Pakeha to get rid of things – the Maori of course, riding those big machines. Swooping round and back, up and down all over the place. Great tools the Maori man had for his carving these days, tools for his new whakairo, but there you are, a man had to eat. People had to have houses, had to eat, had to get from here to there – anyone knew that. He wishes the two kids would stop crackling, their mothers dressed them in rubbish clothes, that's why they had colds.

Then the rain'll come and the cuts will bleed for miles and the valleys will drown in blood, but the Pakeha will find a way of mopping it all up no trouble. Could find a few bones amongst that lot too. That's what you get when you dig up the ground, bones.

Now the next tunnel, dark again. Had to make sure the windows were all shut up in the old days or you got a face full of soot.

And then coming out of the second tunnel that's when you

really had to hold your breath, that's when you really had to hand it to the Pakeha, because there was a sight. Buildings miles high, streets and steel and concrete and asphalt settled all round the great-looking curve that was the harbour. Water with ships on it, and roadways threading up and round the hills to layer on layer of houses, even in the highest and steepest places. He was filled with admiration. Filled with Admiration, which was another word he enjoyed even though it wasn't really a word for saying, but yes he was filled right to the top – it made him tired taking it all in. The kids too, they'd stopped crackling and were quite still, their eyes full to exploding.

The snotty one reminded him of George, he had pop eyes and he sat quiet, not talking. The door would open slowly and the eyes would come round and he would say, I ran away again, Uncle. That's all. That's all for a whole week or more until his mother came to get him and take him back. Never spoke, never wanted anything. Today if he had time he would look out for George.

Railway station much the same as ever, same old platforms and not much cleaner than the soot days. Same old stalls and looked like the same people in them. Underground part is new. Same cafeteria, same food most likely, and the spot where they found the murdered man looked no different from any other spot. Always crowded in the old days especially during the hard times. People came there in the hard times to do their starving. They didn't want to drop dead while they were on their own most probably. Rather all starve together.

Same old statue of Kupe with his woman and his priest, and they've got the name of the canoe spelt wrong, his old eyes aren't as blind as all that. Same old floor made of little coloured pieces and blocked into patterns with metal strips, he used to like it but now he can just walk on it. Big pillars round the doorway holding everything in place, no doubt about it you had to hand it to the Pakeha.

Their family hadn't starved, their old man had seen to that. Their old man had put all the land down in garden, all of it, and in the weekends they took what they didn't use round by horse and cart. Sometimes got paid, sometimes swapped for something, mostly got nothing but why to worry. Yes, great-looking veges they had those days, turnips as big as pumpkins, cabbages you could hardly carry, big tomatoes, lettuces, pota-toes, everything. Even now the ground gave you good things. They had to stay home from school for the planting and pick-ing, usually for the weeding and hoeing as well. Never went to school much those days but why to worry.

Early, but he could take his time, knows his way round this place as good as gold. Yes, he's walked all over these places that used to be under the sea and he's ridden all up and down them in trams too. This bit of sea has been land for a long time now. And he's been in all the pubs and been drunk in all of them, he might go to the pub later and spend some of his money. Or he could go to the continuous pictures but he didn't think they had them any more. Still, he might celebrate a little on his own later, he knew his way round this place without anyone inter-fering. Didn't need anyone doing his talking, and messing things up with all their letters and what not. Pigeons, he didn't like pigeons, they'd learned to behave like people, eat your feet off if you give them half a chance.

And up there past the cenotaph, that's where they'd bull-dozed all the bones and put in the new motorway. Resited, he still remembered the newspaper word, all in together. Your leg bone, my arm bone, someone else's bunch of teeth and fingers, someone else's head, funny people. Glad he didn't have any of his whanaungas underground in that place. And they had put all the headstones in a heap somewhere promising to set them all up again *tastefully* – he remembered – didn't matter who was underneath. Bet there weren't any Maoris driving those bull-dozers. Well, why to worry, it's not his concern, none of his whanaungas up there anyway.

Good those old trams, but he didn't trust these crazy buses, he'd rather walk. Besides, he's nice and early and there's nothing wrong with his legs. Yes, he knows this place like his own big toe, and by Jove he's got a few things to say to those people and he wasn't forgetting. He'd tell them, yes.

The railway station was a place for waiting. People waited there in the old days when times were hard, had a free wash and did their starving there. He waited because it was too early to go home, his right foot was sore. And he could watch out for George, the others had often seen George here waiting about. He and George might go and have a cup of tea and some kai.

He agreed. Of course he agreed. People had to have houses. Not only that, people had to have other things – work, and ways of getting from place to place, and comforts. People needed more now than they did in his young days, he understood completely. Sir. Kept calling him sir, and the way he said it didn't sound so well, but it was difficult to be sure at first. After a while you knew, you couldn't help knowing. He didn't want any kai, he felt sick. His foot hurt.

Station getting crowded and a voice announcing platforms. After all these years he still didn't know where the voice came from but it was the same voice, and anyway the trains could go without him, it was too soon. People.

Queuing for tickets and hurrying towards the platforms, or coming this way and disappearing out through the double doors, or into the subway or the lavatory or the cafeteria. He was too tired to go to the lavatory and anyway he didn't like . . . Some in no hurry at all. Waiting. You'd think it was starvation times. Couldn't see anyone he knew.

I know I know. People have to have houses, I understand and it's what I want.

Well it's not so simple, sir.

It's simple. I can explain. There's only the old place on the land and it needs bringing down now. My brother and sister and I talked about it years back. We wrote letters . . .

Yes yes, but it's not as simple as you think.

But now they're both dead and it's all shared – there are my brother's children, my sister's children, and me. It doesn't matter about me because I'm on the way out, but before I go I want it all done.

As I say, it's no easy matter, all considered.

Subdivision. It's what we want.

There'll be no more subdivision, sir, in the area.

Subdivision. My brother has four sons and two daughters, my sister has five sons. Eleven sections so they can build their houses. I want it all seen to before . . .

You must understand, sir, that it's no easy matter, the area has become what we call a development area, and I've explained all this before, there'll be no more subdivision.

Development means houses, and it means other things too, I understand that. But houses, it's what we have in mind.

And even supposing, sir, that subdivision were possible, which it isn't, I wonder if you fully comprehend what would be involved in such an undertaking.

I fully comprehend . . .

Surveying, kerbing and channelling and formation of adequate access, adequate right of ways. The initial outlay . . .

I've got money, my brother and sister left it for the purpose. And my own, my niece won't use any of my money, it's all there. We've got the money.

However that's another matter, I was merely pointing out that it's not always all plain sailing.

All we want is to get it divided up so they can have a small piece each to build on . . .

As I say, the area, the whole area, has been set aside for development. All in the future of course but we must look ahead, it is necessary to be far-sighted in these concerns.

Houses, each on a small section of land, it's what my niece was trying to explain . . .

You see there's more to development than housing. We have to plan for roading and commerce, we have to set aside areas for educational and recreational facilities. We've got to think of industry, transportation . . .

But still people need houses. My nieces and nephews have waited for years.

They'd be given equivalent land or monetary compensation of course.

But where was the sense in that, there was no equal land.

If it's your stamping ground and you have your ties there, then there's no land equal, surely that wasn't hard to understand. More and more people coming in to wait and the plastic kids had arrived. They pulled away from their mother and went for a small run, crackling. He wished he knew their names and hoped they would come and sit down by him, but no, their mother was striding, turning them towards a platform because they were getting a train home. Nothing to say for a week or more and never wanted anything except sitting squeezed beside him in the armchair after tea until he fell asleep. Carry him to bed, get in beside him later, then one day his mother would come. It was too early for him to go home even though he needed a pee.

There's no sense in it, don't you see? That's their stamping ground and when you've got your ties there's no equal land. It's what my niece and nephew were trying to explain the last time, and in the letters . . .

Well, sir, I shouldn't really do this, but if it will help clarify the position I could show you what has been drawn up. Of course it's all in the future and not really your worry . . .

Yes yes, I'll be dead but that's not . . .

I'll get the plans.

And it's true he'll be dead, it's true he's getting old, but not true if anyone thinks his eyes have had it, because he can see good enough. His eyes are still good enough to look all over the paper and see his land there, and to see that his land has been shaded in and had 'Off Street Parking' printed on it.

He can see good close up and he can see good far off, and that's George over the other side standing with some mates. He can tell George anywhere no matter what sort of get-up he's wearing. George would turn and see him soon.

But you can't, that's only a piece of paper and it can be changed, you can change it. People have to live and to have things. People need houses and shops but that's only paper, it can be changed.

It's all been very carefully mapped out. By experts. Areas have been selected according to suitability and convenience.

And the aesthetic aspects have been carefully considered . . .

Everything grows, turnips the size of pumpkins, cabbages you can hardly carry, potatoes, tomatoes . . . Back here where you've got your houses, it's all rock, land going to waste there . . .

You would all receive equivalent sites . . .

Resited . . .

As I say, on equivalent land . . .

There's no land equal . . .

Listen, sir, it's difficult but we've got to have some understanding of things. Don't we?

Yes yes, I want you to understand, that's why I came. This here, it's only paper and you can change it. There's room for all the things you've got on your paper, and room for what we want too, we want only what we've got already, it's what we've been trying to say.

Sir, we can't always have exactly what we want . . .

All around here where you've marked residential it's all rock, what's wrong with that for shops and cars. And there'll be people and houses. Some of the people can be us, and some of the houses can be ours.

Sure, sure. But not exactly where you want them. And anyway, sir, there's no advantage do you think in you people all living in the same area?

It's what we want, we want nothing more than what is ours already.

It does things to your land value.

He was an old man but he wanted very much to lean over the desk and swing a heavy punch.

No sense being scattered everywhere when what we want . . .

It immediately brings down the value of your land . . .

. . . is to stay put on what is left of what has been ours since before we were born. Have a small piece each, a small garden, my brother and sister and I discussed it years ago.

Straight away the value of your land goes down.

Wanted to swing a heavy punch but he's too old for it. He

kicked the desk instead. Hard. And the veneer cracked and splintered. Funny how quiet it had become.

You ought to be run in, old man, do you hear.

Cripes, look what the old blighter's gone and done. Look at Paul's desk.

He must be whacky.

He can't do that, Paul, get the boss along to sort him out. Get him run in.

Get out, old man, do you hear.

Yes he could hear, he wasn't deaf, not by a long shot. A bit of trouble getting his foot back out of the hole, but there, he was going, and not limping either, he'd see about this lot later. Going, not limping and not going to die either. It looked as though their six eyes might all fall out and roll on the floor.

There's no sense, no sense in anything, but what use telling that to George when George already knew, sitting beside him wordless. What use telling George you go empty handed and leave nothing behind, when George had always been empty handed, had never wanted anything except to have nothing.

How are you, son?

All right, Uncle. Nothing else to say. Only sitting until it was late enough to go.

Going, not limping, and not going to die either.

There you are, old man, get your feet in under that heater. Got her all warmed up for you.

Yes, young fulla, that's the story.

The weather's not so good.

Not the best.

How was your day, all told?

All right.

It's all those hard footpaths, and all the walking that gives people sore feet, that's what makes your legs tired.

There's a lot of walking about in that place.

You didn't use the buses?

Never use the buses.

But you got your business done?

All done. Nothing left to do.

That's good then, isn't it?

How's your day been, young fulla?

A proper circus.

Must be this weather.

It's the weather, always the same in this weather.

This is your last trip for the day, is it?

A couple of trains to meet after tea and then I finish.

Home to have a look at the telly.

For a while, but there's an early job in the morning . . .

Drop me off at the bottom, young fulla. I'm in no hurry. Get off home to your wife and kids.

No, no, there's a bad wind out there, we'll get you to your door. Right to your door, you've done your walking for the day. Besides I always enjoy the sight of your garden, you must have green fingers, old man.

It keeps me bent over but it gives us plenty. When you come for Minnie on Tuesday I'll have a couple of cabbages and a few swedes for you.

Great, really great, I'm no gardener myself.

Almost too dark to see.

Never mind, I had a good look this morning, you've got it all laid out neat as a pin. Neat as a pin, old man.

And here we are.

One step away from your front door.

You can get off home for tea.

You're all right, old man?

Right as rain, young fulla, couldn't be better.

I'll get along then.

Tuesday.

Now he could get in and close the door behind him and walk without limping to the lavatory because he badly needs a pee. And when he came out of the bathroom they were watching him, they were stoking up the fire and putting things on the table. They were looking at his face.

Seated at the table they were trying not to look at his face, they were trying to talk about unimportant things, there was a bad wind today and it's going to be a rough night.

Tamatea Whakapau.

It must have been cold in town.

Heaters were on in the train.

And the train, was it on time?

Right on the minute.

What about the one coming home?

Had to wait a while for the one coming home.

At the railway station, you waited at the railway station?

And I saw George.

George, how's George?

George is all right, he's just the same.

Maisie said he's joined up with a gang and he doesn't wash. She said he's got a big war sign on his jacket and won't go to work.

They get themselves into trouble, she said, and they all go round dirty.

George is no different, he's just the same.

They were quiet then, wondering if he would say anything else, then after a while they knew he wouldn't.

But later that evening as though to put an end to some silent discussion that they may have been having he told them it wasn't safe and they weren't to put him in the ground. When I go you're not to put me in the ground, do you hear. He was an old man and his foot was giving him hell, and he was shouting at them while they sat hurting. Burn me up, I tell you, it's not safe in the ground, you'll know all about it if you put me in the ground. Do you hear?

Some other time, we'll talk about it.

Some other time is now and it's all said. When I go, burn me up, no one's going to mess about with me when I'm gone.

He turned into his bedroom and shut the door. He sat on the edge of his bed for a long time looking at the palms of his hands.

Kepa

GIRLS AGAINST BOYS TODAY, AND SO THERE WERE THE GIRLS with their dresses tucked into their pants, waiting. The boys came out of their huddle and called, 'Ana.'

'We call Ana.'

'Ana Banana.'

Ana could run it straight or try trickery. Straight she decided, and committed now with a toe over the line. Away with hair rippling, eyes fixed on the far corner, that far far corner, the corner far . . .

Boys bearing down, slapping thighs and yodelling. And confident. If Denny Boy didn't get her, Macky would.

'Ana Banana.'

'Anabanana.'

'Banana Ana,' Denny Boy leaving the bunch in a fast sprint, slowing down and lingering for the show of it, then diving for the ankle slap. But not quite. Not quite. Ana was ready for him. She side-stepped and kicked him in the knee, then she was off again.

Infield. No hope of a straight run now, nearly all on top of her. Facing her. Spreading out and facing. Back at the line the girls all screamed, 'Run, Ana.'

'Run.'

'Ana, run.'

'Runana,' over the humps and cracks, plops and thistles. Not far to go, but they all knew someone would . . . Macky. She hit like a slammed door while the other girls all yelled at her to get up, Ana.

'Get up.'

'Up, Ana.'

'Come on, gee.'

'Gee, come on, Ana, get up.'

'Up.'

Macky's fingers were clamped to her ankle but he hadn't got her yet. He hadn't got her three times in the middle of the back and those were the rules. She kicked out with her free foot, but he wouldn't let go, and now the other boys were sitting on her. Thumping One, taking their time for the show of it, Two, caught Three. Howzat?

'Howzat?' The boys were doing some sort of dance, an arms and legs dance, a face dance, a bum dance, and the girls were wild. Sukeys, they called.

'Pick a fast runner next time, sukeys.'

'Cheats.'

'Sukeys and cheats.'

Not that the boys cared, getting together for their next conference. They decided to call Charlotte, just to prove they weren't sukeys. Or cheats.

'Cha-arlotte.'

'Ba-anjoes.'

'Charlotte Banjoes.' They weren't scared.

Charlotte leapt forward and three of the boys ran ahead to help from the front because they knew it would take a united effort. Macky was coming from behind, but suddenly Charlotte halted and put her foot out and he somersaulted over it. 'Go Charlotte, go Charlotte,' the girls screamed. She went off at another angle with only three boys to beat. She charged straight for them, stopped and buckled her knees at them, then changed direction again and went for the line. Safe, with Macky throwing dung at her and the girls yelling, 'All over, all over,' running out into the bunch of angry boys.

Two more of the girls ran across safely while those who were caught went to the sideline to recuperate and to await the revenge time.

'How's that, you fullas?'

'Only three of you fullas left.'

'Shut up, you cheats.'

'Just only three.'

'Who do you call?'

Erana ran out with fists flying. She saw a little gap between Jack and Denny Boy that could be big enough for a side-step foot-change and through, but not quite. She was quickly caught, held and tagged, and so was Becky. That left Charlotte.

'Banjoes.'

'Cha-arlotte.'

'Ba-anjoes.'

Charlotte ran out on to the field and swerved round two of the boys. She knocked another down, knowing there was still a long way to go. Knowing Macky had it in for her and that the foot trip wouldn't work a second time. He was gaining on her and wasn't put off by her sudden balk tactic. Still gaining, and with a strong group up front, Charlotte knew her chances were not good. She tried a change of direction but Macky stayed with her. He was close enough now but seemed to be delaying, and Charlotte didn't know why. Then suddenly she knew. She saw the thistle as Macky brought her down on top of it. Macky wisely held tightly on to both of her legs until help came. It came swiftly.

'One, Two, Three.'

'All out, all out.'

'Howzat?'

'Howzat, you fullas?' but the girls were already conferring and Charlotte was enraged. 'Macky-Blacky,' she called, and she was going to throw that Macky in the tutae for sure.

After him. The slipperiest, the ugliest . . . Charlotte was running alongside and they all knew she would have to do something quick because Macky-Blacky was faster than she was. She kicked his legs from under him and swiped him in the back with her fist. Macky was down with Charlotte on top of him. He wriggled on to his back so that she couldn't tag him; after all he was not only the fastest but also slipperiest so he wasn't caught yet. But Charlotte wasn't so interested in tagging him because there was a big round, soft plop not far away. She dug her knees into Macky's thighs, pinned his arms down and rolled. Now he was on top but still quite helpless. Another

heave and roll . . . a splash and his back was right in it, good
job. 'Good job, Blacky.'

Macky bounced up, and suddenly there was blood pouring
out of Charlotte's nose. Then the two of them were down again
punching and kicking, while all the others shouted at them to
get up.

'Come on, gee.'

'Gee-ee, you're spoiling the game.'

'Jeez, you fullas spoil everything.'

And Denny Boy was really mad. He was still *in*. He hadn't
been caught yet and these fullas must fight. He got through
the fence and had a drink at the creek, then he sat on the stile
to wait. Gee those two fighting, and the rest of them hopping
about and shouting, and he was still *in*. He hadn't had his turn
yet. A-ack they made him sick.

He stood up on the stile . . . and it was from there that he
noticed, far away at the end of the beach where the road began,
a little speck which seemed to roll from side to side. He'd seen
that same speck doing that same thing more than two years
ago. And he knew what it was if only he could remember – now
he remembered. He knew what it was, who it was. It was Uncle
Kepa, home from the sea, lifting his feet high as he walked so
as not to get dust on his shoes. Uncle Kepa who had been to
all the countries in the world and who was bringing them back
a monkey. Denny Boy began to run. Across the paddock, down
to the beach and over the stones.

Back in mid-field Lizzie noticed him going for his life, he
was cunning that Denny Boy. You had to watch Denny Boy,
running off in the middle of a fight like that. He was up to
something. Look at him, running like a porangi . . .

'Uncle Kepa,' Lizzie screamed, and began to run too. The
others were only seconds behind her, calling.

'Come back here, Denny Boy.'

'Cheat.'

'Liar.'

'Stink bum.'

Charlotte, still running, ripped the bottom off her dress

and wiped the blood from her face. Then she handed the rag to Macky who wiped all round his mouth where his teeth had come through his lip. 'You wait, smarty,' she was yelling, 'Come back, tutae face.' But Denny Boy was way ahead. Not even Macky or Charlotte could catch him now. And if Uncle Kepa gave that monkey to Denny Boy, well, watch out.

For some years now, whenever they had thought about Uncle Kepa, who had been round the world thousands of times, millions of times and overcounting times, they would discuss claims on the pet monkey that their uncle would one day bring.

Charlotte said she should have it because she was the eldest, but she would let them all come and see it whenever they wanted to. Denny Boy thought that he should be able to keep the monkey because he helped Uncle Kepa a lot. He cleaned Uncle's tank out, chopped his wood, and looked after his fishing lines while he was away. Becky and Lizzie backed Charlotte's claim because she was their sister and that would make them second in charge. One day Mereana had said that Uncle would be sure to give her the monkey because she was the youngest, and they all stared at her wondering if this could happen. No. Charlotte decided that Mereana was too small to look after a monkey.

Yes. The others were relieved. Mereana wasn't big enough but they would let her – and just then, Macky, who was stretched out on his back looking at the sky, said, 'Uncle Kepa, he's going to give that monkey to me.'

'You?' they all yelled.

'You?'

'You don't even know Uncle Kepa.'

'You haven't even seen Uncle Kepa.'

'Auntie Connie, she only got you last year.'

'Uncle Kepa, he's not your real uncle.'

Macky closed his eyes, 'Uncle Kepa, I bet he'll give that monkey to me.'

'What for?'

'Yeah. What for? He never told you he was bringing a monkey.'

'You weren't here.'

'Auntie Connie, she only got you last year.'

'Uncle Kepa, he'll give that monkey to me.'

'What for?'

'Because I look like a monkey, that's what for. And the monkey will like me the best.'

They all stared at Macky angrily, wondering. 'You always say that's what I look like, a monkey, so that means I do.' Macky got up and started running around on his hands and feet. Then he stood up, stuck his bottom teeth out up over his top lip and began scratching under his armpits. When he could see that they were really worried he ran up a tree and hung from a branch by one hand, making noises like Tarzan's ape.

They watched him without speaking for a long time. Then Charlotte said, 'You don't look like a monkey any more.'

'No,' they all agreed. 'You don't look like a monkey at all.'

'Only when Auntie Connie first got you you did.' But they were worried.

'I think Auntie Connie might give you back soon.' And after that they'd spent the rest of the morning swinging in the trees and gibbering.

Later that day someone had put forward the idea that if they made a house for the monkey and kept it in the orchard then that would be fair, because the orchard belonged to everyone. They had all agreed, each thinking he would find a way out if Uncle Kepa gave the monkey to him.

But now, there was Denny Boy hugging Uncle Kepa. And while it was one thing to be the eldest, or the youngest, or to be lucky and look like a monkey, it was another thing to be first and *smart*. Uncle Kepa was sitting himself down in the lupins at the side of the road to wait for them. He put his arms out and they all fell in. 'Ah my babies, my babies,' he kept saying.

His babies all hugged him then moved back so the monkey

wouldn't get squashed. Where would Uncle keep a monkey? So far they couldn't see a monkey anywhere. All Uncle's pockets were flat and he wasn't carrying any boxes. There was only his bag. Charlotte dug her elbow into Mereana and whispered, 'You ask, you're the youngest.' So Mereana hid behind Lizzie. And Denny Boy, making sure to keep the upper hand, said, 'Uncle, you got us a monkey?'

'Ah no, my babies. Not this time. The monkey, he got away. That monkey, he's too quick for this funny old uncle. Next time, my babies.'

Ah well.

They walked along the beach with their uncle, who rolled from side to side as though he was still on board. Uncle was a big strong man, and he had chased a monkey the length and breadth of some faraway jungle, climbing trees and swinging from branch to branch, but the monkey had got away. It shows you how quick and clever monkeys are.

That evening when Uncle Kepa was sitting in a chair by the stove at Auntie Connie's place with all the kids hanging round, he said, 'Ah that's good. Good to be a landlubber for a while. Good to see all my babies again. All my babies. These the only babies I got.' Then the kids heard Auntie Connie say, 'What about that drop kick of yours over in Aussie?' and Auntie Connie was laughing.

Then Uncle looked at the ceiling and started to laugh too, 'Ee hee, ee hee, ee hee hee.' Uncle Kepa was a great big man but his laugh was high and skinny like a seagull noise. And gee they all had a lot of things to talk about when it was time to go back to school. All about their uncle who was a great big man who went everywhere in the world in a big ship. And who was bringing them a monkey one day. As well as that they'd just found out that Uncle was a famous footballer too, and it made him laugh like anything.

The Pictures

AFTER ALL, SHE AND ANA WORE SHOES TO THE PICTURES NOW, and hers had the toes and heels out, and she'd been promised stockings for the winter. 'I might get me some earrings,' she said to Ana, as though earrings grew on trees.

They'd spent most of the afternoon getting themselves ready for the pictures, heating the irons on the stove and going over the skirts and blouses – pressing and steaming, reheating and pressing. Then they'd taken the basins outside and washed their hair, and now they sat on the stile waiting for it to dry. 'And I might get me a haircut,' Ana said. Charlotte drew in her breath, 'Ana, we wouldn't be allowed.'

'Yes, well. I might get me a haircut anyway – and I'm putting mine up for tonight.'

'So am I.'

'Let's go and try it now. See if it suits us. You do mine and I'll do yours.'

In front of the bedroom mirror with clips and elastic. Charlotte pulling the wire brush through her hair. Pounding the brush on to her scalp, dragging it down through the layers of thick tangles. Scraping up now, and out, up and out. Until the room is filled with flying streamers of Charlotte's hair.

Ana spread the circle of elastic on her fingers and worked carefully, putting the ends of Charlotte's hair into the band. She let the band close, then tied a ribbon tightly over the band and pulled the bundle of hair up and under at the back of Charlotte's neck. She spread the fold so that it rested thickly about Charlotte's shoulders. A clip above each ear to hold the hair in place. Finished.

Charlotte looked into the mirror, smoothing and patting.

Not bad. Not too bad. As long as the elastic would stay, as long as the clips would hold. Ana was hovering, 'It suits you. It does. It suits you.' 'Ye-es. Not bad. Not too bad.' Charlotte could see Macky and Denny Boy peeping round the open door at her but she couldn't be bothered with them, not with her hair done up, and it suiting her. She arched her eyebrows and stroked her hair, 'Get those kids out, Ana,' she sighed. 'Get those nosey brats out.'

'Get out,' said Ana, making a face and slamming the door. 'We don't want any kids hanging round – yes, it suits you, Charlotte.'

'It's okay. Course when I get dressed up. With the skirt . . . and shoes . . . I'll do yours now. Then we'll go over to Linda's and do hers, and tonight we'll wear some old boots on to the road to keep our shoes clean.'

'Are those kids still hanging round?'

Ana opened the door. 'They've gone,' she said.

The boys had wanted it to be a cowboy one but it was going to be a sloppy one after all, with kissing and people singing – La la la . . .

'La la la,' Macky sang with one hand on his heart and the other extended to his love, Denny Boy. 'La la la, will you marry me?'

'No,' Denny Boy sang. 'No I won't, my darling.'

'Thank you. La la la . . .'

'Anyway,' said Denny Boy, flopping down on to his stomach, 'we mightn't be going yet.'

'We'll go. We'll get there.'

'Auntie Connie won't give us any money. I just walked over her scrubbed floor – by accident. Just by accident.'

'What did she do?'

'Picked up her mop. So I took off. She's in a bad mood. For nothing.'

'We better not ask her for any.'

'No . . .'

'What about Uncle Harry?'

162

'He's too mingy.'

'We could hoe his garden for him, and chop his morning wood.'

'Boy, we'd be working all day.'

'And he mightn't give us anything. He might be broke.'

'And we might work all day for nothing.'

'Let's go and see Auntie Myra then.'

'Okay, she might.'

'But she mightn't.'

'But she might.'

And there was Auntie scratching her borders with the rake and all her ducks scrummaging into the loose soil at her feet. Wonder what sort of mood she's in.

'Hello, Auntie.'

'Tena koe, Denny Boy.' Talking Maori ay? Must be in a good mood – not like that Auntie Connie.

'Hello, Auntie.'

'Tena koe, e hoa. Kei te pehea korua?'

'Kei te pai, Auntie.' Talk Maori back to her.

'Yeh. Kei te pai, Auntie.' That'll keep her in a good mood.

'Ka pai.'

'We came over to see you.'

'To see how you're getting on with your flowers.'

'And your ducks.'

'Ka pai ano. Kei whea o korua hoa?'

'Down the beach.' Hope that's right.

'Yes, down the beach. And Charlotte and Ana are do-dah-ing themselves up for the pictures.'

'The pictures tonight.'

'Ah.'

'It's a good one.'

'Yes real good.'

'Kei te haere korua?'

'Not him. Not me, but all those others are going. Everyone else.'

'But him and me, we can't go.'

'Na te aha?'

'Because . . . because . . . Auntie Connie's in a bad mood. For nothing.'

'Yes, just for nothing.'

'Kare aku moni, e tama ma.'

And that's easy enough to understand, she's bloody well broke.

Shit what a waste of a good mood . . .

'Well . . .'

'Well . . . we have to go, Auntie. I hope your flowers are all right.'

'And your ducks.'

'Haere ra, e hoa ma.'

Uncle Harry was hoeing up the dirt round his kumara plants. They could see him from the willows at the back of his place.

'All that and he might be broke, like Auntie Myra.'

'Wait a bit longer. When he gets to the last two rows we'll go and help.'

'If he's broke we'll have to try to get Auntie Connie in a good mood.'

'That's too hard.'

'Mmm. Worse than hoeing up Uncle's kumara.'

'All this trouble and it's only a sloppy love one.'

'Yes. La la la . . .'

'Shut up, he'll hear.'

'Anyway he's nearly finished. Let's go and help.'

'Hello, Uncle. We came to help you hoe up your kumara.'

'Hello, boys. Good on you. Get another hoe from the shed and one of you can have this one. I'll sit down and have a smoke. You two can be the workers and I'll be the boss.'

He sat down and began shredding tobacco along his paper as the boys started to mound the dirt up under the vines.

'That's the way, boys. Heap them up. When we dig them there'll be plenty for you to take home.' Well, it wasn't a bag of kumara they wanted.

'Plenty of potatoes too.' Or spuds.

'Those others are playing down the beach, Uncle.'

'Yes they're lazy.'

'Just playing. But Macky and I, we like to come and help you with your garden.'

'Instead of playing.'

'That's good boys. Keep it up. Careful of those vines.'

'After this we'll chop your morning wood for you.'

'That's the way. Good on you, mates.'

' . . . Uncle?'

'Ay?'

'You know what Charlotte and them are doing?'

'No.'

'Looking at their ugly selves in the mirror.'

'And ironing their clothes.'

'Ironing their clothes ay?'

'They think they're bea-utiful like ladies in the pictures.'

'And their hair is all done up funny like rags.'

'And they got banjo feet and gumboot lips, but they think they look bea-utiful, la la la . . .'

'Hey Uncle.'

'Ay?'

'You know why Charlotte and them are ironing their clothes and washing their hair?'

'No.'

'They're going to the pictures.'

'Ah the pictures. What's on tonight?'

'Well it's a good one . . . a cowboy one.'

'Yes, a good cowboy one, Uncle . . . All those lazy kids are going.'

'All of them ay?'

'Yes all.'

'Well, boys, you've done a good job there.'

What was the matter with Uncle Harry. Wasn't he listening? They'd hoed up two rows of kumara and now they were lopping the dry brush heads off the manuka and tying it into a bundle to start his stove in the morning. They'd told Uncle that all those lazy kids were going to the pictures but he wasn't listening.

'Good, good. Put your hoes away in the shed now, and stick our axe in the block.' Was he deaf or something?

'Got any more jobs, Uncle?'

'No that's all, boys.' Deaf all right. No ears. All that hoeing, all that chopping. And old Uncle No Ears going up his steps and in his door . . .

'See you later, Uncle.' Deaf Ears.

'Okay, boys. Hey, don't you want these?'

Up on to the verandah, pecking the coins from Uncle's big dried paua of a hand. Running, shouting. Shouting . . .

'Thank you, Uncle.'

'Thank you.'

'La la la.'

'La la la.'

Lizzie was coughing again. Mereana ran with her down the track past the garden, Lizzie's eyes bulging like two turnips, her chook hand clawed over her mouth. Running into the dunny and banging the door. Then the coughing. Mereana kept watch outside because they wouldn't let Lizzie go to the pictures tonight if they knew she had her cough.

And from where Mereana waited, she could hear the cough gurgling and rumbling up Lizzie's throat then barking out of her mouth as though Lizzie was a dog. Then after a while the gurgling and rumbling and barking stopped and she could hear Lizzie spitting down the dunny hole.

Coming out now with the bottom half of her face all white and stretched and her pop eyes watery and pink. 'Come down the beach,' Lizzie gasped at her. 'So they won't hear.'

Down through the lupins with the black pods busting, which was nothing really, only a sound. Lying on the beach stones and licking them for salt. Lizzie gurgling and squeaking, and Lizzie was nothing but an old crumpled bit of paper there beside her. What if Lizzie died right now?

'Lizzie, Lizzie! There'll be a lot of kissing, I bet.'

'Mmm. Plenty . . . of kissing.'

'And she'll have lovely dresses, Lizzie.'

'Yes . . .'

'The men will fight over her. Ay?'

'Mmm.'

'But the best one will marry her.'

'Mmm. At . . . the end.'

'And they'll have a long long kiss.'

'At the end.'

Bending over the sea now. Her neck stretched and lumpy like a sock full of stones. Spitting on the water. 'Don't cough, Lizzie,' Mereana called. 'Don't. They'll hear you. They'll make you stay home.'

Oh but it wasn't that. Not the staying home. The cough was too big. Bigger than the sea – bigger than the sky. Now standing up, pulling a big breath in, 'Yes . . . I bet she has . . . lovely dresses.' And another long breath. In. 'There'll be a long long kiss . . . at the end . . . I bet.'

At the gate where the road began, Charlotte, Ana and Linda took off their old shoes and hid them in the lupins, then carefully slid their feet into the good shoes and smoothed the skirts, patted the hair. Ahead of them the others were running along the sea wall yelling. Leaping down on to the sand, running back up the wall, but they were only kids. They didn't want kids hanging round. Mereana and Lizzie dawdling along behind them and that Lizzie barking her head off. 'We'll sit up the back,' Charlotte said, 'so we won't have *kids* hanging round.'

Not that the others wanted to anyway. Charlotte, Ana and Linda stank and had canoes for shoes and rags for hair. What's more, Charlotte and them, they had hairs under their arms and they were growing tits as well, just like cows. Along the top of the sea wall, flying now, and landing in sand. Cold. Sand goes dead at night time, up the wall again. Bits of shell everywhere, winking, on the road getting blacker every minute.

And waiting. At the store waiting. Lollies and a drink, then up the verandah poles, swinging and sliding – except for stinky Charlotte and them. Not Lizzie and Mereana either, Lizzie coughing like an old goat and baby Mereana nearly crying. Then . . .

'Here it comes.'

'Here it comes.'

Two eyes rounding the corner, bowling downhill. Jack had his foot down tonight.

Slowing down. Stopping.

'At last.'

'Yes. At last.'

Money in the tin. Smart the way Jack flicks you the ticket.

But Charlotte, Ana and Linda were waiting till last. What was the hurry? Damn kids. Always in a hurry. Always pushing. Always in the way. Well . . . well . . . Might as well get in.

'Might as well get in, you two.'

'Might as well.'

'Go on then.'

'No you.'

'You first.'

'Go *on*.'

Up the steps. Gum rolling, eyes down. Wondering who's staring. All those big eyes in the bus must stare – or were they? Have a look, look away. They knew it, people *were* staring.

'All looking pretty tonight, aincha?' Jack yelled.

Bloody Jack. And now that Ana. That Ana had started giggling. Charlotte and Linda were wild with her. No wonder everyone was staring. No wonder . . . And look at Linda. Now Linda was going to. Sneaking along the bus with her hand up over her mouth, snorting behind her hand. Gee they made Charlotte wild those two – and Jack. Everyone staring.

Now Linda was looking at her with cow's eyes, rolling her fat eyes at her and cackling like a chook. Then oh! Oh shame. She, Charlotte, could feel all the little dribbles of laughter gathering in her throat – climbing, pushing . . . Pushing. She threw herself on to the seat between Ana and Linda as the sounds fizzed and exploded behind her hand.

The boys who had sat behind the girls at the pictures got off the home bus at the store and followed the girls along the beach road. They were tossing bits of shell into the girls' hair and shoving each other. The girls were giggling and telling each other secrets. Those kids were going to get a good hiding too, running up and down the sea wall. Shouting, 'Give them a kiss.'

'Kiss.'

'Kiss, kiss.'

'Kiss, kiss, kiss.'

Making sure to keep out of Charlotte's way because she wasn't really a beautiful lady you know. You had to watch Charlotte for the left hook and the leg trip, yes.

Ack, those big boys were dumb following Charlotte and them. Whistling between their teeth and chucking things.

'Give them a kiss.'

'A kiss.'

'La la la.'

But no. No kiss. The boys had stopped now that they had come to the end of the road, and they were calling out to the girls.

But Charlotte, Ana and Linda weren't answering. They had remembered something and were walking ahead, not talking, not turning, not looking down . . .

Their hair suited them.

Their skirts suited them.

They had shoes to wear to the pictures.

They might be getting earrings.

And stockings.

And haircuts.

And they'd just remembered.

And now Macky and Denny Boy had remembered too. 'Hey you girls. What about your old boots you hid in the lupins?'

'Your old pakaru boots.'

Then away for their lives over the dark paddocks, through the thistles and plops. Lucky they had a head start. Up over the stile and jump the creek. Lucky they could see in the dark, those smartheads would never get them now – across the yard and in. Canoes for shoes. Rags for hair. Not till tomorrow. They'd kill them tomorrow.

But that's tomorrow.

Yes.

Drifting

THEY WERE UP WHILE IT WAS STILL DARK, RUNNING THROUGH the wet lupins with the tin of herrings, over the black stones to Uncle Kepa's hut. There they put the tin under the step, pushed the door open and went in.

Still asleep. But his morning wood was ready on the hearth. Mereana opened the grate and put the wood in on top of the crumpled newspaper. She lit the fire and moved the kettle over. Lizzie was mixing porridge.

'Hello, my babies. You got our bait?'

'Yes, Uncle. Plenty herrings.'

'Stoke up then. Your funny uncle will get changed.'

They heard him moving around in his other room, then he went outside and filled his basin at the tankstand. Uncle. He had a wash for going fishing, but just as well she and Lizzie hadn't wasted any time washing this morning or brushing their hair. Just as well they'd slept in their clothes to make sure about being early, because Uncle had forgotten to wake up. Get up, straighten the blankets, out over the verandah and away.

Now Lizzie was spooning porridge into three enamel plates.

'Come on, Uncle,' Mereana called.

He came in, making the room small. The skin on his face was mottled with the shock of cold water. His eyelids were rimmed with red as though his eyes had been always shut and forgotten but had now suddenly been slit open with a sharp blade to reveal surprised and bulging brown eyes, the whites all yellowed with waiting. His lashes, too, seemed as though they had this minute been put there, standing stiff and straight like glued bristles.

Mostly Uncle's face was long and thin, with big folds of

skin hanging down, but his cheekbones were round and jutting. His nose was hooked at the tip, with a big bubble of flesh at either side. He wore the top half of a football jersey with the bottom half of a black singlet sewn on to it; and he carried a billy of milk which he had brought in from the outside safe.

The room swung back to its normal size as he sat down, and there was a grey light coming in through the one little window high up in the wall. Uncle Kepa leaned over his dish and stuck his bottom lip way out like a shelf, then rested the spoon with the hot porridge there and sucked. The spoonful of porridge was gone.

'Ah. Ah good, my babies.'

Mereana stopped staring at her uncle and began pouring tea while Lizzie ran to rescue the bread that was toasting by the grate.

The little bit of dirty sea in the bottom of the dinghy swung and eddied with each push. Then away, rocketing down over the stones until the bow crunched into sand at the tip of the water. One more big push and it was flying out into the lagoon with Mereana and Lizzie throwing themselves in over its sides. Uncle Kepa, who had rolled his trousers up and whose legs were *white*, stepped in over the back and sat down on the middle seat to take up the oars.

They were soon through the channel, pulling out over the belt of brown kelp where the sea changed to a dull navy blue, then further still to where the water became thick and green.

The day was alight now. Far away, back on the shore, the sun was sending silver off the roofs of all the tiny houses, and streamers of smoke leaned from the morning chimneys. As they rounded the point they could see the large patches of brown rock below them in the water, while rocks closer to land and not yet warmed and browned by the touch of sun stood black with the cold of night on them, and at their feet was a white lacework of smashed sea.

Out on the water, so far away that it was like being no-where and like being no one, where even Uncle Kepa wasn't big any more, they let the rope down with the bag of stones on it and began baiting their hooks. Mereana watched her sinker break the surface and felt it take her line deep down into the sea. Who would be first? She could see a few feet of line before it disappeared, and could feel a small tingling. A quick glance at Lizzie. Lizzie was looking into the water too. Wondering perhaps who would be first. Thinking perhaps about all the fish in all the sea in all the world . . .

One of them will get on my line. I will pull it up quickly, and I will be first . . . Who would? Uncle Kepa was leaning forward with elbows on his knees. And gee, Uncle Kepa, he was asleep. What if a big fish got on Uncle's line and he didn't know? What if a shark came and bit the boat in half; who would save them? And if an albatross as big as the one in the museum came and took her and Lizzie away, who would fight it? Mereana forgot her line for the moment.

'Lizzie, Uncle's asleep.'

But then Uncle's hand with the line in it shot up above his head. His eyes popped open and he began to pull in. Uncle was first. Mereana and Lizzie watched him bring in his tarakihi then went back to their fishing.

'I got one. I got one, Uncle. I got one, Mereana.' Lizzie's face was all red and she was zipping her line up. Now Lizzie had a fish and Mereana didn't. She could feel some little nibbles on her line but the fish kept going away and getting on Lizzie's and Uncle Kepa's. Perhaps she was on the wrong side.

'Change seats, Lizzie.' But Lizzie wouldn't. She knew the good side. Lizzie used to be her best cousin and her best . . . Got one!

'I got one, Uncle. I got one, Lizzie.'

Hand over hand, hand over hand. Watching in the water. Far down a shadow moving, coming closer. There was her fish. Nearly to the top. Waving in the water like a big shiny hand.

Then, as the fish broke the surface her line went slack. The shadow that had been her fish was speeding back to the deep.

'Never mind, baby. Catch another one soon.'

And there was Lizzie who used to be her best friend pulling

in another one. It didn't get away from Lizzie either.

Never mind. They were there again. Nibbling, pulling, snatching. And if only the boat would keep still for a while, or was it herself? Just her, going up and down, up and down? The sun was above them now, bouncing its heat at them from off the surface of the water. And the sea. The sea was rocking them from side to side. Up and back, up and back . . . Uncle had tied his line to a rowlock. He was taking some old crayfish out that he had brought for bait.

'Waste of good crayfish,' he was saying. 'Waste giving it to the fish.'

He snapped the legs and began sucking the rotting flesh from them. Suck. Suck.

'Waste of good crayfish for those fish down there,' he said. 'Waste of good kai.'

Something was wrong with Mereana. Her stomach was all pinched up and she had no spit left. 'Up and back, up and back,' said the sea. The sun was going on and off and she could hear Uncle saying, 'Put your head over, baby. Put your head over,' so she did. Her throat was stretching out wide. And there she was, sicking on to the sea. She watched the sick floating away like a little white nest on the water.

But what was Uncle doing? Pulling in the anchor.

'No, Uncle.'

She wiped her mouth on the bottom of her dress.

'No, Uncle. I want to catch one. A fish. A fish, Uncle.' Letting it down. Letting the anchor down.

'A little while, a little while,' he was saying. Well that's good. That's all right. Her line tinkled and rang, and suddenly it swam away.

'I got one. Got one, see.' She pulled quickly.

'Got one, Uncle. Got one, Lizzie.' She could see it now nearly at the top. Don't get away. Bigger than Lizzie's. Bigger than Uncle Kepa's. And Uncle Kepa, he was leaning over the side with a gaff hook. Don't . . .

Her line was empty again. She saw her fish flip and dive. Then.

Then there was a great crashing in the water and the sea had turned white. It had Uncle in it.

'Uncle!'

Uncle Kepa's head popped out of the water.

'I got it, baby.' And he held up the gaff with her fish flapping and gasping on it. Her fish. And it was bigger than Lizzie's. Bigger than Uncle's.

He reached over the side and put the gaff with the fish on it into the boat. He turned the boat and took hold of the anchor rope and began easing himself up. Uncle was brave you know. What if a shark came and bit his legs off, or a whale, or a giant octopus like the one that picked up a whole submarine in the pictures. The back of the boat rose as he levered himself up over the bow. He was in. He made it and his legs were still on.

The back of the boat came down with a slap and a wave whacked against its side and splashed in.

'Bail out, mates.'

Mereana and Lizzie took the bailing tins and began throwing the wave back.

'We got it, Uncle. We got my fish.'

'We got it, baby. We got that big fulla.' He was pulling up the anchor now. Never mind.

'These funny fishermen are all wet,' he said.

Out from the point they watched him take his spinner from his fishing bag. He tied the end of the line to the back seat and straightened the boat for a hard pull homeward. Then they were shinning out over the water, which now that they had rounded the corner was quiet and unruffled in a windless afternoon.

Mereana watched the spinner sending out a fine white spray behind them. Would they catch a kahawai as Uncle said? Because fish don't eat paua shells.

'Uncle, kahawai don't eat paua shells.'

With each big pull Uncle Kepa's breath was hissing out between his teeth, 'The kahawai ... he think ... it ... a herring.' Gee, Uncle. Anyone could see it was a paua shell with holes in it spinning on a line. Most of the time Uncle was clever and strong, and he could row fast, and he had jumped in the sea and saved her fish. But now . . . Uncle thought . . .

The kahawai struck. There was a green-silver flash, and spray ribboned up and out as the boat dragged the fish through the water.

'We got one. We got one. The kahawai he thought it was a herring. Gee he thought the bit of paua shell was herring. Dumb, ay, Lizzie? Dumb, ay, Uncle?'

'Dumb, ay, Mereana.'

The lagoon was full of children, waiting to see how good the catch had been.

Mereana and Lizzie were tired that night. They had been up early and out fishing. So many things had happened that the other kids hadn't believed them. They lay side by side on Lizzie's little bed. It was a warm night. They could hear the sea scrambling up the stones.

'Mereana?'

'What?'

'I wonder where your sick is.'

'Something might've ate it.' Because fish were dumb. They didn't know one thing from another.'

'I think it's still there on the water.'

But Mereana was tired. Her eyes closed. Away, away, in a dark place far at the back of her eyes there was a little nest drifting . . . Drifting. Somewhere far away on a dark, dark sea. . .

Whitebait

At most times of the year the creek kept its secrets to itself. In the armpits of its banks eels tucked themselves, and outsized worms made quiet, intricate passages. Brown trout and cockabullies fed against the creek's knobbled belly. And the transients – larvae of dragon, damsel and may fly – waited for the time when they would climb out into air and fly away.

But at this time of the year the creek abandoned secrecy, and as though parting great legs and giving sudden and copious birth, set crowds of whitebait speeding for the sea.

The children had made a net from an old petticoat that Auntie Connie had given them, and they ran with it to the creek. They put the net down in a narrow place facing upstream. The net ballooned in the water, and Denny Boy from up-creek called, 'Coming.' He began to wade towards them, swishing his shoo-shie stick from bank to bank and watching the whitebait race ahead of him.

As he got close to the net the whitebait at the head of the shoal began to turn, trying to escape. But there was no escape. He directed them expertly into the net's open mouth.

Macky and Charlotte lifted the net and took it up on to the bank where they emptied the whitebait into a tin. Then they moved further up-creek to where the water was still clear, to set the net down again.

Later in the morning Lizzie and Mereana were sent back to Auntie Connie's for some eggs and fat and a frying pan. They waited in the willows not far from the house wondering what they should do.

'I think,' said Mereana, 'if we ask her she might . . .'

'But if she's in a mood,' said Lizzie, 'we'll get a flick on the ear and a job to do.'

Just then the door of the house opened and their auntie came out with a bucket of water, a scrubbing brush and a block of sandsoap, and went round to the front of the house.

'She's in a mood,' whispered Mereana. 'I saw her face.'

'She's in a mood all right,' Lizzie agreed.

'So?'

'You get the pan and the fat, I'll get the eggs.'

Run.

To the outside safe.

To the hen house.

Then walk quickly back to the hiding willows with the pan and fat.

Quiet, chookies, quiet. You know me, ay, I'm Lizzie. I gave you plenty wheat this morning, tons and tons. And plenty water. Sh-sh, chookies.

Take the eggs quietly.

Shut the hen-house door. Carefully. And turn the nailed block into position to make sure the door stays shut.

Get behind the hen house and breathe. Breathe out holding the warm eggs gently.

They could hear Auntie Connie bashing the front steps with her scrubbing brush.

The others had made a fireplace and collected dry rushes and sticks, and now they were in the creek again, lifting stones to find crayfish. When Mereana and Lizzie returned, Denny Boy got out of the water and lit the fire. Charlotte washed a stick, strained the water away from the whitebait, whipped the eggs in with them and cooked them in the pan. Macky put fresh water into one of the tins and put the koura on to cook as well.

Pin eyes and pinchers.

They'd never know what a bright colour they had become.

And how many eyes could a panful of whitebait have?

Not one pair of eyes now that would see the sea.

Eyes. Auntie Connie never saw.

Out front banging her steps.

Pull away the pink shells and toss them on the fire.

Hang the hot flesh on your tongue.

Let it burn.

The only way to taste.

To know.

Is to let it burn.

Bite the eyed heads and there's more to know.

Knowing the creek and wind sounds, and the small one-eyed glow that is the fire, the hiding willows and nailed wood block on the hen-house door. And the cocked hen eye, and the lifted curled foot of a hen.

Knowing the whipped bleeding cuts that the cutty grass has made on legs and arms, and remembering a woman with a scrubbing bucket pounding the front steps, back on to the drumming sea.

Suddenly all is made small and known, fitting easily on the tongue before being swallowed with a quick, cooling breath.

Denny Boy took out his tin of cigarette butts and tipped them on to the ground. He unwrapped each one and teased the collection of tobacco evenly along an oblong of brown paper, then rolled his cigarette slowly, using the tips of his fingers and thumbs. They were all watching him. He half shut his eyes and spat carefully on the edge of the paper and rubbed the spit along with his finger.

Charlotte had left her tin behind, in a tree in the orchard. So had Macky and Ana, under the floor in the shed.

Denny Boy smoothed the wet edge of the paper down, leaned into the eye of the fire and lit up.

They watched him draw in and let the smoke out holding the cigarette finely between the very tips of two fingers.

They watched him blowing out with his eyes half shut. And pulling his cheeks in.

Puffing out between lips that were formed into a little circle.

'Give us one.'

'There's no more.'

They watched him lie back and blow dawdling smoke into the trees.

Shoo-shie sticks.

And cigarette butts.

He was King, and as he closed his eyes he heard the others stamping off through the bush to look for thistle. Huh.

Anybody knew dried thistle wouldn't light up properly.

Anybody knew it gave you a mouth ache.

Butts and sticks.

Whitebait and koura.

And smoke going easily into the trees.

When the cigarette was half gone he pinched the lit end off and put it away in his pocket. And later when the others had come back with their thistle stalks and huffed and gasped, and hurt their mouths, and made their throats sore. Then. That was when he would find the other half of the cigarette in his pocket.

And he'd light it and draw in, and hold smoke in him for a long long time, and his half-shut eyes would see them watch. He'd blow out slowly.

Slow and

Blow.

He could hear them somewhere behind him, treading through the rushes.

Kip

THE OLD HALL WAS AS ACCOMMODATING AS TREES. ON THE way home from school, and when they were younger, the kids would stop and bounce their bald tennis balls against its wall – sevensies to onesies, right hand, left hand, whirls and claps. They planted their feet on it doing against-the-wall handstands, their eyes dropping from their heads. The recessed doorway was a ghost house, a witch hole, a tick-a-lock home base.

Dogs sniffed the bottom edges of the building before lifting a leg. Sparrows and starlings scrabbled and fluttered in the spoutings and corrugations, and when the time was right made their nests. It was the birds, dogs and kids that gave the hall its animal smell.

But, while the outside of the animal retained its spots – grey and white dried splashes left by season after season of bird, flat black pennies made by the bouncing balls, patches of dog dribble, and the smeared footprints with toes pointing earthwards – the inside now had a new look. The walls had been painted pale blue. The old stage had new blue satin curtains, and new facings, painted white and edged in blue glitter. The leaking roof had been mended and the ceiling strung with twisted streamers of pink, white and blue crepe paper. From the centre of the ceiling hung the blue moon.

On weekdays with the door shut and no light or sound coming from within, it was still the 'old hall', but on Saturdays it had become the 'Blue Moon' dance hall. And on those nights once the lights went on and the doorman was ready with his tin and his roll of tickets, the band would string out its first few notes and the turning mirrored ball would be spotlighted in blue. Then the floor would quickly fill with dancers all measled with moving blue light.

Bob gave an uneasy lead, striding deep into the corners and not knowing quite how to come out of them again. His arm about her waist exerted no pressure, and the cupped hand in which she placed hers could just as easily have been holding one of the hairless tennis balls they'd kicked goals with, or chucked again and again against walls.

'Apprentice electrician,' he said. 'With my old man.'

'Do you like it?'

'I like it okay. What about you, what're you doing?'

'I'll be leaving school at the end of the year.'

'Then what?'

'Don't know. I might go nursing.'

'You like it all right, do you? School I mean.'

'I'm sick of it. Glad this is my last year.'

'I really hated school. Couldn't get away quick enough myself.'

And just then Mereana had a sudden picture of him at seven years of age standing in front of the class wearing a white shirt and a pair of navy shorts, his fair hair oiled into the shape of a shell. His face was entranced, and shocking to look at, and a sudden stream of pee was running down his leg.

Now after remembering that, it was difficult to speak: he had noticed her shift of memory. 'The band's all right,' she said.

'I hear they're having a singer later on.'

'Probably the same one they had last week.'

'She's all right too.'

His legs at seven years of age had been thin and veiny.

As Lizzie danced past, the blue light turned the red spots on her cheeks to purple. Reuben Hails' large hand on her waist moved her first away then close as they toed round the floor. Looking at Reuben, Mereana could read the contempt that Lizzie was too close to see, and which in any case she had never learned to see. Lizzie's large eyes, fringed by large curled black lashes, rested like two sea anemones just above Reuben's shoulder.

'Your cousin and Reuben are hitting it off,' Bob said to her.

'Lizzie.'

'Yes. I don't remember her so well.'

'She missed quite a lot of school.'

'She was sick a lot, wasn't she?'

'Yes but she's okay now, or supposed to be.' (Her lung was 'cured' – like salted pork.) 'Do you know Reuben well?'

'He's older. Used to be in my brother's class. He thinks the sun shines out of his arse.'

It was a long speech for him. She liked Bob, who had no questions behind the eyes, no hidden slivers of glass in the cupped hand, and the light and shadows spinning across his face came only from the turning spot-lit ball. Mereana put her hand into the triangle that he'd made with his arm as the music frittered away, and he led her to her seat.

'Bob. Bob-ee,' Macky sang in her ear as she sat down beside him. 'La-la-la.'

'Give us a cig,' she said.

He drew in on the cigarette that he was smoking, then passed it to her. 'Last one,' he said. Reuben's elbow crushed Lizzie's hand to his side as he walked her towards them. Macky put his head back and blew smoke balls towards the ceiling. 'Reuben Hails,' he said, 'has got a theory ... about dark-skinned women ...' Reuben turned to Lizzie, twitched the corners of his mouth, and walked quickly away. 'Did you know?'

'You can guess it easy enough,' Mereana said.

'What're you talking about?' Lizzie asked. She was breath-less.

'Throw your eyes in there,' Macky said, nodding towards the supper room. 'Sausage rolls, cakes, sandwiches. Food,' he hooted. 'When are we going to have food?'

'Just watch out for Reuben,' Mereana said to Lizzie.

Charlotte and Denny Boy came over. 'I think the next one's going to be the supper waltz,' Charlotte said.

The sea spread beside them like a length of tossed shot silk. The old bus sailed the sea's curve, its headlights catching the white tips of the waves.

When they got off the bus they could hear the sea niggling at the shore stones, then there was the skirr of sprayed road metal above the grind of the gear changes as the bus backed, turned, and rocked away in the dark. They lifted a hand to Bob whose face and hand appeared briefly at the back window. She liked Bob whose eyes held no questions. The kiss in the bus had made no demands, had taken away nothing apart from a small breath.

'They shouldn't have gone with him,' Lizzie was saying.

'Don't worry about them,' Mereana said. 'Anyway we said to you to watch out . . .'

'I know.'

'Why did you then?'

'Well he said only for a minute. Then when we walked along . . .'

'He wanted to get you in under the trees with him.'

'He got all funny when I wouldn't . . .'

'It's because of his theory,' Macky said to the stars.

'Anyhow what about Charlotte? She was dancing round with him. Smiling and all that, after I came back and told yous what had happened.'

'Don't worry about Charlotte.'

'What's on anyway? Where've they gone?'

'Some sort of party up at Ian and them's place.'

Then as they came nearer to the home gate they heard singing and saw that all the lights were on at their Auntie Connie's place. They began to hurry, over the stile and over the plank across the creek, under the thick dark of the willows and up the gravel path to the door where they studied the row of shoes at the doorstep. Uncle Kepa.

'Uncle Kepa.' The room was warm and beery and noisy as they hurried in to greet him.

As he approached the wharf gates he saw the boy look up and start towards him out of the dark. Then, strangely, he thought he heard the boy say his name.

He waited as the boy limped towards him, and then there

was the boy's face under the light for him to see. And Christ! it was his own face. This was himself approaching. He held his breath. This was himself surely, at sixteen, going off to sea after the death of his grandmother, with some old clothes in a brown paper parcel. This was himself, broad cheeked, full lipped and dark, hair standing up like a kina, clutching his parcel to his side.

But no, this boy was smaller, more stooped, and he dragged a slightly turned shoe over the footpath, down the guttering and across the pot-holed road towards him. Yet under the buttery light it was *his* face, his own sixteen-year-old, young face. He heard his name again.

'Yes?'

'I've looked for you,' the boy said. 'There's no place for me here, so I looked . . .'

'My drop kick,' he breathed out of his past.

'I didn't know . . . so I looked. There isn't any place . . .'

Kepa paused a moment then said, 'There is a place,' and he took the parcel from the boy and pushed it down into his swag.

'You didn't stay long,' Mereana said to Denny Boy. 'At the party I mean.'

'Long enough,' he said.

'What did you do?'

'Me? Nothing.'

Uncle Kepa was pulling himself up out of the armchair. He staggered slightly and almost toppled. Denny Boy and Charlotte stood and took an arm each. 'You haven't ask me yet,' he said.

'But Charlotte did,' Denny Boy said to Mereana. 'Asked you what, Uncle?'

'You haven't ask me yet . . .'

'What did she do? What did Charlotte do?'

'Put a left hook on his jaw. He dropped like a bomb.'

'You haven't ask me yet if I brought you a monkey.'

'A monkey!'

He stumbled towards the bedroom.

'Fell back on Geddy's fence and stabbed himself before he hit the ground,' Charlotte said.

'In here. There, my babies. Funny uncle . . . he found you a monkey.' Then he showed them the boy asleep.

They were looking down at Uncle Kepa with all his years taken off like old skins, and all the engine room grease and callouses and tight muscle removed by a reversal of time from hands and arms.

'Kip,' he said. 'My little one from Aussie.'

He lifted the blankets and got into bed beside the boy Kip, who moved only slightly. 'Funny uncle,' he said, then seemed immediately to be asleep.

ELECTRIC CITY
and
Other Stories

Contents

Waimarie

WAIMARIE CALLED TO MAX TO COME AND UNPLUG THE IRON. She spoke in their own language.

And she told him to have a smoke now, where she could see him. 'Lucy's picking me up,' she said, 'and don't you smoke while I'm out, putting the place on fire. And don't cook. You come down the marae after and have a kai down there, you hear me . . . Get me up,' she said.

For a moment Max stood and looked at her. He had the cigarette out of the packet but he hadn't lit it.

'Get me up,' his sister said again.

So he moved to the settee where she was sitting and took her by the arm, pushing up under her elbow until she stood.

'My stick.'

He unhooked her stick from the back of the settee and put it in her hand.

'Now you do what I say,' she said, and pointed at the tea-towels and tablecloths. 'Put them in the drawer.'

Max put his cigarette down and went to do as she told him.

'And those in the cupboard.' She poked her stick at towels and pillowcases.

'Nothing else,' she said, when he had put the linen away. 'You have your smoke now before Lucy come.'

She picked up Keriata's and Ariana's jeans and T-shirts and took them to put in their drawer. She put her skirt away and hung Max's shirt on the end of his bed, moving slowly to and fro.

Then she changed into her black dress, and while she was waiting for Lucy she hooked long shark-tooth earrings onto her ears.

'Hot,' Lucy said, as she helped her aunt to stand. 'But could get cold.'

'My shawl, there on the settee,' said Waimarie. 'And my bag too. And dear, I want my teeth, in the bathroom, in the glass.'

'You finish your smoke?' she asked Max. 'You put it out properly?'

He showed her the ashtray with the cigarette butt and the dead match in it.

'Empty that in the rubbish,' she said. 'Wash it, and don't turn on any stove or jug. Don't you smoke. Don't cook nothing. And you wait here. When those girls come back you tell them Nanny gone to the marae. Tell them come straight down. Now, what you going to say to Ariana and Keriata?'

'Nanny gone marae,' he said.

'What else?'

'You go down.'

'Straight down.'

'Straight down.'

'And you speak English, don't forget. Speak English or they won't know.'

On their way down the path Lucy said, 'Your garden's good, Aunt.'

So Waimarie stopped and pointed here and there.

'See all my portulaca. Harriet give me it from her old place but not the dark one, the dark one it's from my mate down the road. She got a big one at the back of her place. The yellow one, it's from Robert's wife. And begonia? I get two when I'm in the hospital and when I come home I stick them in the ground and they grow no trouble. That one, that one, I get them from the gala for the school, and polyanthus from the school too – red, purple, pink. But over here it's all from the old place – kaka beak, gladdies, gerbera, hydrangea – it's my own mother's flowers from the old place.'

'Does Uncle Max help you?'

'Useless, he don't know a kotimana from a flower. Nah, I

just sit on my cushion and do what I want to do, then move along. Next day another part, or whatever I want. Well if there's digging Max can do it. He's not so old like me, only handicap, but still strong. My mother's forty-six when she have him and I'm twenty. Well it's me who bring him up all his life . . . Now, dear, get me a leaves from my little tree.'

Lucy picked the leaves and helped her aunt to the car. She opened the door and held the old lady as she eased her way on to the seat. She helped her get her legs in and put the shawl across her knees.

'Lovely car, dear,' Waimarie said. 'Warm, nice sheepskins.'

'Kids bought us the sheepskins not long after we got the car.'

'Who's home with you and Jimmy now?'

'Only Teina. Teina's the only one still home.'

After they'd been driving a while, Lucy said, 'We've got room Aunt, if you want us to have the girls.'

'They won't come,' said Waimarie. 'Won't even go to their own mother. Too haurangi that one. That's why I take them off her in the first place. She give them flash names and that's all. She come here wanting them last Christmas – now she sees them pretty and growing up – but they won't go. "We're stopping with Nanny," they tell her. Anyway all beer talk. She only ask for them when she's haurangi.'

'Yes, I suppose . . . Or Uncle Max. We could have him. Jimmy likes Uncle Max, those two get on like a house on fire.'

'Well it's me who bring him up all his life.'

Lucy pulled over and stopped the car.

'That's true . . . but, if ever you want . . .'

'What time they bringing Bill in?'

'Two. Leaving the undertakers at two, and should be here by ten past. Sit there I'll come round.'

Lucy helped the old lady out of the car and they moved towards the wharenui where others waited in the sun.

'I was here earlier, Aunt,' Lucy said. 'Everything's ready, house is ready. Hone, Mattie and Watson are doing the kai,

193

and there'll be more helpers this afternoon and tonight.'

'Kei te pai,' the old woman said.

Then Waimarie stopped and said to Lucy, 'Later on, dear, later on I want them to come to you, Ariana and Keriata.'

'Kei te pai, Aunt.'

'The house can be for Max, well it's me who bring him up all his life. And . . . someone can come there and live with him. Later on. Dear, I want the girls to come to you and Jimmy.

'Kei te pai, Aunt, don't say anything more.'

Waimarie moved to greet the men at the front of the wharenui.

'You see him out,' she said to one of them.

'Tough breed,' the old man replied.

'Me too,' she said.

'The wicked stay healthy.'

Lucy assisted her up the two steps on to the verandah where those who were waiting stood to greet her.

'You're here,' someone said.

'With teeth.'

'We can get the show on the road then.'

'Where's Uncle Max?'

'Burning our house down might be.' She sat down to wait. 'You all got a warm, nice place here in the sun. Poor old Bill, ah well.'

She looked out over the marae to where the mats had been put down for the casket. The seating was ready for the family coming in and the grass had been cut and the edges trimmed. As she waited she twisted the trail of leaves into a band for her head.

When the group saw that the people were ready at the gate they helped Waimarie to her feet. Lucy put the shawl about her aunt's shoulders. The old lady moved forward to the top step and the group closed in behind her.

There was hot sun on her lifted face, sun which swathed light through her hair and sifted the circle of leaves into layers of green. And then she called their kinsman to his home, called him to the warmth, the protection of the place where he would be wept for.

The light showed the lines on her face to be deep and hard, and light spun off the gold clasps which clutched the ornaments at her ears. These ornaments hung quivering in the brightness, curving the way her jaw curved, light sculpting them against the contour of her jaw. She called the spirits of the many dead to gather along with the kinsman, so that the dead could all be wept for together.

Light mixed the muted colours of her shawl and glossed the dark clothing. And her voice lifted out, weaving amongst the sheddings of light, encompassing the kinsman and his family, bearing them forward.

The Geranium

AFTER THE KIDS HAD GONE TO SCHOOL MARNEY STARTED ON the work. She did the dishes, washed the teatowels and hung them out. She wiped down the table and the bench, and the windowsill and the frame of the window. She cleaned the window and the fireplace, and took the ashpan out and emptied it where she'd been digging. She wiped the hearth with a damp cloth.

Then she put the mat outside so she could sweep and mop out. She liked the mat, which was new. Bob had come home with it the week before and she'd put it in the centre of the room where it wouldn't get marked. She thought Bob might get another mat for by the door, not a flash one, just a little rope mat to step on. She began sweeping, moving from the kitchen to the bedrooms. She was sorry the kids were all at school now, and she thought about having a job. She swept, getting into the corners with a dustpan and brush. Some of the women had kitchen jobs or did part-time cleaning, or did machining down at Hayes.

When she'd finished sweeping she got a bucket of water and a mop and mopped out. She scrubbed the back step and mopped the porch, then opened the window and door to let the breeze blow through, hoping that the floor would dry out quickly before Sandra and Joey came. She was looking forward to mid-morning when Sandra and Joey and their kids might call in on their way to the shops. Before they came she would put on her cardigan to hide her arm.

She went out into the wash-house and began rubbing the clothes that were soaking in the tub. If she had a job she'd get her a washing machine. Not a dear one, just a second-hand.

She'd seen washing machines advertised in the Wanted to Sell column of the paper that came on a Wednesday. Tomorrow. At about two o'clock every Wednesday the woman came with the papers. Tomorrow there'd be another paper. And when it arrived she'd stop what she was doing and have a read, sometimes reading right up to the time the kids came home from school. But she didn't read everything on the Wednesday.

There were all sorts of things to read – stories about people of the district, or about some new building going up. A picture of their street had been in once, showing one of the Works' trucks loaded with shrubs that were being given out to each house.

She liked reading about sports and the different things that people did, and there was a cooking section and sometimes a special section about gardens.

The Public Notices took up two pages and told about meetings and raffles, or where you could buy firewood or coal or an incinerator. Or you could read about garage sales and jumble sales, and where to send clothes and household goods that you didn't want. Sometimes there were notices of market days advertising produce, crafts, jumble, quick-fire raffles, white elephant, lucky dips and knick-knacks. Sometimes there were auctions with everything going cheap.

If you wanted to join a club you could read through the notices and find the one you liked, and anyone could join. The notices said things like 'Enrol Now', 'Special Welcome to New Members', 'All Welcome', 'Intending Members Welcome'. And there was one big ad that always had 'WE NEED YOU' in extra large print.

There were a lot of church notices telling the times of the services, and where you could ring for further enquiries. There were notices about where you could get advice to do with money or marriage or the law.

The schools put their notices there when they were having elections or fundraising, or when it was time for the kids to enrol. Or people could enrol at dancing school to learn ballet, tap or jazz. They could do Tae Kwan Do, aerobics, or collect spoons, just about anything. They could learn something, like swimming or ceramics or floral art.

She liked flowers. She had looked after her shrub and it was starting to grow. Sometimes she'd thought about having a few bulbs and poking them in round underneath the shrub. Or a geranium. She thought about having a geranium which could be red or pink. She liked red, but pink was all right too.

There were three pages about houses in the paper, where it told you about each house, how many bedrooms, what sort of fireplace, if there was a carpet, whether there was a garage or a double garage. Some of the houses were great for kids, some were close to shops or schools, or only a step to the railway station. Some had fabulous views. There were photos of a lot of the houses, and she liked counting the windows and looking to see if there was a chimney or two chimneys, or no chimney at all.

It was good looking at all the advertisements to do with things for the house. And there were clothes adverts about fashion frocks, fashion jerseys, fashion sweat-tops. And baby-knits, fleecy and supafleece, flexiwool, polywool, wonderwool. There were pictures of nightwear and shoes and slippers, and the ads told the sizes and colours you could get. Sometimes you could get 'All Sizes, All Colours'.

Then there were the grocery and meat ads, which had the prices of everything and told you which were special and how much off, or how much for two, and there were coupons and competitions, and how to put money aside for Christmas.

And there were jobs advertised too, jobs for all sorts of tradespeople, for office workers, sales people, machinists, cleaners and kitchenhands. Sometimes people advertised for someone to mind children after school, or to do house cleaning for a few hours each week.

She liked the page where people put in what they wanted to buy or sell – like beds, bikes, lawn-mowers, pianos, washing machines, TV sets or aerials, high-chairs, freezers, fridges, pine-cones, vacuum cleaners.

But she didn't read everything on the Wednesday. She

saved some of the reading for the next day, and the day after that. She always hid the paper away when she'd finished reading so that it wouldn't get put in the fire.

When she'd finished washing and rinsing the clothes, she wrung them and put as many as she could into the bucket ready to take out. She went inside for her cardigan and saw that the floor was nearly dry. If Sandra and Joey came before it had dried properly she'd put paper down, or she could mop again afterwards, just in the places where they'd walked.

The teatowels she'd put out earlier were dry, so she took them down and began pegging the clothes, returning to the washhouse every now and again to refill the bucket. There weren't enough pegs for all the washing and she had to drape the towels over the line without pegging them. She thought she might mention about the pegs.

When the women and kids came she was pleased and put some water on the stove to boil. She buttered some biscuits and put jam on some and cheese on some.

'You do this every day?' Sandra said, stepping on the papers.

'Yeh, what for?' said Joey, carrying the pushchair in so that it wouldn't make marks.

'You kids want a biscuit?' Marney asked.

'Take one and go outside,' Sandra said.

'Take two, one on top. And you come in after, I'll give you a banana.'

'They don't need a banana, tell them to get out and stay out.'

'Yes,' Joey said. 'Keep the bananas for your kids, these ones have been stuffing their faces all morning.'

She poured the tea, then they talked about the curtains some people were getting; there was a curtain bug going round and just about everyone was getting new curtains. They knew who it was taking the milk money too, and it was kids from the next street. Someone had seen them and called the cops, and that's who it was, kids from the next street. That skinny-bone one with the asthma was one of them.

Everyone was getting sick too. All the kids had runny noses and coughs. But not as bad as the one over the road from Sandra who ended up in hospital, but no wonder, spaghetti, baked beans. That's what they lived on, spaghetti, baked beans, spaghetti, baked beans.

Then they talked about some T-shirts they were going to buy for the kids, and about the kids growing out of their clothes. They were going to sort some of the stuff out to give to someone. Some of it was haddit and would have to be chucked out.

Then Sandra and Joey thought they'd better get going.

'Good cup of tea, Marney,' Sandra said. 'You coming?'

'Not today.'

'How come? You're always sticking home.'

'Bob does our shopping . . .'

'But a walk won't hurt.'

'Yeah, come for a stretch.'

'Well I'm a bit busy.'

'Busy my foot. What else you got?'

'Ironing . . .'

'Jesus, it can wait. Be back in an hour . . . a few minutes' walk, have a look around and home again . . .'

'And I might do a bit more . . . out the back . . .'

'Dead loss all right, why not let your old man dig? Anyway, what for? It's all rock, nothing grows.'

'I'll look after the kids if you like.'

'Fat chance, they've got money for lollies.'

'What about baby?'

'I could leave bubby. Yes, good, I'll leave her, and . . . better get going, otherwise we'll never get. You kids coming?'

'We want a banana.'

'Look . . .'

'Let them have a banana, there's plenty . . .'

'Well I don't buy bananas, they never last in our house the way they stuff their faces. In and out, in and out, wanting, asking. I go to the shop today, and just about all gone next day. But you . . . you always seem to have . . .'

'It's Bob, always bringing stuff.'

'Mmm. Not like my old man. Hers too. All they bring home is a skinful of booze, one's as bad as the other. Well look, we better . . . You leaving bubby, Joey?'

'Well . . .'

'Yes it's all right, leave her. When she wakes up I'll mash a banana, make some custard.'

'You sure?'

'Yes.'

'And sure you don't want to . . . ?'

'Nah. Some other time.'

'Okay then. There's a nappy in the bag, and her bottle.'

'Good, see you on the way back.'

Marney washed the cups and wiped the table down. The floor was dry and she collected up the paper and brought the mat in. She put milk into a pot to make custard for Jemmy.

By the time the women came back she'd changed and fed Jemmy, washed the nappy and hung it on the line. She'd taken Jemmy outside to play for a little while, and Jemmy had toddled about on the rough ground, laughing and pointing, and occasionally sitting down with a bump.

'She didn't cry,' Marney said. 'Not even when she first woke up.'

'She's good like that,' Joey said. 'Likes everybody. Easy to leave.'

'Here, we brought you a bit of geranium. Joey's got a bit, I've got a bit. They reckon you can grow it from a bit like that.'

'Good. Good, I was thinking about a geranium. Red too. It's just what I was thinking.'

But she was worried about the geranium, and after the women had gone she thought she might get rid of it. Then she decided to put it in a jar of water and put it on the kitchen windowsill.

After that she went out to do some more of the digging, working quickly to make up for the time she'd spent talking, or playing with Jemmy.

When the kids got home she went in and put the tea on. By then the clothes were dry and she took them in to iron.

The children had had tea and she'd almost finished the ironing when she heard the truck stop and heard Bob calling to the driver. After a while he came in and put the bag of groceries on the bench.

'So you been digging?' he said.

'Yes.'

'What else?'

'It's hard . . . quite rocky . . .'

'I said, what else?'

'The . . . the house . . .'

'What did you do this morning?'

'I got the kids off to school . . .'

'Well come on. Did they have breakfast, did they have a wash?'

'Yes. The kids got up just before you left and they had a wash. Then they got dressed while I was getting their lunches ready. I got them their breakfast . . .'

'Late, I suppose.'

'No, plenty of time. They went about quarter past.'

'And who was here?'

'No one . . .'

'I said, who was here?'

'No one. Just me. Just the kids.'

'Then what?'

'I did the dishes, then I wiped down the table, the bench, round the window, cleaned the window. Then I swept out and mopped out and . . . started on the washing . . .'

'What else?'

'I went and hung it out . . .'

'And?'

'I needed a few more pegs.'

He reached out and gripped her arm, she could feel his fingers bruising her. 'Stop changing the subject,' he said.

'I wasn't . . . I just thought . . . when you get the shopping.'

'Stop grizzling about pegs. If I want to get pegs I'll get pegs . . . What then?'

'Sandra and Joey called in.'

'What did those nosey bitches want?'

'Just called, on the way to the shops.'

'So you all went off to the shops, I suppose?'

'Not me.'

'How do I know?'

'No, not me. I looked after Jemmy while Joey . . .'

'Is that all you got to do?'

'No, but . . .'

'No but, no but. You better not be lying, that's all.'

'They came and got Jemmy and . . .'

'Who's they?'

'Sandra and Joey.'

'Who else?'

'No one . . . No one else . . . Only Sandra's two kids but they ran on home. It was just Joey who came in, Sandra waited out . . .'

'So first you say Sandra and Joey, then you say just Joey. Can't you make up your mind?'

'Joey came in, Sandra waited for her.'

'I better not find out different.'

'And after that was when I did the garden. When the kids came home I started the tea. I brought the clothes in and . . . I've been ironing . . .'

'So, what else have you got to grizzle about?'

'No, I wasn't . . .'

'And what's that?'

'What's . . .?'

'That?'

'That's just a geranium.'

'Where from?'

'Sandra gave . . .'

'Sandra hasn't got geraniums.'

'She did. Sandra. She got it when she went to the shop . . .'

'Shop? What shop? I haven't seen any shop with those.'

'I mean she got it, from somewhere.'

'Changing your mind again?'

'No. It's what I meant. She got it, pinched it off someone's bush . . . or . . . spoke to someone and they gave it.'

'You don't know what you're talking about.' His grip tightened even more on her arm, he was beginning to twist.

'She said to put it . . . in water . . . and might grow.'

Then suddenly he let go and sat down at the table. So she went over to the stove, took a plate from the warming tray and began to dish up food. Her arm hurt. She piled the plate high and put it down in front of him.

'Chuck that thing out,' he said, so she took the geranium and put it into the scrap bucket. She could hear him chewing the meat, sucking at the bones and shifting about in his chair as she waited for water to boil for the tea.

And as she waited she thought about the next day when Sandra and Joey might call in. She remembered that tomorrow was the day the woman came with the paper. There would be new stories and she wondered what they could be about. She wondered what there would be to look at in the pictures of clothes and things for the house.

When she had poured his tea she began stacking the dishes into the sink. She squirted dishwashing liquid over the plates and let the water run.

There would be the week's grocery specials to look at, telling about prices down and cut prices, and with crosses over the old prices and the new prices shown in big print. Some of the pictures of houses would be the same as for last week, but there'd be some new ones too, close to shops, great outlooks, good for kids. And there would be some new jobs but not very many.

She remembered that this was the time of the year that clubs put notices in about meetings, with special welcomes to new members and intending members. There could be new clubs with some different things for people to learn and do.

Then she thought about Wanted to Sell, Wanted to Buy, the page she liked best, where you could read about all the things people had for sale or would like to buy. Sometimes she read that page first, but sometimes she kept it until last to read. And she always read it slowly and carefully so that she wouldn't finish it too soon.

Behind her she heard him sucking his teeth and shifting his chair. She pulled the plug and watched the sink emptying, watched the water turning, heard it rushing in the drain.

The Lamp

THERE WAS A RED LAMP IN CHURCH WITH A LIT WICK floating in oil that showed that God was home. God was everywhere but especially in church where the lamp burned. The lamp sat in a shiny gold basket that hung from a beam by three golden chains.

The playground was empty and the other kids had gone by the time Jeanie and Mereana had finished sweeping the classroom floor for Sister. Sister told them to go straight home, but they thought they would make their visit first, as they did on most afternoons after school.

Sister had instructed all the children that they should visit God in the church so that they would become holy. Visits got their sins forgiven – and all the marks and stains they had on their souls from fighting, forgetting, spitting, swearing, lying, being lazy, talking, laughing, playing with privates, bad manners, bad spelling and having bad companions could be cleaned off if you visited enough, and if you confessed. Your soul was a glowing white ball made of light that was inside your body seated at the base of your stomach. You had to keep it clean.

As well as visits you could store up prayers, genuflections, masses, offerings, blessings, communions, good thoughts and good deeds. If you had collected enough by the time you died you could get a good place in heaven, like a block of sky saved for you, and also it lessened the time that you needed to spend in purgatory getting your sins burned away.

The two girls crossed the playground, went up the church steps and into the porch. It was a little square porch and a good place to play Witchy in the Corner if there were enough of you, and if there was time.

But there were other things to do. They went first of all to shake the poorbox to see if it rattled. It did. There was something inside but it wasn't money. Jeanie slotted in a milk top she had saved, and Mereana found a leaf to put in. Then they went to finger the little books that told about sin and prayer, sacraments, saints, the rosary, families, the Trinity, the missions, commandments, catechism and the Far East. The books were full of big words and the girls tried to read some of them. Some of the books had pictures of holy people with sad faces and eyes looking up to heaven.

After that Mereana tried on a lady's coat that had been left hanging on a hook, but she looked silly. Jeanie tried it on and she looked silly too. It made them laugh.

Well it was all right to laugh in the porch as long as there were no telltales watching, but you didn't laugh in the church. They stretched and twisted their faces to stop themselves from laughing because it was time they went in. They clapped their hands over their mouths and turned their backs on each other, but that didn't work. Laughing wasn't much to do with faces and mouths, or backs. It came from inside somewhere. It came from way down in your stomach, filled up your chest, then exploded out of your face.

And it made you cry. They went over to the books again and found sad pictures of the saints and martyrs to look at, but that didn't help either. It seemed to make them laugh and cry all the more, which was something they would have to be sorry about later and confess. They went out of the porch and leaned over the stair-rail laughing and laughing until the laughter was all gone. Then they went back into the porch with their lips pressed together, and stood in the doorway that led into the church.

They peered into the gloom of the church looking out for Mr Ticklekiss with his mops and brooms. If there were other girls around, like at lunchtimes when there were lots of them, and when there was noise and shouting outside, it was quite funny when Mr Ticklekiss came sneaking up to tickle and kiss them. They'd get up and run along the kneelers and dive under the pews. Their lips would come unstuck and they'd giggle and squeal with Mr Ticklekiss coming after them. Then suddenly Mr Ticklekiss would open a door and disappear. They'd go out later and they'd see him clearing the gutters or weeding the paths. He wouldn't look at them or speak.

But sometimes, like now, with no noise and no people, it was scary, because Mr Ticklekiss was like his mops and brooms. He had no footsteps, and he came out of the church walls or from out of the posts of the church with no noise. He was tall and spooky, and his long, pale hands flapped at the ends of his sleeves as though they had been just sewn there, the way that dolls' hands sometimes were.

Mereana and Jeanie looked into all the corners of the church. They looked at all the posts and hiding places of the church and along all the pews. There was no one – not even Bird Lady, who came every morning and afternoon on her bike with her shawl fluttering and flapping behind her. In church she would kneel in the front pew, as still as one of the statues, with her shawl pulled closely about her.

There was just the quiet, dark church with the statues looking down, and the Stations of the Cross, which were nothing but square shadows high on the walls. There was the terrible gaping loft where the choir sang for high mass on Sundays, and there was the little red glow that was the lamp, which showed that God was home.

The girls reached for the holy water, signed themselves with it and went in. They kept their lips jammed together so that no sound would escape.

They genuflected and went up to kiss the big toe of the crucified Jesus, the toe worn and shiny from being kissed thousands of times. The crucified Jesus had big square-headed nails in his hands and feet, in nail holes surrounded by pink blood. There was more pink blood on his forehead beneath the crown of thorns, and pink drops coming from the spear hole in his side. Mereana and Jeanie really felt sorry for Jesus. He gave every drop of his blood to make them good but they were bad all the same. They looked at each other with sad faces, making sure they kept their mouths shut tight.

Then they knelt to pray the 'Our Father', 'Hail Mary' and 'Glory Be'. They said acts of contrition and kept kneeling even though their knees hurt. Now that their eyes had adjusted to the light they could see the wall pictures which made up the Stations of the Cross. It really wasn't fair about poor Jesus in the garden sweating out his pink blood, then being sold, and whipped and laughed at, and having all his clothes torn away. After that he was made to carry the big cross all the way to Calvary.

But if they prayed hard enough, and did good deeds, then Jesus might think it was worth it. It was like helping him. If they could be really good then they were being like the man Simon, who helped Jesus when he fell. Or they were like Veronica, who went up to Jesus and wiped his face with a towel. Then Jesus put his face on the towel like a photo. If they prayed hard, and were good, and had sore knees, and if they kept their lips shut tight and pressed the palms of their hands together, then Jesus might be able to look down and see it was worth it as he sat up there in his chair beside his father with a new crown on his head. He might smile.

Just then, while they were kneeling and praying, one of the Sisters came in carrying an unlit candle and a window pole. She put the candle down, reached up and hooked the window pole into the ring underneath the basket and pulled the lamp down.

The girls watched as she took out the red glass bowl with the light in it, then put it down on the communion rail where she would put in more of the oil and change the wick. But before she blew the flame out she lit the candle, so that while the lamp was out there was the flame of the candle to show that God was everpresent in the church. It was called perpetual light.

Then when Sister had relit the lamp she picked up the gold basket and the candle and went out. The girls knew that she would be out in the sacristy cleaning the gold basket with Brasso, rubbing to make it shine.

But just now, there was the little glowing lamp sitting on the communion rail, right down low where they could see.

They nodded to each other and stood, moving quietly along the kneeler, out of the pew and up to the rail. They stared and stared at the little flame that showed God's everpresence. They squatted, and peered up through the red glass at the dancing flame. It was difficult to keep their lips tight together.

They stood up again and Jeanie leaned over and blew, very gently, on the flame. It danced and shimmered. Mereana blew too, softly, and the wick began to sail gently in the oil, carrying its little fire.

Jeanie and Mereana looked at each other for a moment, then they both leaned over the little lamp and blew hard, together. And suddenly the flame was gone.

Gone. They grabbed hold of each other and shut their eyes, waiting for the high roof to crack and fall, waiting for the walls to come smacking down. They held on to each other, waiting, listening. God was gone, and now the Devil could come leaping down out of the choir loft and throw them in fires. They clung together for a long time in the silence, then after a while they opened their eyes. Then they ran.

They ran clattering down the aisle, through the porch, down the steps and across the playground. And Mereana, who thought she might get left behind, grabbed the back of Jeanie's tunic and yelled 'Wait!'

They ran out of the gate and down the street, with Mereana yelling 'Wait!' and Jeanie yelling 'Let go, let go!'

At the crossing they stopped, breathing hard, and they stared into each other's wide-open, round eyes. Then they ran again, across the road and along the footpath, dodging in and out amongst the shoppers until they came to the street where they both lived. They stopped there and leaned against a fence, picking grass which they held against their sides to take away stitch.

'We both did it,' Jeanie said, just to make sure.

'Yes.'

Then they sat without speaking, knowing that their souls

had shrivelled inside their bodies, that they'd killed God and let the Devil loose to come grabbing them by the ankles and tossing them into everlasting fire.

They waited. After a long time they knew it was late. Lights were going on in houses.

It was *really* late and they were both going to get hidings, good hidings. For a while they talked about the hidings they were going to get. They didn't care because they deserved it. They wouldn't cry. Tomorrow, in the morning, they'd tell each other how many hits. They'd tell if they cried or didn't.

They began to run along the street that they both lived in, pushing open their gates, running along their paths.

'Count.'

'Don't forget to count.'

'And we'll tell each other.'

'In the morning.'

'We'll tell.'

'Tell.'

'Don't forget.'

'In the morning.'

'Tomorrow in the morning.'

The Wall

THE OLD MAN WAS THE ONLY ONE LIKED OUR WALL, OR THE only one said. Our wall got in the papers.

We saw the woman there with her camera, and a guy was with her having a look, writing stuff on a pad. That's good, us and our wall's going in the paper.

The day the man and the woman came was packing-up day, clearing up our rubbish, loading the gear. Only four of us and Lindsay. The others were already gone off on a new job, footpaths down Tamihana Road somewhere. Footpaths are all right but walls are better. Well to me it's a good wall.

It took three months, and at first we didn't know what the hell. Just hacking away at the bank, mixing concrete, carting rocks. Then Lindsay got us going on it, how to put down a bit of the mix, lay one of the rocks, and keep on going like that. But not just any rock. You have to pick out a good one, the right one, the right size and a good shape to fit in with the one you just done.

We all scrapped over which rock. That one. Nah. Ha, ha, haw, haw, like that. Then try them out to see which one. A lot of times my rock was the good one, fitted in just right, ha ha ha, hee hee, get stuffed. Hee, hee, ha, ha. Haw, haw, haw. It was only easy after a while.

So our wall got started and it was pretty good, only easy, and every day there was this new bit of wall. Not just straight. Higher some places, lower some places, and got a bend in it where the road goes round.

Every morning we mucked around and had a look what we done yesterday. My rock, ha, ha. Mine, haw, haw. Stink one, slack one, ha, ha, ha, then Lindsay yells out to get on with it.

Plenty of people went past, in cars, or walking, but they

never said. Drive past, have a look, keep going. Walk past, have a look, keep walking. Sometimes the kids stand around on their way home from school and have a stare, have a talk. Where you get your stones? Off the truck. But where? Don't know.

But I like the old fella best. He's the only one liked our wall.

At half-past three we sent Jerryboy to get us a paper, two papers, three papers, no, four.

And there was a photo of our wall all right, with a write-up about this headmaster and these parents saying how the kids couldn't see cars and buses because of our wall. Our wall was too built out.

Well too bad, at least our wall was in the paper. And us. Not looking, just loading the left-over rocks. Jerryboy's back, my hand, Pete's shoulder, and Notpeter standing up on the truck. Haw, haw. Ha, ha. Sucker. Hee hee, haw, haw, haw. I took the paper home with me at knock-off. Showed it to one or two. They didn't say much.

Anyway, this old fella came walking down the road one day. Not our side, the other side. Our wall was only about halfway then. He stopped and had a good old jack at us working. After a while he came over. He wasn't that old, just a slow walker with his breaths making a noise. Not rich.

Well, he said, and his hands were clanking round in his pockets like he had keys and ten-cent pieces, and might be a few washers and nails. And he had a big smile like he really liked us and our wall. Black old teeth. Fat stomach. Well good on you. Good on all of you and your wall. Hee, hee, hee, hee.

So Peter got up on the wall and bent his arms up and made his muscles big, pulled a strong face. Patsy swung his bum. Hee, hee, hee, squeal, squeal.

And then Notpeter, who was hosing off the footpath, stuck the hose between his legs and went yah ha, hosing all over the road. Well the old fella laughed and laughed, and squeaked and squealed with his noisy breaths. What a pisser, he shouted, hee, hee, hee. Hey, Pisser, hee, hee, hee, squeal, squeal, big funny mouth, black old teeth. Well good on all of you. Good one.

Good wall. And then he went away, slow walking, big funny grin.

Well I watched out for the old fella after that, but he didn't come past again. Only cars, only kids, and people hurrying. Could be in the hospital. Could be dead. Anyway the wall's done now. Finished. We're back on footpaths again.

But if I saw the old fella, round town, down the pub, anywhere, I'd give him a yell. If he didn't remember, I'd tell him it was us made the wall. And he might say was you the pisser, and I'll say no, that's Notpeter. And he might say was you the strongman? The wrigglebum? No. So I might tell him I'm the one finds the good stones, ha, ha, ha, the right rocks to fit in the right place. And he'll say good one, hee, hee, squeal squeal.

Then I might say come on how about it, I'll shout you one. And he might say good on you, what are we waiting for? Then we'll go.

Electric City

A FTER SCHOOL ANI WENT TO PAY THE ELECTRIC CITY. SHE
hoped it wouldn't make her late for work.

Harry was already home when she arrived. He'd changed
his clothes and cooked chops and chips for them.

'Where've you been?' he asked.

'Paying the electric city,' she said.

'Scoff this and we'll get the two-past.'

They'd almost finished eating when Pania came in. 'Did you
cook any for me?'

'We're late, Parney, you get you some,' Ani said, 'and we
have to leave you our dishes. Do them before Mum gets back.
Make Boo help.'

'He's still playing down the road, brat.'

'And, Parn, there's the old man's receipt for the power, in
the drawer. You tell him.'

On the way in on the train Ani couldn't concentrate on the
notes she was reading.

'Test tomorrow?' Harry asked. He had his book too, but
hadn't opened it.

'Mmm. Bio. And maths Thursday.'

'We used to laugh at him, ay, when he said "electric
city"?'

'Mmm. And I used to think what if he said it at work?
People would laugh.'

'He's got this thing, about paying straight away. He thinks
they'll cut the power off – the power, the phone, TV – or whatever. And he has everything counted out, this for the power,

this for that, this for such and such, and such and such . . . like it's his life.'

'We were little then. Snotters. We used to really crack up.'

Then Harry said, 'I'm leaving.'

'Leaving?'

'School. I'm too old. School's for kids. I want to do something worth it.'

'Harry . . .'

'I know. Big scene. But . . . Well, I skipped classes today and went down to the video shop for an interview. I reckon they'll take me. If they take me I'm quitting.'

'Look, Harry . . .'

'I've had enough. School's for kids.'

'Like me?'

'It's different. You're brainy. But me . . . I can earn heaps, work nine to nine, six days a week if I want. Old man can give up his night job. You can stay home and do homework . . .'

'But you don't have to . . .'

'Nah, I've had enough. The old man won't mind.'

'What about Mum?'

'She'll get used to it.'

The train shuttled through the cutting and they began zipping up their jackets and pushing the notes and books into their pockets.

They had three hours' work ahead of them and they hoped their boss would be there in time to open up, so they could get started early. They hoped they'd get finished in time for the two-to-nine train home.

The train scuttled out of the cutting. It was already dark. All the lights were on – row upon row of street lights winding round and winding upwards.

There were lights threaded about the harbour, and layers of light patterned the sides of the tall buildings. Beside them on the motorway the headlights of hundreds of cars beamed on to the darkening roadway.

'So it's right,' Ani said, 'It's what he means.'

'Electric City,' Harry said.

The train shuffled into the station and they looked out into the long, lit-up shelters under which commuters waited, hunching against the cold.

'Electric City,' she said. 'And you always have to pay.'

Flies

LIZZIE AND MEREANA HAD JUST FINISHED THEIR JOBS WHEN Macky came with his fly.

The fly was on a short piece of cotton, which was all Macky had been able to find.

'Get some of Auntie's cotton,' he said, 'and I'll give you some of my flies.' He showed them the matchbox with the flies in it.

Lizzie went to the machine drawer, took out a reel of cotton and gave it to Macky, but she didn't want any of his half-dead flies. She and Mereana decided to get their own.

The two girls went out and looked under the shed for jars, then carried on down the track to the dunny where there were plenty of flies – like eyes, resting on the dunny walls, or down the hole singing round and round on cellophane wings.

The dunny seat and floor were still wet and stank of Jeyes, and the flies, once disturbed, buzzed and circled and zoomed. They stood still with their jars waiting for the flies to settle again. Then they tiptoed, trapping the flies with their hands, holding them lightly in their fists where they felt like live paper, and where their buzzing sounded louder and deeper.

Charlotte, Denny Boy, Ana and Erana arrived and saw that it was going to be a fly day. They went back to their own dunnies. They had better flies, they said, and knew where they could get more cotton too.

You had to be careful tying the flies. First of all you had to move the hand that covered the jar so that there was a little opening, just big enough for one fly to come out into your other hand. You had to hold the fly very carefully in your fingers so that it couldn't move its wings or legs, but you mustn't squeeze. Then someone had to tie the cotton round the neck of the fly, some-one careful, so that the heads wouldn't pop off.

Well now, there they all were, holding the ends of their cottons, looking up at their crazy flies, which zigged and zag-ged and buzzed and dived. There they all were walking about with their flies, and sometimes the flies were little kites, some-times little aeroplanes. Sometimes they were just silly flies making all sorts of patterns in the air, and you nearly died laughing.

But the main thing was *you* were in charge. You could lengthen the cottons to see whose fly could go highest, or you could shorten the cottons to make the flies wild and crazy, pulling and buzzing for their lives. You could buzz your fly on to someone's neck or face, which made you bust yourself with laughing. You could even let your fly go for a second if you wanted to, then jump up and grab. But the flies couldn't go anywhere you didn't want them to go. You were the boss of the flies.

After a while Denny Boy said that they could have a war and that the flies could be soldiers. Good idea. So they put them-selves into teams and had partners. Someone said 'Go' and they guided the flies into each other, and the flies buzzed and fought and tangled their cottons together. Some lost wings and legs. Some died. You were allowed a new fly if your fly died, but you weren't allowed to stamp on your fly just so that you could get a better one.

At the end of the war Charlotte said that the surviving flies should be allowed to go free. Good.

'And they should have medals,' Lizzie said.

Medals, good. Charlotte snapped the head off a flower and distributed the petals. They tied the petals on to the ends of the cottons and lined up to salute while Charlotte said words.

'Here are your medals for bravery in battle and not giving up. Remember your comrades who lost wings and legs, and those who died. And lost heads. God keep you safe on your journey homeward to your loved ones. Amen.'

Amen. They let go of the cottons and watched the flies as they rose, trailing their little red medals. They waved until they thought they couldn't see them any more – or thought they could, or weren't sure. They waved just in case.

Then they turned back to the rest of the flies, dozens still crawling in the jars.

'We could send messages,' Ana said.

All right. They needed paper for messages, and pencils.

'Get the bum paper,' Macky said.

So he and Ana and Erana went to the dunny and tore the white edges off the newspapers, while Lizzie, Mereana and Charlotte went to find their school pencils.

Messages. They wrote messages in tiny writing on tiny scraps of paper that would not be too heavy for the flies to carry. They wrote Help, Save Our Socks, Save Our Sausages, Juju Lips, Tin a Cocoa, Tin a Jam, Denny Boy's got a Big One, Sip Sip Sip, Ana loves JB, CR loves TM, Bite your Bum, Macky loves Ma Fordyce.

Ma Fordyce? That made them think of writing some messages to Four-eyes Fordyce. Good idea. Fordyce has got a face like a monkey gorilla. Fordyce has got kutus. Fordyce is an old bag and a slut. Fordyce stinks, she's got a hole in her bum.

And while they were writing the messages they talked about Monday when they would all be sitting in school, and Fat Fordyce would be screwing her face up, nosing into their lunches, prodding their heads and poking their necks. And then a fly would come in, ten flies, fifty flies. Four-eyes Fordyce would be surprised and go pink. She would catch the flies and untie the messages. She would read them and go red like a tomato or a plum, or orange like a pumpkin. She would screw her mouth like a cow's bum and go round banging her strap, on desks, on seats, on anything, and she would be shouting, 'Who did this? Own up. Own up. Who did it?'

And they would all flick their eyebrows at each other, tiny, tiny flicks that only themselves could see, but they would keep their faces sad.

They finished writing and tying their messages and then lined up with their flies facing the direction of the school. They let go their cottons and waved and saluted as the flies lifted the messages over the lemon tree, over the manuka and away.

There were still a lot of flies in their jars, so they took a piece of cotton each and tied a row of flies along each piece. They thought of using short pieces of cotton to join the rows one below another, which was a good idea. It wasn't easy, and some of the flies died, but at last the convoy was ready.

It took all of them, holding carefully, to launch it. They let go and off went the flies, crazily, pulling this way and that. It made you laugh your head off. It made you die.

There went the flies slowly rising . . . dropping . . . rising. There they went . . . up . . . drop . . . up . . . yes. Yes, they were up. Up. You ran after the flies, over the grass, through the flowerbeds, through the bushes. Go flies. Up . . . Yes. Go. There they went, higher, higher. Go flies . . . Up. Goodbye. Go to Jesus. Go to Jesus, flies. Goodbye . . . Goodbye . . . Goodbye.

Going for the Bread

AFTER SCHOOL, WHEN HER MOTHER GAVE HER THE BREAD money and the bag, Mereana said that she wanted to go to the shop the long way because of girls.

'You can't go the long way,' her mother said. 'Too many cars, and too far. Go down the track. Be careful crossing the Crescent.'

'I want to go the road way,' Mereana said.

'What girls?'

'They tell me names.'

'Like what?'

'Like dirty.'

And then her mother was angry.

'Well are you? Are you dirty?'

'I don't know.'

'What do you mean, don't know. Of course you know. Course you're not dirty. We wash, don't we? Got a clean house, clean clothes?'

'Yes.'

'And don't you cry, you stop it.' Her mother was angry. 'You go down the track. And . . . if anyone says . . . anything, don't look at them. Walk straight past. You hear?'

'They might hit.'

'They won't . . . just cheeky and smart, that's all. Straight past, do what I say.'

'Yes.'

Then her mother stopped being angry. 'Bubby'll be up soon. We'll come to the top of the track to meet you. When you get to the Crescent keep on the footpath. Be careful crossing.' Then she said, 'You buy us something nice with the two pennies.'

Mereana liked the track and she could run all the way down without stopping, down the steep places holding on to the broom bushes to stop herself from sliding, over the rocky places, along the top of the bank, through the onion flowers. At the top of the bank she could climb down using the foot-holes that the big children had made, but today she kept to the track so that she wouldn't get dust on her clothes.

Sometimes she would stop there at the bottom of the track to watch the big children playing soccer with a tennis ball, but there was no one on the park today. She crossed the green and went up the path to where the Crescent began.

At the top of the path she stopped, looking out for the girls, but there was no one on the road, no one on the footpath. She began to hurry, not looking at gates, or people's letterboxes, or people's houses, but just looking straight ahead. No one played hopscotch on the footpath, no one skipped on the road.

It was when she rounded the corner that she knew the two girls were there. They were sitting up on the terrace looking down.

'It's her,' she heard one of the girls say, and the other girl called out a name.

Mereana didn't look at the girls, but walked quickly looking straight ahead the way her mother had told her.

Then one of the girls called, 'You're not allowed past here,' and called her the name again.

Mereana didn't look and didn't stop, and the girl said, 'We'll take your bag and throw it in the bushes if you go past here.'

She kept going, looking straight in front of her.

As she passed them the two girls came scrambling down the bank. The bigger one snatched the bag from her and ran ahead, pushing it into a hedge.

'There,' the girl said. 'Leave it there. If you get it we'll cut you with glass.'

But Mereana was going to the shop for her mother. It was her mother's bag, and the money was in the bag wrapped in a piece of paper. Anyway, the girls had run off now. They were climbing the bank again. She didn't look at them, and when she got to the hedge she pulled the bag out and walked quickly.

Then she heard the two girls scramble down the bank and come running up behind her. They pushed her over. One of them held her while the other one cut her with glass.

Mereana's mother was frightened. She thought she should take Mereana to the doctor, but how? She couldn't take her bleeding in the bus, not while she had baby as well. She could afford a taxi one way, but it would take her ten minutes to get to the phone box and back, and she'd have to leave Mereana and Kahu by themselves while she went to ring. Also, it was baby's feed time and he was starting to yell. If she did go to the doctor, how would she get home again?

She had another look at the cut. The bleeding had almost stopped. It wasn't as deep as she'd first thought, so perhaps there was no need . . . But it could leave a scar. She didn't want her children to have scars, didn't want their father coming home from overseas and finding his children with scars.

'Babe, will I ring us a taxi and take you to the doctor?'
'No.'
'When I've fed Bubby?'
'No.'
Well all right, the cut wasn't too deep, a lot of blood though, and the scar would be just on the edge of the hair-line. It would probably fade.

And another thing. She was scared about going and telling the mother what her kids had done, but she wasn't going to let them get away with it. She sat Mereana in a chair and told her to hold the facecloth against the cut.

'I'll feed Bubby,' she said. 'Then I'll help you to change your dress.'

There were bloodstains on her own clothing too, and mud on her skirt where she'd slipped on the track. She had almost dropped Kahu. The front of her blouse was wet where her milk was coming through. She undid her buttons and put the baby to her breast. He stopped crying, sucking deeply, swallowing noisily, pale milk overflowing at the corners of his mouth.

She had tried to go down the track when she'd heard Mereana crying but she'd slipped, just letting herself slide to make sure of holding on to Kahu. Otherwise he'd be hurt too, bleeding and bruised. His father hadn't even seen him yet. She sat the baby up and he brought up wind, and she saw that he had a splash of mud in his hair.

Then she was angry again. She stood up, wrapping Kahu in a rug.

'Come on, Mereana, we're going to show their mother what they did. Can you walk, Babe? Can you bring your cloth?'

'Yes.'

She moved very carefully down the track, holding Kahu in one arm while she grasped the broom stalks with her other hand. Mereana moved down behind her. When she was almost to the bottom of the track she stopped and changed Kahu to her other arm.

As they rounded the Crescent the two girls were playing up on the terrace, and when they saw Mereana coming with her mother they ran up the path and into their house. There was blood in the guttering and the glass was still there.

When the door opened Mereana's mother couldn't think what to say for a moment. Then she said, 'This is my daughter. This is what your two daughters did to her. Here's the piece of glass.'

'Get off my steps,' the woman said, 'Don't come here with your dirty daughter and your dirty lies,' and she shut the door.

Mereana and her mother went back down the path, and as they went they heard the woman yelling and running through the house. They could hear her hitting with something heavy, and there was shouting and screaming and doors banging. The two girls were getting the hiding of their lives. Their mother was in a rage, and it seemed to Mereana's mother that the woman was somehow frightened.

Kahu was beginning to cry again. He'd only had half a

feed. They were all muddy and bloody, in a real mess. She was frightened too, and angry.

But there was something she knew now, something she'd made up her mind about. No one, ever again, was going to push her kids in the gutter, cut them, muddy them, make them bleed. She would never send them out alone again, not for bread, not for anything. They didn't have to have bread every day. Once a week she'd get a taxi and the three of them would go to the shops and get what they needed.

And one day the war would end.

The Urupa

WHEN THE CHILDREN WERE ALMOST AT THE TOP OF THE hill they started bagsing. Macky was the first to bags their cousin Henry but Charlotte yelled him down. He gave in, and tried for Uncle Tamati instead. But Macky couldn't have Uncle Tamati either, Macky didn't even know Uncle Tamati, only by photos. Uncle Tamati fell out of a train long before Macky came to live there. Denny Boy got Uncle Tamati.

Ana got Auntie June because Auntie June had given her a bracelet – and Erana got Bubby Pauly because Bubby Pauly was her own sister.

Lizzie got Granny Wiki and didn't need any help from Mereana or anyone.

None of them had ever known Granny Wiki, but at Auntie Connie's place there were photos of Granny Wiki with long plaits coiled about her head. They all knew that Granny Wiki used to walk out in the sea to get crayfish, bobbing down under the water while her big dress billowed up like a huge balloon on the sea. She would pop up with two crayfish in her hands and walk home. They knew Granny Wiki's favourite songs too, and had heard Auntie Connie and the others sing them plenty of times.

None of them had known Auntie Lola either, who had been brought back dead from somewhere. She had twins on top. The twins were her own newborn grandchildren. Charlotte and Denny Boy said that their Auntie Betty, Auntie Lola's daughter, had come there with her dead twins to put them on top of Auntie Lola. The twins were together in a box, Denny Boy said, smaller than a box for shoes. Well, Denny Boy could be telling lies.

So Macky and Mereana would have to share Auntie Lola and the twins, or otherwise go into the old part of the urupa. They didn't like the old urupa because it was too spooky and a lot of the people there had died of a sickness that swelled them up and turned them purple. As well as that there was an old woman with wetas in her hair who came out of the ground sometimes and laughed at you, and chased you with a big stick. When you came home from the pictures in the dark you had to stop before you got to the track that led past the cemetery. You had to wait there until everyone caught up. Your legs shook and you held on to each other. Then someone shouted 'Ready Seddy Go!' and you ran and ran, yelling and crashing along the tracks through the lupins, your eyes stretching out into the dark. If you were the last one and were left behind you screamed and cried.

When you were well past you had to lie down, or bend with your head almost touching the ground, getting your breaths. And you gasped and said, 'Had it, had it,' and 'Made it, made it.'

At the top of the hill they put the bottles of water and the flowers on the ground and sat down to rest.

After they'd rested a while they went over to Cousin Henry and put their ears down to listen in case Cousin Henry shouted, the way he had when he'd had his fever. Henry could call out to them and they could all dig. Or he could be trying to climb, as he did when he'd had his fever, scrambling out of bed and trying to get up the walls. They could reach their hands down and haul him up. They called and stamped on the ground. Then they listened, but there was no answer to their call, no one thumped in answer to their signals.

They listened for Bubby Pauly too, but Bubby Pauly didn't cry or talk. She could've forgotten them by now. Then they listened for the twins, but you couldn't expect . . . because the twins hadn't been born properly. They could fit inside a match-box, like two matches.

What about Auntie June then, who had come out of

hospital and had her bed shifted to the front porch at Auntie Connie's? None of them had been allowed in to see Auntie June, but they could stand on boxes outside the porch and talk to her through the windows. Sometimes Auntie June would sit up against her pillows, and she'd have on one of her fine-knitted bedjackets that Auntie Myra had made, huddling over her needles like an old black spider, looping the wool up over her spider-leg fingers and letting the web of knitting heap into the hollow of skirt slung between her knees.

Auntie June was so pretty with her shiny eyes, her bright lips and cheeks, her long black hair spread on the pillow.

'Don't fight over the windows,' she'd say, 'or I'll go back to sleep.'

So then they'd just have to let Charlotte and Denny Boy have the best windows and the best boxes, while the rest of them got wherever they could.

Then Auntie June would make them sing. 'Sing or I'll go back to sleep,' she'd say. 'Sing "Blue Smoke". Sing "Red Sails in the Sunset".' Which was as though everything was colours, floating and drifting.

So they would sing 'Blue Smoke' and 'Red Sails', and sometimes Auntie June would join in, in a high lovely voice. After that they would sing their school songs, or some of the songs from the *Lifebuoy Hit Parade* that Charlotte and Ana had copied into an old exercise book.

After a while Auntie Connie would come in with soup and Auntie June would say, 'Yum yum, pig's bum.' Auntie Connie would fix the pillows and put the tray down, and Auntie June's little wrist and hand reaching from the webby sleeve of the bedjacket to take up the spoon was just like a little spoon itself.

Auntie Connie would shoo them all away, and they'd jump down from the boxes and run before they were given jobs to do.

Then one day the ambulance came for Auntie June so they all went to say goodbye. They weren't allowed to go close and could only wave. Auntie Connie was holding a towel to Auntie June's mouth. Auntie June's fingers were out of the blanket wriggling, waving a little goodbye to them. The ambulance was white with two little crosses, like little red sails, one at each side.

Well, they listened for Auntie June, but they didn't expect ... because she'd already waved. They listened for Uncle Tamati too, but how could he? He'd been smashed to bits, all in pieces on the railway track.

And anyway it was time to get on with it. Charlotte and Ana began to divide up the flowers. Charlotte needed dahlias and asters for Cousin Henry because she reckoned he liked purple and red, and he would want green leaves and yellow snapdragons as well. Denny Boy needed dahlias too, and snapdragons and some green stuff. Ana wanted the stocks, just the pink and white, but she thought she might as well have the purple too, and some green leaves. It wasn't fair if Charlotte and Denny Boy had all the green. Charlotte told Denny Boy to give some of his leaves to Ana. Erana wanted one of everything, except marigolds because they'd gone to sleep. And it wasn't fair because Charlotte and Denny Boy had all the asters. Charlotte gave her one. All the dahlias too. Denny Boy gave her one. Lizzie took the remainder of the snapdragons, and there were marigolds left for Macky and Mereana. They could have the whole lot.

So then they all went to their different places and threw away all the brown stalks of flowers that had been there since their previous visit. They swished the green water that remained in the bottom of the jars with a stick, tipped it out, then refilled the jars with water from the bottles they'd brought with them. They began arranging the flowers.

But Macky had the sulks, and he was sitting in the grass beside Auntie Lola's stupid grave. His lips were pinched together, and every now and again Mereana could hear long breaths coming out of his nose. He was pulling the petals off the stupid marigolds. Their bottle had toppled over and the stupid water was pouring out all over the place.

Mereana watched him for a while. She was angry with Lizzie who was a pig, a dog and a rat. There were a few weeds on Auntie Lola's grave so she pulled them out. Then after a while she began picking up all the marigold petals that Macky had let fall everywhere, and began scattering them over the grave.

She started at the top where Auntie Lola's face was, and worked down. Macky saw what she was doing. He watched for a while, peeping through his eyelashes.

Then he began to help, because it looked good, and it was a good idea. Yes. It was much better than banging a stupid jar at the top, a stupid jar in the middle, and a stupid jar at the bottom and bunging flowers in them – as though you were punching someone in the face and in the stomach, and booting their legs.

They worked down over where Auntie Lola's chest was, over the middle and the box of twins, right down to her feet. It took a long time. Then they climbed down the bank to where there were taupata bushes growing and picked bunches of leaves. They placed the leaves all round the edges of the grave, making a border of green. It looked beautiful. It was a good idea.

The others finished and walked round looking, talking about what they'd all done, but Mereana and Macky didn't join them. Instead, they sat down where they were and blew noises through the folded taupata leaves. They could do taxi horns, quacking ducks and seagull noises, as well as a variety of farts.

When the others came to see what they'd done they didn't look up. They kept on blowing through the leaves and only looked at Charlotte and the others through their eyelashes.

Well, Charlotte was wild. She didn't say anything but she was wild all right. She stamped off down the hill. Denny Boy said, 'Smartfarts,' and went off after Charlotte. They heard him calling, 'Smartfarts, smartfellas, fartsmellers,' as he went.

The others stood for a moment or two looking, but they were all wild too, except for Lizzie. Lizzie danced and coughed and said, 'Gee, it's a good idea, a real good idea. It's lovely the way you've done . . . it's like a birthday. And . . . I reckon they like it. See, Ana, Erana.' But Ana and Erana had gone off after Charlotte. They were wild.

Macky and Mereana sat and explained to Lizzie how they'd taken the petals off the flowers and started sprinkling them at the top, down over the chest, twins, legs, feet – and then made a frame right round with taupata leaves. Good idea. Lizzie reckoned Auntie Lola liked it.

It was time to go. They picked up their bottles and began to hurry downhill. From halfway down they could see the others standing in the sea washing the bottles and washing their hands. So they stopped running and dawdled a little, giving them time to finish their wash. Because Charlotte would be still wild and she'd push them in the sea. Denny Boy might ankle-tap. Then they'd get a hiding from Auntie Connie for having wet clothes.

They waited until they saw the others making their way back up the beach and through the lupins, then they went down to the sea to wash.

Bloody cold too. Just as well they hadn't let Charlotte throw them in. Cold, and they were hungry as well. They began to run, up over the beach and through the lupins.

But they'd forgotten that the others might booby-trap them. Charlotte, Denny Boy, Ana and Erana had tied the lower branches of the lupins together across the skinny tracks, and the next minute Mereana, Macky and Lizzie were tripping, flying, falling on their faces, and the bottles were spinning away into the bushes. They could hear Charlotte and the others laughing in the lupin tunnels.

Anyway it was nothing. Macky and Mereana didn't care because it just proved how good their idea was. Lizzie didn't care either, and she was going to do that idea next time. She reckoned Auntie and the twins liked it.

They got up and tidied their clothes, found their bottles and went running. They were cold. They wanted a feed. They wondered what sort of a mood Auntie Connie was in.

Butterflies

T HE GRANDMOTHER PLAITED HER GRANDDAUGHTER'S HAIR
and then she said, 'Get your lunch. Put it in your bag.
Get your apple. You come straight back after school, straight
home here. Listen to the teacher,' she said. 'Do what she
say.'

Her grandfather was out on the step. He walked down the
path with her and out on to the footpath. He said to a new
neighbour, 'Our granddaughter goes to school. She lives with
us now.'

'She's fine,' the neighbour said. 'She's terrific with her two
plaits in her hair.'

'And clever,' the grandfather said. 'Writes every day in her
book.'

'She's fine,' the neighbour said.

The grandfather waited with his granddaughter by the
crossing and then he said, 'Go to school. Listen to the teacher.
Do what she say.'

When the granddaughter came home from school her grandfather was hoeing round the cabbages. Her grandmother was
picking beans. They stopped their work.

'You bring your book home?' the grandmother asked.

'Yes.'

'You write your story?'

'Yes.'

'What's your story?'

'About the butterflies.'

'Get your book, then. Read your story.'

The granddaughter took her book from her schoolbag and
opened it.

'I killed all the butterflies,' she read. 'This is me and this is all the butterflies.'

'And your teacher like your story, did she?'

'I don't know.'

'What your teacher say?'

'She said butterflies are beautiful creatures. They hatch out and fly in the sun. The butterflies visit all the pretty flowers, she said. They lay their eggs and then they die. You don't kill butterflies, that's what she said.'

The grandmother and grandfather were quiet for a long time, and their granddaughter, holding the book, stood quite still in the warm garden.

'Because you see,' the grandfather said, 'your teacher, she buy all her cabbages from the supermarket and that's why.'

The Hills

I LIKE IT WHEN I GET TO THE TOP OF THE ROAD AND I LOOK out and see the mist down over the hills. It's like a wrapped parcel and you know there's something good inside.

And I like being funny. When someone says something I like to have something funny to say back, because I like people to laugh, and I like laughing too. A funny man, that's me.

'Man' might not be quite the right word – but 'boy' isn't right either. 'Boy' means little kid, 'boy' means dirty with a filthy mind. It means 'smart-arse'. A 'boy' is a servant and a slave.

Well, I've been grubby and smart all right but never a servant or a slave. Mum bossing me and getting me to mow grass and mop floors doesn't make me a slave or a servant. That's just something for me to moan about because I don't like doing my share. Anyway, I'm not a slave or a servant. I'm just myself. One day I'll call myself a man, and I won't just be an old 'boy' like my father.

He's gone. I've got an uncle that I really like, Mum's brother, and he's funny too. Jokes don't stop him being a man.

Some teachers don't like my jokes and they think I'm a pain, but I get on all right with a few. Once when I was in the third form I drew a neat moustache on myself. I got told off and had to go and have a wash, and I got picked on by that teacher all the time after that.

When I was in the fifth I grew a real moustache and trimmed it up, and I had about six hairs of a beard as well. Well, my form teacher got screwed up about it and ordered it all off. 'The mower's broken down,' I said, and I got into a heap of trouble. Anyhow I think someone must have stuck up for me somewhere along the line. I got moved to another form class and nothing more was said about my whiskers.

They're not sharp hills, or pointy. They're bums and boobs, with cracks and splits. They're fat and folding. I like it when the wrapping comes off.

One day I wore a big long coat to school. It was an old coat but hadn't been worn much. It was just a coat that my old man had left behind, the type of coat that a lot of men wore them. Gaberdine, my mother said. She said I looked like a drongo.

The first thing the coat made me feel like doing was marching. I don't know why, because it wasn't like an army coat at all. It was big for me and down to my shins. I marched along the street and when I saw Wasi and Georgina I stopped and saluted and they fell in behind. Good on them. Off we marched for a while, until Wasi started talking about something interesting. We stopped acting up and strolled along the way we usually did.

Then when I got to school I thought I could be a flasher. So at each change of class I walked last into the room and went 'Zoonk!' I didn't flash anything of course, except for grey shirt, grey jersey and a pair of baggy cords. Some laughed and some didn't. One of the teachers grinned and yelled out 'Police!', and the whole class cracked up. I liked that. I had a good laugh too. Sometimes you just need a change from grey shirt, grey jersey, pair of baggy cords.

When the mist comes down to cover the hills I don't think grey. I think of parcels and coloured wrapping, and clothes and tits and bums. Then I have a good laugh at myself and think that I'm only a boy after all. I don't mean a servant or a slave or a smart brat. I just mean 'boy' in a different, youngish way.

Then something can happen to you that's too much for a boy. You can't be a boy any more afterwards. And when it's gone for good, and you're sure it's gone, you can feel sorry. It wasn't you that did it or wanted it. It was something done to you.

You get used to the police, stopping, searching, hassling

you around. They say something smart and you say something smart back. But you know you shouldn't get too smart. You have to hold back. You know they don't like you to be clever because it makes them scared. So you let them mouth off and you have to bite your tongue, which isn't easy for someone like me with jokes on his lip all the time. But after they've gone you can have a bit of a laugh – name please where are you going where've you been do you know so and so where do you live whose shoes you got on up against the car search search.

Mum doesn't like me drinking. She says there's nothing wrong with the old man, only drinking. He's all right she reckons, kind, tidy, just useless and a drunk, and she's glad he's gone. We get on better without him, she says. But anyway my mates and I enjoy drinking and parties, and I tell Mum she shouldn't worry about me.

When school finished last year, me, Wasi, Georgina, Steven, Louanna, and Georgie's brother and a few others went to the pub to celebrate. Louanna and Steve weren't coming back to school. I thought I might leave too but hadn't made up my mind. Georgie's brother was the only one old enough to be in the pub. We didn't have much money but Lou and Steve had enough to shout a couple of rounds. It was good. We were having a good time.

Then Steve went out to the toilet and didn't come back. Wasi went to have a look, and when he came back he said that the cops were outside talking to Steve.

Lou and Wasi and I went out to have a look, and on the way we were cracking jokes about Steve leaving school and going straight to Rock College. Ha, ha. There was a cop car outside with two cops in it but no Steven.

We looked round but couldn't see him, had another look in the toilets and he wasn't there, so we went back outside.

I went over to the car and looked in the window. I knew Steven wasn't in the car but I said, 'Have you got our mate Steven in there?' Then I was slammed in the head with the door, jerked to my feet with my arm up behind, and hung over the bonnet of the car. They went down and through my pockets and one of them said, 'Take him in.'

'You can't do that. What for?' That was Louanna yelling at them.

'Get home, girlie,' one of them said. He threw me in the car and started up.

Louanna started booting the car and shouting, 'What about me, look what I'm doing.'

'Shove off,' one of them said, and away we went.

'What for?' I said. I'd got over the bang on the face by then, and just thought that it was the same game, only rougher than usual. They'd drop me off any minute as long as I didn't get too smart.

'Shut your black face,' one of them said. 'You'll know soon enough.'

Well some are polite and some aren't, even though they are mostly all playing the same game.

'Abusive language,' the other said, 'and resisting arrest.'

I was just drunk enough to say, 'I thought it was for under-age drinking.'

'That too,' they said.

And then I was just drunk enough to say that anyway, they were the ones being abusive telling me to shut my black face.

'Why?' the same one said. 'You've got a black face, haven't you? You're a black, aren't you?'

Well he had me there. If I pointed out that I was brown it was like denying blackness, like saying you're halfway to white.

'It's not an offence, is it?' I asked.

'No offence me saying what you are then, is it?' the smart one said.

I could see they weren't going to let me out of the car. Sometimes the game can be quite amusing, something for a laugh later, but I was slacked off with their game this time.

At the station I was charged and asked a whole lot of ques-tions. I just answered the questions and tried to point out that I wasn't drinking when they saw me, I wasn't in the pub when they saw me. I was sober by then. Anyhow the sooner I got out the better, I thought, so I decided I should keep my mouth shut.

The smart one went out for a minute or two then came back in. He held the door open and jerked his head, so I followed him through into another room where I was grabbed and searched again. Then suddenly I was thrown across a bench, my trousers were pulled down and I was searched up the behind.

That's what I meant when I said something can happen, and you can't be what you were after that. I said 'searched' but I didn't know at the time that what they were doing was part of a search. I thought I was being raped. I didn't know then – or if I'd heard of it I'd forgotten – that people sometimes hid things up there.

Afterwards I remember feeling sick, and going out and my mates being out there waiting, and us all going to Georgie and her brother's place. I remember crying. They all thought I'd been beaten up and I didn't tell them any different.

They wanted to ring my mother but I said no. I didn't want her to know. Steve and Lou were staring at me. I don't know what I looked like.

'What do you want? What will we do?' Louanna asked.

'I want to have a bath,' I said. 'I want to go to sleep.'

I stayed in the bath a long time, and when I got into bed I stayed awake a long time.

In the morning Georgie said, 'We rang your mum just to tell her you were staying the night.' She waited a while. And then she said, 'You sore?' So I told them what happened.

But I didn't tell Mum when I got home. I told her I'd been caught under age in the pub and had to go to court. She banged me on the arm and then she cried.

Later that day I went outside and walked up the street, and when I got to the top of the road I wouldn't look out at the hills.

The hills could've been clear, or the mist could've been down or it could've been just lifting off. I turned and went back home. I remember wondering if I would ever look there again.

Fishing

WHILE THE OTHERS WERE OUT GETTING PAUA AND KINA, Ria fished. She'd picked ngakihi off the sea rocks, then taken the line and bait to a place where there was weed. The waves were green there – not heavy, and not breaking until right on shore. On shore they broke, tracking up over the stones.

She thumbed ngakihi out of their shells and baited the hooks, then unwound some of the line and walked to the edge of the water, whirling the traces. She cast, and the line shot out, dropping close to the weed.

From where she sat she could see the others, some out diving off the dinghy to pick kina off the sea bed, others snorkelling about amongst the rocks getting paua. That was the way the younger ones liked to do things, yet she knew if they'd waited until the tide was down they could've walked out and got all the paua they needed, in water that was just knee deep.

Further out past the divers, the children were jumping off Chicken Rock, struggling in the breaking waves and climbing up again. In the shallow water younger children were pushing a log about, and babies paddled and played, watched by mothers who really wanted to be getting kina and paua, or out jumping off Chicken Rock. If she'd stayed there with them she would've watched the kids and given her nieces a break. But today she'd decided to go off on her own and fish.

There were a few tugs on her line and then the biting stopped. She began to pull in, knowing that the bait would be gone, bringing the line in swiftly so the sinker wouldn't snag. Ngakihi was soft bait but would have to do until the water was shallow enough for her to get paua. She baited up and cast the line again – not straight, not far, but the spot was worth a try.

Looking back, she could see the old man sitting under the big umbrella. He would be watching, thinking about the place, thinking about how he knew the shape of the sea bed right there. She knew he would like to have told someone about when the crayfish were thick, about when you could, at this time of the year, have looked down from the hills and seen the large red mass moving shoreward, which was crayfish coming in. She would have listened to him tell about how they'd pulled the weed aside with long-handled spears to find the crayfish that had backed themselves into narrow cracks in the rocks. The old man liked the umbrella.

Out on Chicken Rock the children were facing out to sea, waving. There was the sound of a motor, and then a boat came into sight and began weaving its way in. She couldn't see clearly but knew it would be her cousin May, with her husband and their family, coming to catch what could be the last good tide of the summer. The boat stopped close to shore and the children got out, then it rode out again to where May and Maru would set their nets.

The fish were biting all right, but she wasn't hooking them. She pulled in and baited up again.

Now the kids out on the rock were calling, looking shoreward this time. They would be tired by now, wanting someone to bring the dinghy out to get them. She watched as someone rowed out and nosed the boat up against the big rock. The children climbed down to be taken ashore, too exhausted and too hungry to swim for it. They were soon back on shore, running everywhere picking up sticks. They wouldn't be given bread until the wood had been gathered. Not long after that she saw smoke rising against the backdrop of cliffs. The divers were wading in with full bags.

At low tide she went to look for paua. There were several there on the stones and she collected three. She washed and shelled the smallest one, intending to eat it. Then she decided she wouldn't eat until she had caught her fish. She wouldn't eat, and she wouldn't go back to drink tea. Knowing that her line would snag in such shallow water, she lay down, sheltering where the stones had piled, and waited for the tide to flow again.

For some time there was little activity in the incoming tide. Then suddenly the fish were there again, biting and pulling, and she knew it was just a matter of time.

It was colder now but the kids were back in the water again – the mothers too, getting their chance at last. Cassie was helping the old man up to the car, wanting to get him home before the cold set in. The old man liked being able to come there by car.

By the time she caught her fish it was late afternoon. It was a small fish, but she was satisfied. All she'd hoped for was to catch one fish on this, the last good day of summer. She took it down to the water's edge where she cleaned and scaled it.

Then she knew there was something else for her to do, because how could you be really sure of coming there again next summer? And why should you come if you didn't let the place know you? It wasn't enough just to hold at the end of a line. The mothers were right about needing to go beyond the shore.

She walked out into the half-tide and let herself gradually into the water. She squatted for a while with her skirt floating up about her, then she pushed forward and down, pulling herself along the stony sea bed for as long as her breath lasted. When she came to the larger rocks where the weed grew thickly, she stood and pushed her way though. Once in the clear water again she lay on her back, letting herself go the way the water moved her. It was a familiar place, and she knew she could lie there like that quite safely.

She lay there for a long time watching the sky redden as the sun went down.

Back on shore she picked up her line and the little fish, and walked quickly back to where the others were sitting round the fire, or getting ready to go for the nets.

They were amused at her one little fish, that it had taken her most of the day to catch. She knew they were wondering why she would spend all day on her own, without food, then come back wet and cold with just one little fish, especially when she knew there would be plenty of fish once the nets were brought in.

But it was her cousin May who said to her, as though they were picking up a conversation that could have begun years before, 'Because if you don't, it's like you won't any more. It's like if you sit under the umbrella once, then that's it. You have to still know, and you have to do enough . . . to carry you over. You have to be in there because you don't want to be just waiting by the edge.'

Kahawai

ALL RIGHT THEN. ONE MORNING I GOT UP LATE AND HURRIED to the kitchen. He was up before me and would have the jug boiling, the pan plugged in, the bread popped down, I thought.

Instead he was in the front room looking out.

Because the gulls had gathered out at sea, under cloud, and were chasing, calling, falling to the water. Up, chase, drop. Screaming. There's fish, he said. It brought juices. Kahawai, beating green and silver through purple water, herding the herrings which excited the gulls, which excited me . . .

Could we . . . ?

Be sick?

We could.

Have we got . . . ?

Bait?

We have.

Have we got two-stroke?

No.

Get breakfast, get changed, get two-stroke.

Have we got spinners?

No. Someone borrowed.

Don't need spinner. Can trawl the heads of soldiers.

Then the others came in.

Well . . . what? Have yous got a holiday or something? Or what?

We're sick . . .

Of work.

And the fish are out there, nose to tail.

Yes, we heard.

The birds.

Saw splashes. But . . .'

It's only us who don't go. Sometimes. Or don't get up. Right? Because of hangovers, or laziness, or going somewhere else. Or from not being back from somewhere. Only us have sickies. Right? But anyway . . . Good. Good on yous. Kahawai, yum. Make some bread too. Yahoo.

Lines, bait, knife, hooks, sinkers, jerseys, towel, apples, can of two-stroke, putt-putt motor, rowlocks, oars. Push the dinghy out and sidle out past the weed.

He winds the rope and pulls, tries again and then we're away putt-putting out over the navy blue, under cloud, stopping for a while to remove the sinkers from the lines and to bait the hooks with the heads of soldier fish.

Then away again to where the gulls swarm above the swarming kahawai that herd the swarming herrings. But he and I are not a swarm, we are only two of us. One fish each will do.

Then we are in the middle of it, the darting, leaping little fish crack open the dark water, leap and splash, the gull's eye singling out one, the eye of the kahawai on another. Gulls swooping, following, rising, diving, rising, swallowing, turning, following. And the kahawai zigging, zagging, leaping, shooting through the water, beating silver on the surface of it. Hundreds. But for us two will do.

We trawl our long lines with the putt-putt on slow, putt-putting through chaotic water under the screeching canopy.

Of birds. One of them is eyeing the bait, the head of the soldier, and is following. I stand spread-legged and wave one arm. No. Go. Silly bird. It's dead meat, hooked. Krazy Karoro.

Krazy Kahawai too, for that matter. And Krazy Kataha. KKK. And what about Krazy Kouple in a boat? KKK and KK. I wave. Shout. Go, Karoro, go. So Karoro drops back, but still follows, still wants.

And then, Got it, he says. So I stop waving, stop shouting, plonk myself down. He switches the motor off so that he can pull in . . . number one. Pulling . . .

What have we got here?
One little kahawai, my teacher dear.
Kahawai, Kahawai, nicky nicky nacky noo.
That's what they taught me
When I went to . . .

Pulling . . . Pulling in over the side . . .

Flip flop she flied,
Flip flop she flied,
Flip flop she flied,
She went up to heaven and flip flop she flied
Flip flop she fliedy flied flied . . .

Krazy Kahawai flapping, slapping the tin boards of the boat,
bouncing in the wet sack on the tin bottom of the boat. I pull
in too so that my line won't tangle in the motor while we start
up again.

    Off. Putt-putting full out to catch up with Karoro again.
They have moved further out now, dinning and diving. We
trail the heads of soldiers, turning to run with the fish . . .

Kahawai, Kataha, nicky nicky nacky noo,
That's what they taught me . . .
Hat on one side what have we here?
One little chin chopper, my teacher dear.
Chin chopper, snot catcher, eye basher,
sweaty boxer, nicky nacky noo
That's what they taught me when . . .

Karoro. Again. Eyeing, swooping. I stand, wave, shout. Not
for you. Shoo. Wave and shout. Go. Blow. Karoro backs off,
then moves up again. I pick up an apple, throw it, and Karoro
turns, circles, returns. Krazy Kamikaze Karoro. I pick up the
towel, swing it, and Karoro, nervous, drops back, still wanting,
still turning the eye.

    But then, is beaten to the bait by Kahawai. Number two.
Got it. He switches off and I sit down pulling in swiftly . . .

One little kahawai, my teacher dear,
Kahawai, Kahawai, nicky nicky nacky noo,
That's what they taught me when . . .
Kahawai, Kahawai, nicky nicky nacky noo,
That's what they . . .
What have we here?
One great big kahawai, my teacher dear,
Kahawai, Karoro, Kataha, Krazy Kouple,
nicky nicky nacky noo,
That's what they taught me . . .

Bring it in over the side, hand into the gills, push the hook. Look Karoro, hook, turn your eye. Not meant, not bent for a feathered throat. Open the bag and . . .

Flip flop she flied,
Flip flop she flied,
Flip flop she flied,
She went up to heaven and flip flop she flied
Flip flop she fliedy flied flied.

And now, the gulls, the fish have moved out again, too far for a tin boat and a putt-putt on a cold day. It's Kold, and two will do. One flick and we're moving again, turning, the Krazy Kouple. Kold. Heading home.

As we come to the weed in the shallow water we switch off, lifting the motor, and row in swiftly. Kold. We step out, ahh, into water, kold hands gripping the sides of the boat. Can we lift it? We can, rushing it up over the stones. Rest, then again. Again, blue knuckled. And lift. Can we? On to the trailer? We can.

Then back to the edge we go with the two fish, scraping fast, because it's kold. The scales leap. We slit the white bellies, pulling the insides out, flinging. Kum Karoro. They come, dance on the surface of the sea, snatch the innards and fly up gulping. We wash the fish and the water runs red-salt-blood. We hurry with the trailer, home, to be dry and warm.

When it is time I put bread in the oven. He cuts up fish, puts it in the big pot with a good fist of salt, watches so that it won't boil fast. We scrub and slice vegetables and put them on to cook.

Then the others come, lifting the lids of the pots. Did yous? Yous did.

Opening the oven door.

Did yous? Yous did. Yum.

When it is time we lift the fish carefully into bowls and strain the water into a jug. We break up the bread on the board and heap the vegetables on to dishes.

Then we sit down to celebrate.

Hospital

There's something being hauled up from inside her – up and out of her throat – something sharp and cutting, and live. She is puffed up and big – this one of her. The other one of her is small, sitting cross-legged on air, still and serene, watching.

It's fish, bunches of tarakihi with splayed fins, tearing the insides of her, tearing her throat, ripping her stretched mouth – and then falling in heaps about this swollen, inert one of her, pale, bloodied and flopping. She can smell the sweet, green smell of live fish. There are voices and noise.

The other one of her, sitting unmoving in the shadows, is telling her something – not about fish, fins, falling, bleeding or noise, but about the pain – warning her not to let it go. Above all the clamour and the fish stink, there is the precious, grinding pain that she mustn't let go – must keep . . . keep . . . keep . . . The other one of her, sitting still in the shadows, is warning her, so that in the sudden stillness she won't let herself slide . . . or shift . . . or drift . . .

Without the sounds, without the movement, there's only the solid pain to hold.

Taking hold. It of her. Her of it. And then slipping. She slipping. It slipping . . . Out through her feet? No. The other one of her, sitting straight-backed and unmoving is telling her to reach . . . reach . . . threatening that if she doesn't, then someone else will get her pain, as a legacy. Someone else will have, as inheritance, what only you should . . . you should . . . you should . . .

'Who?'

'Your daughter.'

'No. I have it, have it now, safe, and keep it to my bloated, bloodied, groaning, fish-woman self. Don't speak . . . of daughters. No more slip, slide. No slipping, sliding. Just hold, hold, holding . . . until it is . . .

Time.

Shouting.

A name.

Her name.

Faces.

She knows one of . . .

Voices.

She knows one . . .

'How . . . feeling? Feeling? How . . . feeling?'

Sore. She knows she hasn't said it.

'Feeling?'

She finds breath, pushes it out. 'Sore,' but it is only a whisper.

'Yes, I'll bet. Anyway, good enough . . . let you . . .'

Rest.

And she's looking down on a bare world where naked people crawl on a dry earth searching . . . for kai.

But there is no kai. It's a world of sand, and the figures crawl like insects over its surface, thin-limbed, large-eyed, dry, flaky.

'Looking down from where?' she calls to the other one of her.

'From where you are.'

'Don't want . . .'

'But anyway, there it is. There they are.'

'Don't want . . .'

'Otherwise who else? Who will see? Who will know?'

'Dreaming.'

'Not dreaming.'

'Dreaming.'

'Not dreaming.'

Waking.

There are patches of light, smudges of dark, circling. Green counterpane and two arms. Hers. Her two arms on a green counterpane. A tube going upwards. Blood.

'Warm enough?'

'Yes.' It is only a breath.

'Lost your voice, hmmm?'

'Blood.'

'And look, flowers. Nice, ay?'

But she knows there's no place for flowers.

Or fish. No place for the pop-eyed tarakihi, hands pulling, hooks, lines, seaweed, sharp fins. No seas or rivers. Only . . . insect people with long hands, and feet that are hand-like. They crawl with their noses close to the ground. They cry into the ground, long fingers scratching at the earth, long toes spread, finger-like, patterning the sand.

'Don't want to see.'

'Want or not, there they are. Otherwise who?'

'Dreaming.'

'No. Not dreaming.'

'Dreaming.'

'Not dreaming.'

Awake.

Voices.

Faces.

' . . . nice wash . . . feeling now?'

'Scared.' Has she said it? Her two arms on a green counter-pane. A tube going upwards.

'Water.'

'Fluids, to keep you going. Nice flowers, ay?'

But she knows there's no place for flowers. No seas, no rivers, only . . .

'Burning.'

'Sore I bet . . . But you'll feel a bit better tomorrow. We'll take the drip off later, and we'll shift you down to a ward room in the morning.'

She's on a trolley, in a corridor. Wheels click over the linoleum, fast, past windows . . . windows . . . windows . . . Wheels, win-dows, wheels, windows – like in a tunnel, in a train.

The wheels slow down, they stop by glass doors. She's making way for a wheelchair which has been tilted on to its back wheels. They are wheeling in . . . a pig?

There was one in a barrow, trundled through the streets, covered with apples. A prize. Only two ears and the snout with its two great snout-holes showing.

No. Not a pig. It's a woman. Her neck, crusted with dry blood, is arched back over a pillow, and her stretched nostrils are packed up with cotton.

'Now a cup of tea, love? Sit you up a bit. Mr Siers is coming soon. Better without those drips?'

'Yes.'

'No voice yet, hmmm? No water passed either. Well, drink up plenty – for the waterworks, get the plumbing going. We'll sit you out on a chair later, on a pan, see if that works. Nice carnations, ay?'

But the flowers are shocking and wrong-coloured – shocking red, shocking pink and shocking shiny gold. The stalks are bright, lime green. For a moment a woman stands by the door and the patterns on her dressing gown move away from the gown itself, shimmering . . . or else there is a trick of light. If she asks about the flowers – do they brighten, darken, do they shift and change, or about sharp fish, or the insect-shadow-people that move over the surface of the turning sand-bone world – will her questions come out wrong-coloured too? Will she yell instead, scream? She slides down off the pillows thinking about what she can safely say. She can say, 'Yes,' or 'No,' or 'No voice.' Open your eyes.

'A bit better today?'

'Yes.'

'What's happened to your voice?'

'No voice.'

'Well, don't rush it.'

Sister lifts the covers back, opens the gown, folds it away

from the dressings and the surgeon touches gently about the bandages.

'What about the waterworks?'

'No.'

'No? We'll try her on some Mist. Pot. Cit., Sister, that should help. A bit sore round here?' He touches gently.

'Yes.'

'Lift the dressings a little? Yes, it's fine.' Looking down, thoughtful, kind. 'Eating?'

'Not yet, Mr Siers, but we'll see what we can tempt her with at lunch. And we'll get her moved over by the window.'

'Good, I'll look in again tonight.'

'Drink up as much as you can. See. Big jugful, drink the whole lot, that should do the trick. It's nice.'

Yes. It is nice. Lemony and cold, with a faint fizz. If it didn't work, what happened? Did you swell up and pop, like a frog?

'Nurse.'

'What is it, love?'

'Can you shift the flowers?'

'To?'

'The shelf in the corner.'

'You won't see . . .' Nurse frowns, but she takes the vases, lifts them onto the shelf.

'Is that okay?'

'Thanks.'

She can hear the trolleys rumbling down the passage bringing midday meals.

'Now, dear, they're bringing roast beef and vegetables,' Sister says. 'Is that all right? Or would you like poached eggs, a bit of pie?'

'Just the vegetables, Sister, thanks.'

'Good, and some gravy?'

'Yes please.'

'Good. Got your appetite back now, have you? And

pudding? Fruit and rice, and I'll tell Nurse to put some cream on. Do you like cream?'

'Yes, thanks.'

'Good, love. I'll pop back and see how you're getting on.'

The dinner nurse comes in, beaming, with a tray.

'Here you are.'

Salt and pepper in glass shakers, and cutlery wrapped in a napkin. On the plate there is a ball of mashed potato which is pale and metallic-looking, a ball of red pumpkin, a spoon of emerald peas and a mound of navy blue silverbeet. There's a topping of reddish gravy.

She could ask what has happened to colours, or what has happened to her. Instead she asks the nurse to put the tray on the locker. The nurse looks unhappy.

'Would you like something else instead? Sister said . . .' So she relents. 'Leave it, Nurse, I'll try.'

'Good. Pud's coming. Enjoy your dinner.' Away beaming.

She puts a forkful of the potato to her mouth, swallows, and eats two of the peas. Then she leans back on the pillows. In a minute she'll have a mouthful of the drink, then try again. Someone coming.

'Not hungry today?' It's the pudding nurse with a little bowl of something golden.

'Could you put this tray up on the locker, please, Nurse?'

'What's happened to your poor voice?'

'Nothing's the same.'

'What about pudding?'

'Put it on the tray for me, please.'

'Get into it later, will you?'

'When I've had a drink.'

'Will I pour you some?'

'Thanks.'

She has a mouthful of the drink, reaches out and puts the glass back on the locker. She removes two pillows and lies down to sleep.

We left you, dear, let you sleep. Now we'll get you tidied up. You got visitors coming?'

'Yes.'

'That's nice. Let them do the talking. Look after that throat of yours. You can just nod and smile, like the Queen. We'll wheel you over the other side first, by the window. Right? Then we'll get you out onto the chair for a few minutes while we make your bed. And you'll have time for a little wash and a brush up. We're bringing you a room-mate later.'

'Good.'

Out of the window there are rows of petunias, many times darker than what she's known. They are purple-black, black-blue, red-black, brown-black and black. She won't ask what's happened to colours.

Trolley. A gowned, masked nurse is pulling on gloves.

'We'll put a catheter in, dear. You'll feel better after that, able to get a good night's rest. Have you been at all since . . . ?'

'No.'

'Did they try you out on the chair?'

'Mmmm.'

'Run the tap?'

'Yes.'

'What about the lav, did they take you down?'

'After visiting.'

'Not much voice there . . . Now this won't hurt . . . that's it, we're in business. Well now! No voice, no plumbing, how's the rest of it?'

'Healing up fine, Mr Siers said.' It was one of the things she could safely say: 'Yes.' 'No.' 'No voice.' 'Healing up fine.'

'Crikey, I should've brought a drum down to flow you off into. I've filled one bottle, and now this one's halfway. Must've been sore, poor you. Anyway, should feel a lot better after this . . . I know what, I'll get one of the nurses to bring a bowl in when I've finished and you can have a little wash. You can get pretty sweaty and worried having bits and pieces poked in, taken out, tubes all over the place . . . Taking it out now. That's it. How does it feel?'

'Much better.'

'And tomorrow they'll have you walking a bit more. Then you'll be away laughing, what do you think?'

'There'll be no stopping me.'

'Good on you. Now me, I'm taking this lot away, and going to get me out of this gear. Have a good sleep. And anyway, they'll give you something, won't they, to help you sleep?' Her voice floats back from the corridor above the noise of the trolley.

'Nurse'll be along with a bowl – for a wash. Goodnight.'

In the morning she doesn't know whether she has slept or not. She has the feeling of not having slept, of having listened for many hours to the groans and mutterings of the woman next to her, of having been aware of the night nurses coming in, playing the torches discreetly over the two of them.

'I came in with a nose bleed,' the woman says, 'and they did a Caesarean.' The woman has been propped up on pillows and she lies back against them with her eyes closed. Her fingers play along the edge of the counterpane. It's a relief to hear the woman speak.

'What did you have?'

'A girl. I think she's dying.' Tears run down from under the woman's closed lids.

'What did they say?'

'They're doing their best. They'll wheel me down . . .'

The woman begins to breathe deeply as though she's fallen asleep again.

Later that morning she is taken to the lavatory to perch and a few drops of urine leak away.

'That's only spillage,' the nurse says, 'not the real thing.' She's little and rosy and talkative. 'Lean back, relax as much as you can.'

So she lets herself sag, deepens her breathing, waits.

'You can leave me here if you like.'

'No, we'll give it another couple of minutes. Don't want you pegging out on us.' It's true that she's feeling dizzy. 'If it's no go, we'll get you back to bed. You can drink some more fizz, have another cup of tea.'

When she gets back into the room the woman is being helped back into bed.

'How's baby?'

'It's sad for a baby to just lie there, with no one,' the woman says.

'What did they say when you . . . ?'

'Next twelve hours should tell . . . Just tubes, sticking plaster, things . . . Just a tiny baby, in a little glass bed.' The woman's voice becomes a whisper.

She turns to look out the window. What did it matter about flowers, about colours, when there were more important things. You were the only one to tell yourself what you saw. It was only you who knew, so what did it matter. The woman's being there was helping her – the woman's night moaning and snoring, the tears, the baby, naked, alone, perhaps dying in the little glass canoe.

It was something to think about. It helped, which didn't seem right or fair.

'No clothes for baby,' the woman says. 'Nothing ready. I wasn't even six months. It's never happened like this before. Always gone full term . . .'

'Someone will . . .'

'Not the father, he hasn't been in. Couldn't even find him to bring me here. My nose was pouring, messing my clothes, messing the taxi . . .'

The woman begins to cry again. 'It's just baby's clothes. Without the clothes it's like I'm not expecting . . . to take baby home. There's nothing from the last one. Gave it all away long ago. It's like not expecting baby . . . to live.'

So the woman needed baby clothes so that she could know through the next twelve hours that she was expecting to take her baby home.

'I got clothes,' she says to the woman. 'Two drawers, naps and all. I don't need them.'

The woman is silent, wondering perhaps if the clothes are not needed because a baby has died.

'My baby's eighteen months, walking round, I won't be having more now.'

'I'd like the clothes,' the woman says.

'My cousin's coming in an hour. She could bring them if I ring.'

'Getting round and taking notice now, are you?' the nurse asks as she helps her to a phone.

'Are you busting?' the nurse says from behind the trolley, from behind the mask.

'Feels like it.'

'A bit more voice than yesterday?'

'Yes.'

'Good-oh. Here we go.'

Later that evening two ministers come in to pray with the woman. They put on purple gowns and mantles.

'I been in to see baby,' one of them says. 'I prayed with baby. Baby's holding her own. Before that, all afternoon, we been with the koroua. And after our karakia, going back to pray with him.'

They begin the prayers, and somewhere beyond the window a bird starts to squeal intermittently. The chanting is restful. She doesn't hear the ministers leave.

The woman hasn't slept. 'The bird kept on all night, now it's gone.' Only her lips move. Then there's movement in the doorway, a glimpse of purple in the half-dark.

'Kua mate te koroua,' the minister says, and moves away.

'I thought it was baby. Instead it was the koroua. When I heard the bird I thought it was a message about baby. I suppose if it was baby they would have come for me. I was waiting for them to come.'

'Who's the old man they're talking about?'

'From up home. Last year we had his ninetieth birthday, up home. Tino ngawari te koroua ra, real gentle.' Tears slide across the woman's temples and into her hair.

'Last night, in the night, I was glad about the clothes.'

'Great, that's wonderful.'

'Only a trickle.'

'Two trickles and a drop, but you're on your way. Away laughing. Perch there and concentrate for a while and we'll see what happens.'

She waits. Finally she is peeing into the bowl, forever.

'Milestones,' the nurse says. 'And they take out a few clips in the morning. Right?'

'Right.'

'You'll be a box of birds when I come back on tomorrow.'

There's a world spinning, dust-covered, where stick people search, finding nothing.

People are calling her name.

People calling.

Someone . . . wiping her face.

'Passed out on us, love? Not too pleasant getting the clips out. But those were the worst ones. You'll hardly feel the next lot. Mr Siers'll tell you when he comes. Do you want a drink?'

'No thanks.'

'Voice gone on you. A bit shaky are you? Well let's leave you flat like that for a bit, tuck you in so you can have a good rest before visiting.'

She lies flat and straight with the blankets tucked in tightly. The screen curtains make a wall about her, and when she blinks her eyes, dark smudges move about the space like flying clods. Am I here flat and face upwards, or there sitting upright at the edge? Edge? But you do not question. Curiosity can become a plan to escape. From where? From what? You do not question, but instead lie still, planning what ordinary things to say to visitors, ordinary things that help, that keep you where you are.

She tells her visitors about the old man, the woman, the baby, the clothes for the baby, the clips, her voice, her bladder. They tell her she doesn't look good, that she'd looked better yesterday.

'There could be a draught,' someone says, 'from the window.'

The woman is wiping her face with a towel as she is wheeled back into the room. Her eyes are red and puffy.

'It's good what they can do,' the woman says as she's helped into bed.

'Is baby all right?'

'She's pulling through. They said she's a strong little thing . . . As long as nothing develops. But . . . they lost one this morning.' The woman begins to cry again. 'The mother never held him . . . alive. The family didn't . . . We talked about our babies yesterday, the other mother and me. Yesterday she sent her husband off to get a bassinet. It was like me with the clothes. You have to have baby's things, a name for baby, otherwise it's like waiting to see.'

For some time the woman is quiet, then she says, 'Before I saw her I called her Cynthia. Don't know why. It's not a family name. It just came, out of nowhere, but I wanted her to have a name. She had to be somebody, with a name, with clothes. So I been calling her Cynthia when I go down.'

'Did it suit her, when you saw her?'

'Suits her good. Cynthia suits her just right. Father mightn't like it, but too bad, she's already Cynthia.'

She wants the woman to go on talking.

'Who does she look like then?'

'Nobody, just herself. She's tiny, but got big hands, like our other girls – long hands, with long, pointy fingers. The other one, the one that died this morning, was little, like Cynthia, but had tiny, tiny hands.'

Was that it then? Was it the long-hands people who inherited the earth? Was it the tiny-hands people who escaped? No. Keep talking.

'Is your bladder okay today?' the woman asks.

'Dribble dribble, but it's better than nothing.'

'And your voice's gone funny again.'

'Fix up one end, then the other end packs up.'

'I'm getting some clips out in a day or two . . .'

'It's no picnic . . .'

'But I don't seem to care about anything. I don't even want to look outside.'

She decides then that she will tell the woman.

'They put me over here so I could look out,' she says. 'I couldn't believe . . . the flowers were all strange, and different-coloured. Dark and bright. I got scared.'

The woman doesn't speak.

'All the flowers, these ones too. And the food. Strange. I was scared, but now . . . I don't care.'

'At night,' the woman says, 'there's people come and sit on me, on my feet, on my chest.'

'I thought they'd ripped fish out of my guts, dragged them up my throat, out of my mouth.'

'It's tubes. They do it to babies too . . . People, every night, and I stay still, keep myself awake, until they go.'

'Sometimes I see what it might be like outside, now, or some other time. There are two of me. One showing the other, making her see. It could be a dream, but it's more like seeing. It *is* seeing. It's like a world with nothing. People with no kai, no clothes, nothing. Just dirt.'

'I been trying to grow a garden, and the only thing good is turnips.' The woman sits forward in her bed smiling. 'And tomatoes. I had a real good crop. Ha!'

So it's all right. She's told the woman and the woman hasn't seemed surprised, hasn't noticed, possibly hasn't heard.

She watches the woman lean back into the pillows.

'But I don't really want to think about the garden,' the woman says, 'or home, or anything out there. Most of the time I lay here and think about Cynthia, wait for them to tell me how she's doing, wait for them to take me down. I've got this idea that if I don't think about Cynthia she might slip. Don't want to sleep at night. And . . . when *they* come in the night I don't know if it's good or bad, if they help me – or if they've come for Cynthia. I just wait . . . just keep awake. After a while they go.'

'Do you see?'

'Only feel.'

'Who is it, then?'

'Don't know. People belonging to me, the old people, I suppose. Anyway, it wouldn't be strangers. So I wait it out, keep my mind on Cynthia and just wait.'

In the quiet that follows they hear the trolleys at the other end of the corridor.

'You been eating,' the woman says, 'this morning, I noticed.'

'I tried to eat most of it, then missed lunch. The food looks plastic and different . . .'

'You been having a hard time.'

'At first I was scared, but not now, because I know I'm really as tough as guts. Underneath I'm as tough as guts. No, it's you. You're the one who's having a hard time. It's different . . . if it's a baby.'

'Cynthia's coming through. She's strong. But I can't help crying, because it's like she has to make it on her own . . . no mother, no family, no clothes on her, no blanket – just machines, tubes, sticking plaster. Anyway it's only machines and tubes that's kept her going, it's good what they cando. I suppose they wonder why I'm always crying my eyes out.'

Cold meat, lettuce salad, tomato and two slices of bread. She finds she can put colour on, or take it off. There's a trick to it. It doesn't matter because later she'll stop doing it, stop being able to do it. She'll be home, too busy to think about it. She's determined to eat the food, and takes a bite out of the slice of bread. While she's eating she'll talk to the woman . . . about tomatoes.

'We had a good crop too, tomatoes. Must've been a good year.'

'I was out picking,' the woman says, 'and that's when my nose bled, pouring like a river.'

Red. Blood, fruit, river, what can she do? What should she do? She wants to scream, to go to the woman, ask what it's all about. Where are we? What can we do?

'Good. That's good.'

She will eat – cut the tomato and eat it, cut up the meat, chew, swallow. While she's eating she'll talk to the woman. In a couple of days she'll go home.

The skirt is too big but she pins a tuck in it. She puts on her coat and shoes.

'I can go too, in three days,' the woman says. 'I'll come in each day until I can take Cynthia home.'

'How long before . . .?'

'It could be another three weeks.'

'Cynthia's doing fine.'

'She's strong.'

'We'll meet again one day.'

'We will.'

She walks the long corridor wearing a warm coat over a pinned-up skirt, passing window after window, like watching a train. There's rain on the windows. She looks down on old buildings, a busy road. She descends in a noiseless lift and walks along more corridors.

At the door she feels the cool air on her face. There's slanting rain, and she walks out on to wet pathways between beds of glossy flowers and shrubs, to the car. The wheels turn on wet asphalt, swishing through the rain. And she thinks that only the rain and sun know that buildings can become rubble, that roads can become dust, that somewhere along the road are people, bare as bone, turning each stone and each grain.

Ahead of them is one corner, and another, and another. All she wants for now is to come to each one blindly – and not to know what is round this bend, the next, the next one after that.